voyeur

fiona cole

D1713760

voyeur

Cover Designer: Najla Qamber Designs
Cover Photographer: Alex Sens
Interior Designer: Indie Girl Promotions

This is a work of fiction. Names, characters, businesses, places, events and incidents are either the products of the author's imagination or used in a fictitious manner. Any resemblance to actual persons, living or dead, actual events, or locales is entirely coincidental.

Playlist

I Wanna Get Better – Bleachers
Mess Is Mine – Vance Joy
HAPPINESS – NEEDTOBREATHE
Moment of Weakness – Tenille Arts
Haunted – Taylor Swift
Looking Out – Brandi Carlile
Dreams – Brandi Carlile
Sober Up – AJR (feat Rivers Cuomo)
Dream – Bishop Briggs
Iris – The Goo Goo Dolls
Hurricane Drunk – Florence + the Machine
OK – Robin Schulz (feat. James Blunt)
Work – Jimmy Eat World
The Cure – Lady Gaga
One Foot – Walk the Moon

Dedication

To Rachel and Georgeanna.
Ride or die, bitches.

Chapter One

Oaklyn

"What do you mean the money's gone?"

"I'm so sorry, honey. The water heater broke, and we thought we were okay, but then the car broke down. Our savings were empty, and the car couldn't be fixed, so we had to get a new one or your dad couldn't get to work. Then rent came up and the check ... was just there."

My hand squeezed the phone, I now couldn't afford, as I tried to control my anger and panic. "Mom, that's my tuition money I was supposed to live off of."

I couldn't believe the check was sent to the wrong address. I updated the address as soon as I moved into my tiny studio apartment. Yet, somehow, it was sent to my parents in Florida. My mind raced with regrets and cursed my bad luck. I'd just been there last week for Thanksgiving. Why couldn't it have been delivered then? Why couldn't they have sent it to me without opening it?

What the hell was I going to do?

"I'm so sorry, honey. We panicked and made the wrong decision. We—we can sell the car. We'll figure it out."

Inside I screamed *"Yes!"* But I knew I couldn't make them do it. How would they survive if my dad couldn't get to work? And while college was my dream, I'd still survive without it. I should've been mad, and I was, but I couldn't take it out on them. I'd done nothing but watch my parents struggle from one paycheck to another, and I knew if I asked, she would've sold the car back. Only god knows what would happen then, and I wasn't willing to take that chance.

"No, Mom. Don't do that."

"What are you going to do?"

"I don't know," I said, sagging against the wall of my friend's dorm. I'd stepped outside to take the call, but on the brink of tears, I wish I'd have stayed inside where no one could see me crumble.

"Can you get another loan?" my mom suggested, her voice filled with hope.

Nothing could stop the laugh I choked out. Another loan? I'd applied for every scholarship, grant, and loan to get to school. I'd busted my ass in high school in hope of scholarships flooding my bank account. And they did, but it hadn't been enough. I'd also taken any of the loans offered to me through FAFSA.

You didn't have to go out of state, my subconscious whispered. Well, it was too damn late now. I'd wanted to get away, leave the rut I'd been stuck in at home, and I'd found the means to do it. Too bad those means were gone now. All ten thousand dollars of it. Eight thousand to pay for my last semester—damn out of state fees—and another two thousand to live on until the end of summer.

"No, Mom."

"I'm so sorry, baby.".

I knew she was—I could hear it in the crack in her voice, but I just couldn't give her the forgiveness she needed in that moment. My dream was crumbling before me, and I couldn't focus on anything else. With tears clogging my throat, I got off the phone and went to hide in my friend's dorm.

"How's mommy and daddy," Olivia joked when I walked through the door. But as soon as she looked at the defeat on my face, hers morphed into one of concern. She jumped up and rushed to me. "What happened? Did someone die? Is everyone okay?"

Her arms wrapped around me, and I dropped my head to her shoulder, letting the tears fall. "They . . . " I sniffed and tried to work past the tears. "They spent my tuition money."

"What?"

I couldn't say it again, so I simply nodded.

"Fuck, Oak. That's . . . Fuck."

"Yeah."

She didn't say anything else, just led me to her twin-size bed and held me as I let it all out.

I hated being overly emotional. I tried to be efficient with my feelings and sitting there crying wasn't going to get me anywhere. Sitting up, I wiped my cheeks and took a few deep breaths.

Olivia got me a water from her mini fridge and leaned back against the wall.

"You could always sleep here. I'm sure we could get away with it."

I seriously considered saying yes. My fingers tapped the pink bed sheets, looking at the minimal floor space and remembering her other roommate. She probably wouldn't love the idea of another body taking up space.

"God, Olivia," I said, falling back on her pillows. "Why didn't you accept the penthouse suite when you first started college?"

Her laugh was easy and just as bubbly as she was. "I know, I'm such a bitch."

Olivia came from a rich family who wanted to put her in a penthouse apartment off campus. All she wanted was a dorm room, so she could really experience college life. Her father begrudgingly accepted as long as he was able to hire a driver for her.

All I wanted was a dorm room but couldn't afford the added cost above my tuition. So, I was stuck in an apartment off campus. It was no penthouse, that was for sure. It was barely an apartment. More like a shoebox. I had a semi-decent car to get me from point A to B, and a bus stop close by in case it went from semi-decent to broken down. I'd made it work. Maybe I could look into selling the car for some extra cash.

"So, what are you going to do?"

"That's the million-dollar question. I'll start by looking for a job, even though most are taken by all the holiday workers."

"But you already do student work at the Biology Department. When will you have time to work another job and still be able to study?"

"Sleep is overrated." I succeeded in making her snort since we both loved sleep dearly. "I can always sell my plasma . . . maybe my eggs."

"I will kidnap you before you sell your precious possible babies."

"Aw, thanks Liv. You're a true friend."

She blew me a kiss and put on a movie for distraction. At least an attempt at a distraction. But even as we laughed and ate popcorn, my mind was swirling with possible places to apply for work. I'd start looking for any job possible as soon as I leave the dorm. I joked about losing sleep, but I'd sacrifice a lot more than that to stay in college.

A week later and I still hadn't found another job. Every possible position that may have been open was snatched up by the seasonal workers. It was three weeks before Christmas, and if one more person told me I should have applied before Thanksgiving, I'd scream.

"I have an appointment at the Bursar's Office tomorrow to beg for some kind of help to come up with a solution," I explained to Olivia over lunch. "In the morning, I'm going to run by the bank and see if I can take out another loan."

"You know, I could talk to my da—" Olivia started, but I cut her off.

"No. I will not take money from you."

"It's a loan. And you wouldn't have to pay interest."

I was already shaking my head before she finished. We'd had this conversation before, and I was adamant about not entering into a financial relationship with her. I'd seen my parents borrow money from a friend, and it tore their relationship apart. They lorded the loan over them, and took advantage just because my parents had owed them money. When they finally paid it all back, the friendship had been too damaged to repair. Nothing good ever benefitted a relationship when the exchange of money occurred.

I couldn't have that happen between me and Olivia. She was too important to lose. "It's bad enough I let you buy me lunch today."

We sat at the corner table at the school's largest dining hall. I was content to eat another pack of ramen, but she'd dragged me here and bought my entry before I could say otherwise.

"Just eat your damn food. You know it's good," she grumbled.

I took a bite and stared at her, but she was looking down, her long blonde hair hanging like a curtain around her, hiding from me. When she finally looked up, she looked nervous. Her lips were pinched and her eyes wide.

Alarm bells went off in my head. "What?"

She set her silverware down and sat up straighter, as if she were preparing for battle. "Listen," she started. "I have an idea. It's really good money, but you have to have a *waaaay* open mind about it."

"Okaaay?" I dragged the word out, trying to prepare myself. "You know I'm desperate and will do just about anything."

Her tongue slicked across her pink glossed lips and she swallowed. What the hell was it?

"My uncle—kind of the rogue agent of the family—owns a club."

I dropped my fork and sat up straight, trying to think of a club that wasn't a strip club. "What kind of club?"

She cocked her head and looked around as though searching for the right words. "It's not really a sex clu—."

"I am *not* standing on a street corner to make money. I'm desperate, but not ready for prostitution."

"No. No, no, no." Her hands rose up, halting that line of thought.

"Think of it more like . . . performing." She paused. "Sometimes naked."

I blinked, several times, waiting for her to tell me she was kidding. Something. Anything to explain what the hell she was talking about. I sat there, mute, unable to form words, unable to ask questions. Unable to anything, really.

"It's called Voyeur." Caving under the silence, she picked up her fork and moved food around her plate before spitting the rest out on one breath. "People come to watch other people do things. It can range from showering to . . . performing with someone else."

Olivia looked up through her lashes, giving me time to digest what she'd just said. I sat there, dumbfounded. Words swam around in my head, but none of them would coalesce to form complete sentences. There was one that stood out, however: *Maybe.*

"He said over Thanksgiving he had to fire a girl for sleeping with a customer on the clock which is a big no-no. I've heard it pays really good money. It's also a bar. Maybe you could work as a bartender, but you wouldn't make as much."

Voyeur. I knew that word. Saw it on some porn site maybe? Read it in a book? It's when someone likes to watch others. Usually in sexual activities.

Could I let someone watch me?

When the immediate answer wasn't no, I let my thoughts expand. *Maybe* was morphing into *possibly.*

I wasn't a virgin or a prude. I'd experimented with the boyfriend I had in high school, and then other boys my senior year when we broke up. I wasn't going to pretend that I knew all of it since I was only nineteen. But I wasn't so naive and inexperienced that the thought shocked me.

"With your body and looks, you would probably be a shoe-in."

I laughed. "Thanks, Liv."

"What? You've got the whole girl-next-door thing going on. If the girl next door was a sex kitten." She curled her fingers into claws, making me laugh with her rawr. "You're fit and petite. People like that."

"Petite and fit is a nice way of saying no boobs."

"Hey, you've got a good handful."

I laughed when she held up her hands like she was measuring. "Besides, it's not a strip club. I've overheard that the more natural and normal you look, the better."

"Overheard?"

"Well, my uncle doesn't talk too openly about it when I'm around, but he gets loud when he drinks."

Biting my lip, I considered my other options. They felt weak and unstable. So did this, but at least if I didn't make it to next semester, I could say I tried everything.

"Okay. I'll check it out."

That night I sat across from a tall, blond man with crow's feet stamped around his eyes, the only thing showing his age. Otherwise, his slim build hinted at a youth he no longer possessed. His blue eyes matched Olivia's, and I could see the family resemblance. He wasn't at all the Ron Jeremy look-alike I'd expected. His casual looks and easy smile had set me at ease.

I'd been there for almost half an hour answering questions and telling him about myself. When he would stop to write things down or turn to his computer, I clasped my sweaty hands together and looked around the dark office.

I didn't know what I was expecting, dildo statues on the shelves? Pictures of naked women? Books on Kama Sutra?

Actually, there was one on Kama Sutra on the shelf, right next to *Moby Dick* and *Little Women*. Hell of a selection.

"There's no paying for sex," he said firmly, pulling me back to the rules he was discussing. "I don't run a prostitution ring."

"That's good." One side of my mouth tipped up in an awkward smile, showing off how uncomfortable I felt. He just laughed and continued.

"The rooms change for different themes throughout the month. A bedroom is kept constantly, but sometimes there's an office setup, a bathroom, a classroom, a bar. Pretty much anything you could think of. There are also various rooms based on what you're willing to do. Some rooms, like BDSM, require training before you're allowed to work in them. I keep my workers safe. All clients sign an NDA protecting your privacy. You will also sign an NDA so they're safe as well. They pay a lot of money to be here, and it's important I provide a safe environment for them."

The more he explained, the more comfortable I felt. This wasn't some run-down strip club where everything was a free-for-all.

"Clients can watch in an attached private room through a one-way window or sit in the provided chairs inside the room. But no one touches the performers. Ever. You don't touch the clients. Ever." His blue eyes held me in place and I nodded. "You will have a panic button close by and a guard outside the room should you need them." His long fingers flipped a page. "Any questions so far?"

"No, sir." The words were barely whispered. Each rule he read off made me feel better, but also increased my heart rate at the possibility that this would happen. Was I excited? Scared? Nervous?

Definitely all of the above.

"You can call me Daniel. Or Mr. Wit."

"Okay."

He looked back to his list of rules. "There are no cameras or recording devices of any kind. Phones are left in the locker room or at the door. You can perform up to three times in a shift, and the rest of the time, you will be working the bar and common area. You will fill out a form upon arriving and clients will be able to look through the performers in a computer system. You may not always be selected."

He passed the sheet over to me to look over and instructed me to sign. It had the fifteen dollars an hour base I'd make when I was there, as well as the range I could be paid for each performance. Based on the hours we discussed and the prices next to each performance, I had the opportunity to make almost a thousand dollars a week.

I gripped the pen.

I was signing an agreement of the rules.

Because I was going to be an employee at Voyeur.

A sex club.

Goose bumps sprang up across my skin. The scrape of the pen across the paper sounded loud in the quiet room. But it felt like I'd reopened the door to my education, and that made the smallest of smiles twitch on my lips.

"Okay, Miss Derringer. The final process requires you to submit to an STD test as you will be interacting with other employees, and we keep everyone safe. Then, another of my associates will look you over for me."

Look me over? My expression must have given away my alarm because he chuckled and rushed to explain. "Her name is Agnes. She does this part to prevent me from getting sued for sexual harassment. But I can't have you going out without her approval. I hate to say it, but the job is based on looks. While you look good in clothes, I need to know you don't have a swastika tattoo on your ass for as much as you'll be naked."

The reminder of my nudity made me swallow. I was comfortable in my own skin and never hesitated over nudity, but anyone would be nervous to strip down for a stranger and perform.

"Personal upkeep is also continuously checked on. We need our employees clean and healthy, so we do regular checks." He extended another paper across the desk. "Here's the list of things that you can sign up to do. Feel free to look it over."

My eyes almost bugged out of my head when I looked at the sheet with a list and check boxes on it. "This is the checklist you'll be filling out each time you begin a shift to let members know what you're comfortable performing that night."

Anal.

Caning.

Solo Masturbation.

Joint Masturbation.

Vaginal Penetration.
Non-consensual Play.
Daddy Play.
Asphyxiation.
Dry sex.
Multiple partners.
Oral sex. (Male)
Oral sex. (Female)

I remembered back to when I thought I wasn't a prude. Or when I said I'd experimented. Apparently, I skipped the caning experimentation phase and couldn't say I was sad about it. Doubt began to creep in.

"Don't let the list alarm you. These are at your own discretion, and I try to provide something for everyone. We have a wide clientele, and we keep it a judgement-free zone. If you're unable to do that, then we should stop here."

"No. No. I just . . ." A nervous laugh bubbled up. "No judgment. Different strokes for different folks. I'm just not sure I'm ready for a gang bang."

Daniel was pretty damn handsome when he smiled. "Fair enough." He leaned back in his chair and folded his hands on his tight stomach. "We try to make our employees as comfortable as possible and try to provide realistic scenes for our customers. Therefore, we usually pair up the same couples each time. Next time you come in, I'll be sure your partner will be here so you two can meet. Jackson is off today."

He stood, and I did the same. "Let's find you a locker and introduce you to Agnes."

I stared at his broad back as he walked toward the door and one thought raced through my head.

I'm in.

Chapter Two

Callum

"You need to get fucked, man." My best friend, Reed, stated this like a decree.

I bit back my initial response, which was that I wished that I could, and grunted instead. I was in no mood to encourage him. Unfortunately, it didn't seem to work.

"You've been so damn focused on your job."

"I like my job."

Reed took a long pull from his beer bottle, eyeing me with skepticism. I mimicked his motions and held his stare with one of my own.

"I don't know why you didn't take that bigwig job back in Cali when we graduated. I mean, I know I'm pretty, but you didn't have to stay here for me."

Nothing would ever get me back to California. I got out of that state as soon as I could. My parents still lived there, but they knew my stipulations and came to visit me instead. They knew my demons wouldn't let me rest if I ever went back.

"I like it here," I said, defending my decision. "It's too sunny and there's no snow in California. At least not in Sacramento. Cincinnati suits me."

"I suppose I just sweeten the deal," he joked.

"Nah, I'm really just here for your wife and her delicious meals."

He rolled his eyes. "Speaking of Karen, she told me you gave her friend a peck on the cheek and bolted after your date." He said it like I'd made her tuck and roll out of the car. "Listen, Cal. I say this with all the love, but Lucy is Karen's slutty friend. The woman loves sex, and I was sure you would've taken her home."

I nudged my spoon up to better line up with the knife centered on the napkin as I thought about how to answer. Reed had been my best friend since college, but he didn't know everything there was to know about me. He didn't know my secrets, and I wanted to keep it that way.

"She was nice. Just because we went on a date doesn't mean we need to have sex."

"How long has it been, Cal? A year? More?"

"Reed," I said, my tone warning him to drop it. I didn't want to answer that question because it had been a lot longer.

"It's been more than a year since you broke up with what's-her-face. I know you've dated, but when have you gotten laid?"

I took another drink of my beer, looking around at the other patrons of the restaurant avoiding meeting Reed's eyes.

"You. Need. To. Get. Laid," he said again.

"I get plenty of action." I didn't need to explain what kind of action I was referring to.

"No, you *see* plenty of action."

"We all have our kinks," I said avoiding that topic. "I'm sure you let Karen tie you up all the time."

He didn't take the bait and pushed on, letting out a growl, throwing his hands up. "You frustrate me, man. Look at you." Reed gestured to me across the table. "Women flock to you. They dig all those muscles you go to the gym for. Karen raves to me about your eyes." He fluttered his lashes and put on a woman's breathy voice. "Callum's eyes are so blue. They're so bright."

I laughed. "Jealous?"

"Yeah right. I satisfy my wife plenty. You're just an enigma." His eyes flicked to his left before leaning back. "I bet you don't even realize the girl approaching our table has been watching you the whole time. She's probably just coming over to be disappointed when she asks you out and you say no."

I may not have been eager to be intimate with women, but that didn't mean I didn't date and appreciate a woman's company. It didn't mean I wasn't attracted to them. I'd noticed the blonde across the room almost as soon as she walked in. My lips twitched when I thought about how I was going to make Reed eat his words.

I took one last swallow of my beer and then set it down, exactly back on the wet ring it had left on the center of the napkin. Satisfied with the fit, I leaned back and mimicked his position.

"Hi," the woman said once she reached our table. "Excuse me, but I noticed you across the restaurant, and I just couldn't leave without coming over to introduce myself."

Her voice was soft and feminine, and I could imagine sharing conversations with her. I rotated my body toward her to get a better look. She was beautiful. Tall and slim in her black pants and flowy cream shirt. She looked professional—organized.

I shifted my lips into my most charming smile and extended my hand. "Hello. I'm Callum."

"Shannon." Her slim fingers slipped in my palm, feeling soft and fragile.

"Nice to meet you, Callum." She tucked a strand of hair behind her ear and cleared her throat. "Well, I don't want to keep you, but I wanted to see if you'd like to get coffee sometime."

I glanced quickly to Reed, making sure he was watching, satisfied by the smirk that was going to crumble.

"I'd love to have coffee with you, if you want to give me your phone number."

"Yes. Yes, of course. I left my phone at the table but let me write it down and you can message me with yours."

When she bent over and scribbled her number with the pen the waiter left behind, I smirked at Reed. I had to fight letting a laugh slip out when he mouthed, *Fuck you.*

I cocked an eyebrow and turned my attention back to Shannon.

Maybe she'd be different than the others. Maybe she'd be the one to help me move past my nightmares.

Chapter Three

Oaklyn

After stripping down to the most minuscule pair of undergarments I'd ever known, Agnes gave me the approval I needed. Afterward, I went to the doctor they told me to use, and I got my STD test done. Lying on the table, a young female doctor between my legs, I wondered if she knew I was there because I needed to be clean for my performances. I wondered if she cared or judged the work I was going to do? Either way, she didn't let on and I left the office, called only a few days later to let me know everything came back clean. No shocker there since I always practiced safe sex.

After finding out I was good to go, I'd headed to the Bursar's Office armed with a whole new plan and plea to get me through the semester. To say I was lucky was an understatement. The man who listened and saw me almost break down in tears had helped me immensely.

We set up a payment plan to get my semester paid for before spring break, and he also found a spot for me in another work study program in the physics department. It seemed an easy solution since I was already in the building for my work study in biology.

For the first time in a couple of weeks, I felt like I could breathe, as though a weight had been lifted from my chest. The semester was going to be hard, but I wasn't scared of hard work. My determination would keep me going. And next year, I'd be more careful. It would be easier. I just had to focus on these next few months.

However, I still kept my feelers out for other jobs, hoping to find something less . . . just less than Voyeur.

Less than the black pumps and Santa dress I currently wore. My breasts lifted to perfect display.

"Derringer." Daniel called my name as he walked in with a tall, shirtless guy. To say he was attractive was an understatement. He looked like a modern-day James Dean and my jaw almost dropped taking in his bare chest and tight black jeans.

"My eyes are up here," he joked.

"Be nice, Jackson." Daniel issued a warning before speaking to me. "This is your new partner, Jackson."

He reached his large hand out and I lamely placed mine in his, watching it get lost in his long fingers. "Hi, I'm Oaklyn."

"Hey, Oaklyn. Can't wait to make out with you."

"Stop scaring her, Jackson." Daniel glared at Jackson before turning toward me. "We keep it professional around here. Yes, there will probably be sexual acts between the two of you but think of it as an acting job. There will be a probationary period of sorts with you two to make sure the chemistry is there, and if it doesn't work out, you'll try another partner. So, don't let Jackson scare you. He's one of the nicest ones I know." He turned his attention back to Jackson. "Don't get yourself into a harassment suit. I'd hate to lose you."

Jackson put his hands up in defeat. "Alright. I'll lay off." He turned to me with earnest eyes and a warm smile, different from the sexy smirk from earlier. "It's nice to meet you, Oaklyn. If you have any issues, just come to me, and I'll help you out."

"Thank you," I answered.

"But we probably should get together to talk soon. Get comfortable with kissing each other so it all seems more natural."

"Yeah. Okay."

My nerves had crept in and limited me to simple one- and two-word answers.

"I have paperwork calling my name," Daniel said. "I'll leave you two to it. Oaklyn, come to me if you have any issues or questions."

And then it was just Jackson and me in the room.

"Nice outfit, Derringer," Jackson broke the silence.

Outfit was an understatement. More like barely-there lingerie that resembled Mrs. Clause. "Thanks," I responded dryly.

Jackson shined his perfect smile at me, and I couldn't fight the smile back. Somehow, he'd already begun putting me at ease around him.

"You nervous for your first night?"

"A little. But a little excited too."

"That's good. It's better to just think of it like acting in a play—to remove yourself from the porny feel of it." He closed his locker and leaned against it, staring at me. "You going to select any partner work tonight?"

"Umm." I looked down and fiddled with the white fur lining the bottom of my dress. "I don't think so."

"Maybe next time." He stood to his full height and looked me over before walking toward me. Each step he took, my eyes grew wider and wider until he stood right in front of me. I watched, frozen, as his hand came up to cradle my cheek and he leaned down to press his lips to mine. They were soft and lush and not at all demanding. When his tongue flicked out at the seam of my mouth, I opened and met him halfway, tasting the fresh mint.

I had expected the kiss to go further, to shoot to my core and set off sparks along the way. Instead, it was comfortable. Friendly. He knew exactly how confused I was when he pulled back and took in my face.

"It's a good feeling to have, Oaklyn. We'll be better partners if our feelings for each other are mild."

I nodded and muttered an okay. He gave me a quick peck and a slap on the ass before heading out.

"See you out there, Derringer."

I walked to the entrance of the employee lounge and grabbed an iPad to enter what I was willing to do that night. A giggle burst up as I started checking things off. The situation of sitting there in a slutty Santa costume, picking out what sexual acts I was willing to do in front of strangers was too funny for that moment.

Bypassing all the partner work, I select almost every solo performance possible. Except anything that required anal masturbation. Pretty sure I wasn't ready for that just yet.

I placed the iPad back on the charger and snagged a bracelet that looked like a Fitbit. It would buzz to let me know if anyone had selected me for the night.

Walking into the lounge, you'd never know the things that went on behind closed doors. A black modern bar with glass shelving was off to one side. Booths lined the opposite wall. A sprinkling of bar-top tables ringed the dance floor. Dim lighting lent a secretive air to the place. The piped-in music fluctuated between a variety of genres, but all with an upbeat tempo, filling any silence and absorbing any conversations going on nearby.

The only thing different between this and any other upscale club, was that the employees walked around in lingerie or other seductive outfits. I made my way to the bar and asked Charlotte, who was wearing a slutty clf costume, what she needed help with.

"Keep a pad on hand to take orders as you walk around. Eventually, you want to get better about remembering without writing them down. But for now, if you could run these to table twenty, that would be great."

The next few hours passed in a blur of taking orders and passing out drinks. Jackson helped the time fly by playing twenty questions each time we passed each other. I found out that he was twenty-two and had worked at Voyeur for two years. He was bisexual and not into being dominated but dabbled in dominating himself. His favorite color was green, and he liked Tic-Tacs, but only the orange ones.

Surprisingly, I hadn't gotten any lewd comments, and no one tried to touch me. Sure, men—and women—looked and flirted, but no one had crossed the line or made me feel uncomfortable.

"These people pay a lot of money to be here. If they wanted to flirt and get handsy, they could go to a strip club for free two blocks down. People tend to be more respectful of the rules when they're dropping over a grand a month to satisfy a specific kink of theirs," Charlotte had explained when I'd mentioned it.

She laughed when my eyes bugged out. "Jesus. I hadn't realized how much the membership fee was."

My bracelet began to vibrate. The feeling traveled up my arm, sending an electric shock to my heart and jolting it into action. Lifting my arm, I looked at it like it was a bomb about to diffuse. I went blank, unsure of what the next step should be. Even though I knew. We'd gone over it. Go to the iPad and check the specifications of the request. Accept or reject.

Charlotte patted my shoulder. "Hey, hey, girl. You got one."

"Yeah," I said softly.

"Don't be scared. It's like your virginity. The first time is the worst, but still fun, and it only goes up from there. And you don't have to do anything you don't want to do."

I nodded, and she turned my shoulders to head where I needed to go. "Now go get 'em, tiger."

I went to the iPad and pulled up my file to find the request, almost sagging in relief to see what it was.

Couple session.
Male: 58
Female: 55
Request: Solo Performance
Comments/Specifications: Like you're coming home for bed, lay down and start reading a book. Then begin to masturbate but show nothing. Just your hand moving under your panties with your legs spread. Make enough noise, but not overly fake.
In room or privacy room: In room.

As for what could have been given to me on my first go, this was a gift. It wasn't too much exposure and something I could pretend I was actually at home for. How many times did I read a book and end up playing with myself before falling asleep? Plenty.

This was just like that. Sort of.

I went to the back hallway that led to all the rooms and saw the tag hanging on the knob indicating the couple was already in the room.

"Don't forget your panic button if anything should happen," Tim, the security guard who was placed outside my door explained. "I placed it on the nightstand for easy reach should you need it. I'll be right out here the whole time."

"Thank you."

Taking a deep breath, I gripped the knob before turning it and clearing my mind.

Ignore the couple in the corner. Focus on you and the scene.

I walked into a normal bedroom. A dresser with a mirror set up on the wall next to the door, littered with all kinds of basics you'd find in a bedroom. Brush, books, makeup, perfume. A bed on the far wall with a basic hotel-like set up and a nightstand on each side. I'd been told each room included a fully dimmed alcove where the voyeur would sit, and though I didn't look, I knew my couple was sitting in the alcove to my left.

Instead of focusing on that, I went to the dresser and took off any jewelry I had and avoided looking in the mirror, unsure if I was ready to see what I'd find staring back at me. I brushed my hair and then flipped through the books, selecting one and heading to the bed.

I pulled the covers back but lay down on top of them after fluffing the pillows behind me. My eyes skimmed the words, not taking anything in as I tried to determine the appropriate amount of time to pretend to read before fingering myself.

The nervous laugh that bubbled up at the thought almost escaped. I clamped down on the inside of my cheek to keep myself in check, then I rolled my hips and rubbed my thighs together. I shifted the book to one hand while the other worked its way down my body. Repeating the motion of my hips, I slowly drew my heels up toward me and spread my legs wide, letting my fingers play with the edge of my lace underwear. Each graze along the edge of the fabric sent shocks to my core.

Were the couples' eyes glued to my movements, desperate for more? Were they touching each other? Was he mimicking my movements? Teasing her with soft grazes against her core? I didn't dare lift my eyes.

When my fingers sunk beneath the fabric, I let out a moan, surprised to find how turned on I actually was and that I was wet. I made my motions big, to make sure the couple sitting directly across from my spread legs could see what was happening.

When I heard them for the first time, it almost pulled me out of the moment. A swish of fabric, her soft moan, his heavy grunt. I kept my hand moving, my hips pushing up, but my mind was slipping.

What were they doing? Who were they? Did they like what they saw?

Her breathing increased, and the repeated rustle of fabric led me to believe they were having sex.

Were they even watching me anymore? What would I see if I lifted my head enough to peer into the shadows?

My core tightened at that thought, and I closed my eyes and pictured it. I pictured her straddling his lap and grinding on him as he stared over her shoulder and watched my thighs shake from pleasure.

Using my rush of moisture, I pushed my fingers inside my pussy and moaned. I pulled back out and circled my clit, wondering if she had turned to watch me too, and I moaned again.

The rustle of clothes sped up to a rhythmic thrust that I used to time my motions, keeping pace with them. Her cries became louder and mine matched hers. Not that I was particularly loud but had to remember their request for sounds.

But soon they were real, and I was coming. My walls squeezing around my fingers as my thumb worked harder across my bud. Almost as soon as I was done, with ringing still in my ears, I heard them climax, his loud groan pulling another spasm from my core.

I gathered myself fast, unsure of how to finish the scene. They hadn't specified and laying there with my hand stuck in my underwear seemed like too much, but I knew they were supposed to leave first.

With one last breathy gasp, I pulled my hand out and rolled to my side, bringing the book with me. I slipped under the covers and pretended to read. While they prepared to leave, I stared at the words on the page and a small storm brewed inside me.

I'd come.

I'd *enjoyed* it.

I *liked* being watched. It spurred me on more to imagine them watching, getting off to what I was doing.

In all my thoughts about what I'd agreed to do, my nerves had been the only ones I'd been concerned with. I never imagined that I would like it. Would I like being with Jackson? Would I begin to crave him too? How far would I be willing to go?

When I heard the click of the door, I sat up and watched the minute hand circle around, waiting two full rotations before I got up to leave. As soon as I walked out of the room, I went to the iPad and removed my options. I was done performing for the night, too overwhelmed with my first performance to continue. Instead I stuck to Charlotte's side and distracted myself with orders and customers, knowing I would eventually need to process the surprising reactions I had in the room.

But it could wait.

"I had a great night, Cal. Would you maybe want to grab a drink at my place?"

I thought over Shannon's offer, knowing it was more than a drink, knowing I should say yes, but my body already breaking out in a sweat at the idea. "I've got an early morning, but maybe next time." I added a smile to soften the rejection.

"Next time." Her hand trailed down my chest as she stepped into me outside her car door. I moved my hand to her waist, as she probably expected, and leaned down to meet her halfway for a kiss.

I watched her eyes close and wondered what she saw behind them when her lips touched mine. She pressed close and I moved my mouth against her softer one, enjoying the connection, but unable to lose myself in it. Before it could become more, I pulled back with a peck, watching her eyes dreamily open and a small smile play across the flushed lips I'd just tasted.

With a flirtatious smile and heated look, she turned to open her door and said, "Call me," before getting in. I nodded and stood back until she pulled out of the parking lot, but I wasn't sure if I would.

I got in my own car and drove home. The keys jangled too loud in the empty house, echoing against the walls, reminding me I was alone. I didn't bother turning on the lights after I placed my keys in the bowl and set my wallet in line with the corner of the entryway table. Instead, I let the moonlight streaming across my hardwood floors through the open blinds guide me to the wet bar in the corner of the sitting room. I poured a shot of expensive bourbon. I didn't keep too much alcohol in the house after the way I struggled with it as a teen, but tonight wore on me. I poured another before sitting back against the stiff cushions of the couch.

This house was too big. I thought maybe if I had a house with so many rooms, a house that begged for a family, it would push me to fill it. Yet there I sat, in the dark, sipping bourbon, on my barely used couch in my barely used sitting room.

My mind wondered to Shannon and what she would think if I'd taken her up on her offer to go somewhere for drinks, preferably one of our houses. She was a beautiful woman. A slim body and medium height. Her breasts full and the cleavage she'd had on display alluring. She gave the vibe of a good girl who'd want to do dirty things in bed. Would she understand my desire to watch? Would she like it?

I adjusted my hardening dick as I thought about bringing a woman to Voyeur to watch with me. Torn between watching the performance and watching her bare breasts heave in excitement.

Yet, I hadn't taken Shannon home, because thoughts were just that. Enough to turn me on, but I was realistic enough to not act on them.

The quiet was getting to me, leading my mind to shadows I didn't want to visit. I needed to get out of the house. I tossed back the last bit of bourbon and moved to the kitchen to wash and dry my glass, putting it away in the cabinet before grabbing my keys and heading out. My parents would be in town next week, and I wouldn't be able to satisfy my desires while they were there.

Confidence surrounded me as I walked through the door to Voyeur, entering my ID number into the program, even though it was unnecessary since everyone knew me. I waved as I passed some of the guards and regulars that had been there longer than me. When I reached the bar, I ordered a beer, remembering my two drinks at home. The bartender, Charlotte, set my bottle in front of me and left to attend to others. I grabbed my drink and turned to scan the crowds, trying to find someone I wanted to watch tonight.

Just as I brought the cold glass to my lips, I spotted her walking out of the back hallway. Her light brown hair looked mussed, fanning out behind her as she walked, like she'd just rolled out of bed. A flush stained her cheeks all the way down to her chest, making my eyes trail over her perky breasts, barely a handful. My mind raced with thoughts about what she might have just done, how she would have looked.

Instantly, my cock hardened as I stared at her slim body weaving between the patrons. She wore a minuscule Santa nightie and black, thigh-high stockings that made her legs look much longer than her short body could handle. She kept her head down for the most part, but when a woman stepped back, bumping into her, she glanced up with a smile that punched me in the chest. Her lips were full on her petite face and her smile almost too big. It was beautiful.

I stared as her features pulled me in, entranced me as I mapped every inch. Something about her ensnared all of my senses and wouldn't let me go. I couldn't put my finger on what it was. Maybe physical attraction? It felt bigger than that, like a planet that was pulling me into its orbit.

Too soon she slipped behind the wall I knew led to the employee's lounge. I took one last quick pull of my drink and abandoned it, half full, at the bar before heading to the iPads where I could make my selection. Flipping through who was working for the night, I searched for her face. An urgency I couldn't explain hit me. An excitement I hadn't felt before lit a fire through me. I needed to watch her tonight. Watch her do anything as I wrapped my fist around my cock, imagining it was her, until I came.

When I found her picture, an asterisk stood beside it and my chest deflated. The asterisk was to let people know that she was no longer able to perform for the night. *Fuck.* Had I just missed her last performance? Had I missed my chance for the night?

Squeezing my sweaty palms into fists, I closed my eyes and took a deep breath. This wasn't me. I didn't let such strong emotions carry me away and affect my body like they were now. Another deep breath and I swiped my palms against my slacks. Then I opened my eyes and looked down one last time at her seductive eyes in the picture.

Continuing to swipe, I decided to find someone else to watch. I needed something harsh and angry to get some of the added frustration out that had suddenly taken over. I didn't want the tediousness and teasing of BDSM, just rough. Finding a couple, I marked my preferences, noting that I'd be observing from the private room behind the one-way mirror.

Having made my choice, satisfaction rushed to the base of my spine, hardening my cock even more.

Reed could comment all he wanted about my sex life, but I had a plethora of options laid out before me.

Who cared that I couldn't bring myself to do any of them?

Chapter Four

Oaklyn

I'd never masturbated so much in my entire life as I had in the past two weeks. Each time seemed more intense than the last. Charlotte was right, the first time was the hardest, and it got better from there. She'd laughed and said, "I told you so," when she saw me filling all three performance slots every night I worked.

A lot of clients had been similar to the first, only wanting the illusion of peering into something hidden, without actually seeing everything. But then there were some that wanted me topless and playing with my nipples, or not wearing any panties, or using a vibrator or dildo. Sometimes, I lay completely naked, exposed to whoever watched me or under the spray of the shower. Whatever they requested. My heart seemed to beat the fastest when they were completely hidden behind the dark glass in the connecting room.

Tonight felt different though, and feeling brave I'd left the option open to work with Jackson. Not that I was sure I'd take it, but I did it anyway, just to see how it would feel to have the option. So far no one had asked, and I felt both happy and sad about it.

The night had been pretty slow. People were probably still recovering from New Year's Eve a few days ago, but it looked to be picking up when I rounded the corner from the back carrying the box of napkins Charlotte had asked me to get for her.

Good. I needed the distraction. The holidays had been hard this year because I couldn't afford to go home. I loved Christmas with my whole extended family and watching *National Lampoon's Christmas Vacation* alone on my couch had been depressing. My parents had called, and everyone wished me a Merry Christmas, but it almost made it worse.

I had to pull back from talking to my parents after that. I didn't want to resent them for the current situation, but I did, and showing how mad I was wouldn't help anything. I knew they were sorry. I knew they would take it back if they could. I knew, and it didn't help calm me at all. Instead, I'd rather avoid them. At least for now.

And it was the new year. I'd start school soon and that was the biggest positive to focus on. I was achieving my goals, no matter what. *That* was my silver lining. Reaching the bar with a new resolve to focus on the positive, I set the napkins down with a smile.

Looking up, I noticed a man with a dark head of hair at the far end of the bar. He jerked away when I noticed him. Intrigued, I wondered if he'd been watching me. Maybe he'd be the one to request me tonight. The idea sent a thrill of excitement zipping through my body. He seemed large under the dim lights. I could see the breadth of his shoulders, straining against his charcoal suit, and how he sat farther above the bar top than the other men sitting around him.

Shadows hid his face, but I could see his long fingers gripping the glass before him. I imagined those fingers gripping his cock, stroking it as he watched. I pushed the napkins off to the side and began to round the bar, wanting a better look at him. Maybe if I would check to see if he needed something, flirt a little. Maybe I could entice him into watching me. I rarely saw the faces of anyone who watched me, and it didn't bother me. It made it easier to detach. But something about this man made me need to see his face. Each step closer caused a flutter in my stomach. The possibilities were making me more excited than I'd been since I started.

When I was just five bar stools away, a body blocked my progress.

"Oaklyn." The way Jackson said my name, matched with his smile led me to believe he wasn't about to ask me for the time.

"Yes, Jackson?"

He dragged a hand through his hair. "So, I was requested for a couple's session, and they specifically mentioned you."

My heart thumped in my chest. This was it. This was my opportunity to try something out with Jackson. I looked down at my watch and saw that I hadn't been notified of a request.

"But why didn't they fill out my form too?"

His smooth smile slipped a little. "Yeah. About that. You, uh, didn't have the things requested on your availability, so mine was filled out since I'm listed as your partner."

"What was the request?" I'd opened a partner option up but limited it to kissing and some heavy petting.

"It's just sex." When my eyes bugged, he held his hands up trying to stop my panic. "Before you freak out, the note says they'll pay double the regular cost of the performance."

My jaw snapped shut and I let those numbers roll through my mind. Just that one performance, at double the price, would cover almost all of my supplies for the semester. Just the thought of having sex with Jackson, who I barely knew, in front of someone made me lightheaded. I knew eventually, I'd make my way to it, but I figured I'd have time to work up to sex.

My skin seemed to be alive with fire the way it heated at the idea, but my heart seemed to be pumping too fast. I didn't know if it was because of excitement or fear.

"Look, I wouldn't ask if the money wasn't so great. Also, it's been requested as lovemaking, so that usually entails below the covers. Kind of like all the times you've been getting off hidden by your underwear. I don't have to penetrate. I can pull your thigh over mine and hide it."

"Were there—" I had to clear my throat past the ball of nerves. "Were there any other requests?" I asked staring at this throat, watching his Adam's apple bob.

"Um, just some oral. For you. I give you oral sex, but I can pretend to do that too," he rushed to assure me.

The possibilities swirled in my mind, and I calculated the amount of solo performances I'd have to do to make the same amount of money. In the end, agreeing to this was the smart decision to make.

It wasn't even real sex. I just had to be naked in front of Jackson and, honestly, that didn't bother me. I wasn't even sure what did bother me.

That I'd like it, a voice rang out in the back of my head.

Squeezing my eyes closed, I nodded in agreement before I could change my mind. "Yeah. Sure, Jackson. Just let me know when."

"Now."

"Now?" I didn't know why I was shocked like the time made a difference in what was going to happen. I just figured I'd have more time to mentally prepare. Then again, maybe just letting it happen and not mentally preparing was better. Jackson looked like he was holding his breath, and I shook off my nerves and put him out of his misery. "Okay. Now is fine. Okay."

Two strong arms banded around me and lifted me off my feet. "God. Thank you, Oak. I promise it will be the best pretend sex of your life."

Once my feet hit the ground again, I gave him my hardest stare. "It better be."

He laughed and grabbed my hand, leading me toward the back hallway, to hopefully the best pretend sex I'd ever have.

We broke apart to go freshen up before we entered the room, letting the voyeur get settled. Once the light had been switched to green we'd decided to enter making out, like we were a couple coming in from a late night.

"Ready?" Jackson asked once we stood outside the door.

"As I'll ever be."

"Remember, it's just a performance. Not real. Try not to fall in love with me." He finished with a wink.

I remembered the lack of fire between us, grateful for how much easier this would be. I shook off my nerves and rolled my eyes. "I'll try not to."

"Panic button is on the nightstand should you need to use it," the guard said. "I'll be out here the whole time."

Jackson leaned down and pressed a kiss to my lips with his hand on the knob. My lids fell closed as I breathed deep through my nose. Then a strong arm wrapped around my waist and I was being tugged into the room. My hands dug into his hair as I pushed myself close to him. He kicked the door closed and hoisted me up with both palms on my ass.

I opened my lips and tasted the mint on his tongue before he began trailing kisses down my neck. When he'd reached the bed, he gently lay me down and slowed the frantic pace we came in with. It took all I had not to let my gaze flick to the large, dark glass off to my right.

Being with Jackson was more than I'd anticipated for the night. But imagining someone on the other side—a man—with his cock in his hand as he watched me, sent a spike of adrenaline through my limbs. I wasn't even sure it was a man. I hadn't looked at the sheet. It could've been a woman or a couple, but the image of a man fueled me, gave me the picture I needed to focus and get amped up.

I was distracted by my white T-shirt being lifted and pulled over my head, leaving me in a barely-there white lace bra. Jackson stripped himself of his own white shirt and then fell to his knees on the floor at my feet lining his face up perfectly with my chest. Holding my gaze, he lifted his hands to my breasts, swiping his thumbs along the hardened tips before hooking them in the cups and tugging them down.

He didn't immediately look at my bared breasts, but continued to look into my eyes, conveying a comfort that I could trust him. I was thrust back into remembering when he kissed me the first time. It had felt nice, I'd enjoyed it, but nothing about it urged me to demand more. The same stretched between us at that moment.

It was a performance. Like actors in a play. Some nights, when working there felt like too much, I reminded myself of that. Voyeur was a job, and I was an actress.

My body still reacted when his mouth dropped to suck on my nipple. My core still squeezed when he began unbuttoning my jeans and tugging them off my legs. My muscles still trembled as he pushed me back on the bed, hoisting a thigh over his shoulder and planting his mouth at the top of my mound.

My whole being seemed to be vibrating with nerves of excitement, of fear. What if the customer knew that Jackson wasn't actually eating me out, but just pretending to? What if they demanded their money back and this was all for nothing? His head dropped lower, skimming my folds and I forced myself to relax. It had to appear natural and I used the tension to arch my back and moan. When his tongue flicked out to slip between my folds and graze my clit on his way back up, I let out a real gasp and one hand shot out to grip the sheet as the other dug into his hair.

I wanted to ask him what the hell he was doing. Remind him that we agreed on pretend and not him actually tasting me. But when he didn't do it again, just tortured me with anticipation of the possibility as he moved closer and closer to my slit, I instead focused on acting natural. This needed to appear natural. I picked up my breathing, my writhing, my moans until I tightened my whole body in a fake orgasm.

It wasn't hard considering I had Jackson's head between my legs. But my mind wasn't on him. It was on whoever watched me behind the glass. Add in the soft touches against my folds, and I felt like a live-wire ready to detonate for real.

Soft kisses worked their way up my body to caress my nipples. Jackson's large hands framed my hips and pushed me further across the bed until my head was almost hanging off the other side. He tugged the cover out from under us, pushing it down and bunching it up at my hip to attempt to block the direct view of us having sex. He crawled between my legs after grabbing a condom, never taking his eyes off of mine.

He didn't let them rove my body and stare when he didn't need to. He respected me and the situation, and we performed. We did our job.

When he finally undid his pants just enough to free his cock, he looked down to roll the condom on, and I couldn't help but look too. Jackson was big. He was long, thick, and perfectly straight. It matched his body perfectly.

Giving him the same respect as he gave me, I quickly averted my eyes, giving him an adoring look as I scanned up from his sculpted abs and defined chest. I stroked my hands up the smooth skin of his arms and gripped his shoulders. He lifted my thigh and then reached to grab his cock to situate it.

Hopefully, to the viewer, it looked as though he was sliding inside me, when in reality, he pressed himself between my folds and began to thrust. The long glide of him brushed against my swollen clit and I knew, despite pretending, I was going to come from the friction alone.

His forehead rested on mine as his thrusts became harder, until he fell into the crook of my neck, picking up the pace. Faster and faster he stroked across me. His hand gripped my thigh tight, holding it in place. All of it swam through me and consumed my body.

But my mind? My mind was focused on the stranger behind the glass. For all I knew it could be an older couple, not even watching as they fucked like bunnies. But in my mind, it was the man from the bar. In my mind, he'd been staring at me and wanting me all night. In my mind, he approached me and took me home and was the man above me. His broad body flexing with each thrust, pushing inside me, filling me up.

I didn't even know his face, but when I began to come, it didn't matter. All that mattered was holding on as groans of pleasure vibrated the skin of my chest and my body struggled to ground itself back to the bed. Jackson pressed his head into my neck as he groaned out his own release, pushing hard against my sensitive clit, drawing a few more aftershocks from my orgasm.

"Thank you," he whispered against my skin once he'd finished, anchoring me to the moment.

I gave him a barely-there smile as he rolled to his side, shedding his pants and tugging off the condom filled with his cum. I forced myself to look away, the picture seeming more intimate than what we'd just done. He leaned back down and shifted us until we laid under the covers, my head resting on his shoulder.

He kissed the crown of my head, but my gaze didn't leave the light by the window. It was still green, meaning someone was still in there. Was this the part that made them come? The aftermath, the connection? Was this what they liked to watch?

I stared at the light until my eyes burned. I wasn't even sure how long I'd been watching before it finally switched to red and I blinked, looking away.

"So," Jackson started. "Best pretend sex you've ever had?"

"You weren't supposed to actually lick me," I reprimanded with little heat.

"I had to at least have a taste. Your wetness was too alluring."

"Stop," I laughed and slapped his arm.

"I won't do it again. No matter how wet your pussy gets against my chin."

I laughed.

I laughed at his question.

I laughed at the bizarre situation of lying naked with a man I just pretended to fuck.

I laughed because I enjoyed it. I enjoyed the idea of the man behind the glass coming as he watched me.

I laughed because I didn't know how to handle these feelings and laughing was easier.

Chapter Five

Callum

"You taste so fucking good," I said into her thigh. She arched up, searching for my lips back on her pussy. I kissed up and over one hip, across her mound and down the other side before slipping my tongue through her wet slit. Her moan fueled me. Using my thumbs, I parted her like a flower, opening her to my mouth, and burrowed my tongue inside her, loving the way her cunt squeezed me.

Her panting grew heavier when I concentrated my tongue on her clit, flicking it faster and harder, stopping occasionally to circle the tight bud and torture her. I loved her whimpers and moans, the way she rose up to fuck my face. Her sweet, tangy cum coated my chin and I savored it, loved having her all over me as her groans of pleasure stroked my skin. I watched her breasts rise as she arched, tightening her whole body through her orgasm, and I sucked up every drop.

"Please," she whimpered. "Please, Callum."

"Do you want me to fuck you?" I rose up between her slim thighs and gripped my aching cock, rubbing it up and down her slit, coating myself in her cum. "Are you ready for me to fill this wet cunt with my cock?"

"God, yes. Please."

I slipped inside, her lips wrapping around my length as her warmth enveloped my aching cock. I leaned down to suck on her nipple, biting at the tip as I buried myself deep inside her. I grinded against her, loving the way my balls felt pressed against her soft ass.

Then I pulled back, kissing my way up her neck, and thrust back in. I nipped at her parted lips, slowly fucking her harder with each thrust. Her whimpers brought a smile to my face.

Brushing her light brown hair back from her face, I stared down into her golden eyes. "Are you ready for me to really fuck you now?"

My body jerked up in bed, sweat chilling on my skin, the sheet kicked down past my knees. My hand wrapped around my aching cock, squeezing it tight, the head angry and purple and desperate for release.

I couldn't believe I dreamed of her. I couldn't believe I woke up still hard and with her still on my mind. I couldn't believe it didn't morph into a nightmare.

I fell back onto my pillows, but didn't let go of my cock. Gray light filtered in through the curtains. I had to be up soon, but I wanted to finish this rare moment. I wanted to bask in the fantasy my mind had granted me. Closing my eyes, I blocked all of it out and took myself back to the room. I remembered the way my hand dug into the wall as the other worked my cock, keeping pace with each whimper that escaped her parted lips. Keeping pace with the way her tits bounced on each thrust.

Fuck, her breasts were only a slight handful, but the way they shook, the rosy tips taunting me, begging me for my tongue. I groaned like I had in that room, desperate to feel her fingers dig into my arm, finding purchase to hold on to me as I fucked her. God, it'd never been so easy to place myself into a scene I watched play out before me, but I had. I imagined her thighs wrapped tightly around my hips. I imagined how hot and wet she'd be on my cock, the way her pussy would suck me back in with its tight squeezes, desperate for me to fill her back up.

My fist worked faster, my muscles straining, aching for the orgasm I wanted to find inside her tight cunt. I wanted to grind my balls on her as I emptied everything I had inside her, feeling her pulse around me as I leaned down to feast on the sound of her pleasure.

Shocks rippled down my spine into my balls and white ropes of cum shot out, landing on my chest and abs. I moaned through it all, hearing her moans again. This time mixing with mine.

My cock jerked at the non-existent sound, the idea enough to cause more ripples of pleasure to rack my body. Slowing the motion of my fist, I looked down at my softening cock and the mess on my body, not feeling sad or ashamed.

I'd never been so entranced with a performer before that I woke up jerking off to memories of her. Especially in my dreams. Usually when I jerked off, it was to a porno and the face was blank. Not this time. This time the girl was beneath me, the image so perfect, my chest filled with euphoria just with remembering it.

It was a good way to start the first day of a new semester, with a positive feeling wrapped around me. I lay there for another few minutes until my alarm went off, and then finally got up to shower and prepare for the day.

I nudged the syllabus a quarter-inch up the desk, so it lined up with the corner and the worksheet beside it. Then I pulled my pen from my bag and set it evenly between the two sheets. Just as I was about to organize the dry erase markers by alphabetical color, the first student walked in.

I greeted him with a smile. "Welcome to Astronomy."

He gave me a tired nod and moved to the back of the class. I was sure nine in the morning felt much earlier for college students. Especially on the first day.

Perched on the edge of my desk, I greeted each student who walked through the doors. This semester I was teaching astronomy for the non-physics majors. They tended to lack the enthusiasm of the students who were ready to begin their knowledge of the stars. I made sure my love of the subject came through enough to spark an interest for all of them. If the teacher wasn't excited about the material, then why would the students be?

Most professors dreaded teaching the non-majors, but I saw it as a challenge to try and convince just one student to love the stars, planets, and everything in between.

"Hello, welcome to Astronomy."

More head nods and a few wide eyes from the girls walking in. I'd been teaching for three years now and was used to it. I was younger than most of the professors in the school, and I wasn't oblivious to my looks. So, I ignored them and kept my smiles polite and my attention short, not wanting to encourage anything. I looked out over the class and saw almost all the seats filled. Only a few more minutes and then I'd begin.

"Hello. Welc—" My throat closed up over the words when I went to greet the next set of students entering the room.

Two girls. One a blonde I'd never seen before.

The other?

The other was her. The girl from Voyeur. In my classroom. As a fucking student.

As *my* student.

Blood pounded through my veins; the whooshing sound blocking out the chatter and movement of the classroom. My vision narrowed, and I focused solely on her. She was smiling, laughing at something her friend said.

She looked so much the same and yet so different. At Voyeur, she walked with an air of confidence, of maturity. Sometimes wearing only lingerie. But as she strode in wearing her skinny jeans and over-sized sweater, she looked so much like a student that I was kicking myself for not seeing how young she was before. Even worse was that most students in my class were freshmen, but I had to hold out hope that maybe she was older. Maybe a senior just getting her last requirements? I cringed, feeling like a pervert for getting off to an eighteen-year-old.

Fuck.

My lungs seemed to be collapsing inside my chest, making it impossible to take a breath deep enough to control myself. Forcing my head down, I stared at my shoes and counted the laces along the top. Anything to help get myself together. When I was able to fill my lungs, I forced a smile and looked up.

"Welcome to Astronomy."

She faced me from her seat and smiled. I waited for the recognition—dreaded it. Not that she could say anything due to the NDA, but I couldn't even begin to fathom the complications. But the recognition never came. As soon as her attention was on me, it was gone. She looked back at her friend who nudged her and whispered something while staring at me.

I didn't even want to imagine what she was saying.

The last of the students straggled in and everyone got settled. I tried to move my attention everywhere, but it inevitably kept going back to her. I watched her take out her pen and then her notebook, mesmerized by her slim fingers gripping the plastic.

I knew what those fingers looked like when they were squeezed in ecstasy.

God, I'd come so hard when she cried out in her second orgasm, her small fist against her partners back. Her legs flexed with tension. I'd gripped my cock, pumping harder and harder, unable to hold back the groan to match the sounds she'd made.

Shaking my head, I pulled myself from the memory and moved around the desk to my seat before anyone noticed my semi-erection.

Student. She's your fucking student.

After mentally listing the names of different galaxies to help get me back on track, as well as taking a deep breath, I was ready to stand and start class.

"Good morning. I'm Dr. Pierce and you are in Astronomy 101. This is the elective for non-physics majors, but maybe by the end of the year, I can convince you to come over to the dark side."

A few students laughed at my mild humor while others muttered, "Yeah, right." Typical responses.

"Since it's the first day, we'll just cover the syllabus, introduce ourselves, and then I'll let you back out into the wild."

I grabbed the stack of papers and handed them in handfuls to the students in the front row, instructing them to take one and pass them back.

It didn't take long to go over the basics; grades, attendance, exam dates, and class expectations. And I'd managed to do most of it without staring at her. I didn't even know her name yet.

Once we were done, I resumed my position against the desk and thought of a way to get the information I desired.

Knowing how old she was seemed to be the most important piece of information, and if it meant I had to ask every student, then so be it. "Okay, let's go around so everyone has a chance to introduce themselves. Tell me your name, so I can cross you off the attendance list. Then your age, what year you are, and your major."

"How old are you?" a brunette asked from the front row. Her question elicited giggles from her friends, and I smiled obligingly.

"I'm twenty-nine, and I've been teaching here for three years. When I was an undergraduate, physics was my major." I gestured toward her. "Now, why don't you go ahead and get us started."

We went around almost the entire classroom before she finally spoke. Her voice was soft and seemed to reach across the space between us as if to stroke against my skin.

"I'm Oaklyn Derringer, and I'm majoring in biology with the intention of going into physical therapy."

"And your age?" I felt like everyone would know why I was asking, would be able to hear the slight tremble in my voice, and I fought the blood rushing to my cheeks down.

"Duh. Forgot that part," she said with a laugh. "I just turned nineteen. I'm a freshman."

Freshman.

Nineteen.

The flush that had threatened me moments before was no longer an issue. All the blood seemed to have left my body. The next three student's answers were blocked by the ringing in my ears. Their smiles and faces unseen as I stared at nothing, trying to make myself breathe.

A freshman. I'd jacked off to a fucking nineteen-year-old freshman. My stomach turned, and guilt seemed to fight a path through me. But watching her walk out of my class once I'd dismissed them, remembering her dusky peaked nipples on her perky breasts, the guilt evaporated, replaced by desire and need.

I didn't trust myself. I needed to avoid her as much as I could. I was sure I could handle seeing her in class only. But I had to avoid her at Voyeur. Maybe I'd explain the situation to Daniel and have him tell me when she wasn't working.

The easy solution would be to just not go back, but I needed Voyeur too much to stop going.

It would be fine. I would just keep reminding myself of her age and that she's my student and I'd resist.

It would all be fine.

Chapter Six

Oaklyn

I will survive this.

That was going to be my mantra for the next few months. I'd worked late at Voyeur last night, then had classes, and now I was shoving a peanut butter and jelly sandwich in my mouth as I hauled ass across campus to the physics department. It was my first day there and I'd feel like a giant tool being late. Especially since I was only added on last minute by the grace of the worker in the bursar's office.

Second day of classes and it already felt overwhelming, but I had to remember that it would even out, and I'd get used to the crazy schedule.

As I opened the large door to the cream stone building, I had to wonder if I'd run into Dr. Pierce. I couldn't help but think about him. Remember the intensity of his light blue eyes, even more startling under the almost black hair, as he'd seemed to stare a hole right through me. I'd tried to ignore it, telling myself I was imagining things and he gave the same look to all his students, but it seemed impossible not to feel it.

A part of me had begun to wonder if I had something on my face. I'd even turned to ask Olivia, and she'd looked at me like I'd grown a third eye before quickly shifting her attention back to Dr. Pierce. Not that I could blame her. He was extraordinarily attractive and young and not at all what I'd expected going into the first class of my second semester. I couldn't help but wonder why he was a teacher, but immediately shut it down, feeling silly for thinking that someone so attractive should be living a bigger life.

He'd seemed to have a passion for the topic as he'd explained some of the things we'd cover. It made his intensity all the more distracting. At least the class would hold my attention if for no other reason than I'd like staring at his lips move as he spoke.

I almost hoped I didn't see him in the department while I was scheduled to work. That way I wouldn't have to face what might be developing into a silly crush on a far superior specimen—my professor.

With a smile on my face, I shook off my thoughts and pushed open the door to the main physics office. A heavy-set woman with white hair and a sweet smile greeted me from behind a desk.

"Hello. How can I help you, sweetheart?"

"Hi. I'm Oaklyn Derringer. I'm here to work as the student aide this semester."

"Oh, of course." She got up from behind her desk and walked around to greet me. "I'm Donna, the secretary for the department. Why don't you set your stuff right here by my desk and I can show you around and introduce you."

It was a fairly short tour. Only a small hallway on one side with three rooms, one of which was a conference room, and then another exit. On the other side was the dean of physics office, and in the middle of the two was the secretary's desk in a small waiting area that held about four chairs and a plant.

"I'm so glad you're here. We lost one of our older students last semester and weren't sure if we'd get another. Physics tends to be a smaller community. Are you a physics major?"

"Oh, no. I'm a bio major with hope of doing physical therapy."

"Well, goodness. What brings you here?"

I answered with a laugh. "Desperation?"

She made her way back around the desk and sat, chuckling at my response. "Either way, I'm happy to have another lady around here."

I sat when she gestured to the seats closest to her desk and waited as she pulled up her computer.

"Let's see. You'll be assisting Mr. Erikson. He runs the labs, so you'll help prepare and clean the supplies. And Dr. Pierce."

My heart both dropped and beat a little harder at hearing his name. But I tried to ignore it, not wanting to embarrass myself by stuttering or blushing or something equally as dumb.

"The other teachers tend to have student workers that they have worked with for a while. Hudson, the student who left, had helped Dr. Pierce the most, so you'll be filling his shoes. But no worries, Dr. Pierce is a very kind man."

"Did I hear my name?" a male voice called from the short hallway. And then, there he was. Tall and so broad his shoulders seemed close to touching each wall. He looked at Donna with a charming warm smile. One that you'd give your grandma.

"Sure did," Donna said. "I was telling our new student aide how nice you are since she'll be helping you and Mr. Erikson this semester."

She gestured toward me, and I offered the best smile I could muster, knowing it looked just as forced as it felt.

Deep breaths. Don't blush. Do not blush!

His eyes swung to mine and he froze. Only for a moment, almost an unnoticeable moment, before he moved again and greeted me.

"Yes. Ms. Derringer. We met yesterday in class." His smile was polite and distant, although I was certain he'd had more of a reaction than he was currently showing. "What brings you to work in the physics department?"

A part of me wanted to joke about desperation again, but I answered as truthfully as I could. "Just trying to pick up more hours to help with tuition."

"Good. A hard worker." He nodded his head and then turned back to Donna. "I have a meeting in ten minutes, but then I'll be back. Is there any way you could copy these for me for tomorrow?"

"Of course, Dr. Pierce. I'll make sure Oaklyn has them to you by this afternoon."

He didn't look my way again as he said thank you and disappeared behind the door with his name beside it.

"Well, let me take you down to Mr. Erikson. He's in the lab equipment room. I'm sure he can get you situated and show you the ropes. When we're done down there, I'll show you how to work the copier."

I followed Donna out of the office and down the hallway three doors before entering the equipment room. It was full of glass beakers and flasks, and machines I'd never seen before, nor had a clue what they did. Mr. Erikson was an easygoing guy, if not a little quiet and nerdy. He had thick glasses, a soft voice, and he stuttered over words sometimes. But I couldn't complain. I preferred silence to a Chatty Cathy.

Mr. Erikson explained the rules and then left me with a sheet of paper to use to inventory the materials. Seventies rock music played softly in the background, and my time working seemed to fly by. Before I knew it, we'd inventoried the whole room and three hours had passed. Only a couple more, and I'd be able to head out for a night not filled with performances.

Waving goodbye to Mr. Erikson, I collected my backpack and headed down the hallway to make Dr. Pierce's copies.

With a warm stack of papers in my hand, I knocked on Dr. Pierce's door.

"Come in," he said, his deep voice reaching through the door.

"I have those papers you asked for."

He looked up from his work and stared at me through thick-rimmed glasses. "Oh. Yes. Thank you. If you just want to set them there, please."

I placed the papers on the corner of his desk and stepped back, watching him shift them to line up with the edge of the desk.

"Nice glasses."

"Thank you. I hate them. I'm twenty-nine and already need readers. Makes me look like an old man," he said with a deprecating laugh.

"Hardly," I chuckled. The word slipped from my lips without thinking it through. Swallowing hard, I looked down, unable to see his reaction. "Anyways, did you need anything else? I'm here for about another hour."

His eyes flicked around the room like he was searching for tasks that may need to be done. "Actually, yes. I have those boxes of papers stacked over there. They're already marked, but I need them alphabetized and filed away."

My eyes widened when I saw the five filing boxes piled next to a cabinet. He must have noticed because he laughed and attempted to reassure me.

"You don't need to get them all done today. Maybe just shoot for one box. A professor who retired last semester left me some of his journals and research files."

"That's a little bit more than some."

"If you'd have seen the rest, you wouldn't be saying that. Boxes were stacked almost to the ceiling in his office. In multiple piles."

"Well, it's a good thing you only got away with five. Otherwise, I'd be here until you retired."

He laughed, and I became a little mesmerized by his smile. The creases in his cheeks. The small dimple in his chin a little more apparent as the skin stretched across it.

When he looked up, I averted my eyes, feeling like a child caught staring. "Well, I should get started then."

We worked in a companionable silence for almost an hour. He would leave, but immediately return. Every once in a while, I'd turn to find him looking at me, and he'd just smile or nod before returning to his work. He probably just wanted to make sure I didn't mess anything up. He seemed very meticulous. I'd look over and watch him shift a pen to line up with the paper, or make sure every piece of paper sat the same distance from the edge, just small things. I had to force myself to stop looking before I got caught staring again.

"Well, I'm heading out," Donna said, popping her head in through the doorway. "Callum, don't work this poor girl too hard."

"But I thought you told me she was my indentured servant forever," he said, furrowed eyebrows directed at Donna.

She narrowed her eyes back. "I would never," she said, turning to wink at me. "Have a good night you two. Callum, I'll see you tomorrow. Oaklyn, I'll see you Friday?"

"Yes, ma'am."

"Okay. Have a good night."

When she left, Dr. Pierce leaned back in his seat and stretched his arms above his head. I had to pinch the skin between my forefinger and thumb to force myself to look away from how his light blue dress shirt stretched across his broad chest.

"I guess we should call it a night. Didn't realize it was already after five."

"Oh, wow. Time flies when you're filing papers."

"Most thrilling job out there."

I liked his quick banter and easy responses.

"Thank god, since I'm going to be doing it forever as your indentured servant. Don't lie, you actually have all those boxes stacked in a room waiting for me."

He smiled and put his hands up. "You caught me."

"Well, I'll be back Friday to pick up where I left off."

Before grabbing my things, I placed the lid back on the box and cleaned up my area.

"It's late. Do you need an escort?" Dr. Pierce asked.

I giggled like an idiot, opening my mouth before thinking. "I'm good without a male escort."

"Oh, uh. I . . . uh, didn't mean it like that."

"I know. Sorry, I have a weird sense of humor." My cheeks burned from saying something so stupid to my teacher. But when I looked at him, red tinged his cheeks too. And he was still laughing.

"Next time I'll definitely clarify. I'd hate for Donna to give me a speech on offering to be a male escort to a student. Don't tell her, but she scares me a little."

"Nonsense. Donna is an angel."

"An angel who can put this whole office of males in their place." We both laughed at the image. Once we'd gathered ourselves, he asked again more clearly. "Do you need someone to walk you to your car?"

"No, thank you. I'm just running to my friend's dorm right across the way."

He nodded. "Okay. Just be safe."

And with a wave, I was out the door, having survived the first day working for Dr. Pierce without drooling all over him.

I walked the short distance to Olivia's dorm and she greeted me, letting me in, before taking me to the common area with her other friends. Joining the study party, I pulled my books out knowing I wasn't going to get anything done. We started talking as soon as I sat down, and I had no doubt it would continue until I left.

"So, how was your first day in the physics department? Did all the geeky guys fawn over you? Were there any hot geeky guys? Please tell me there were."

I laughed at her rapid-fire questions. "I didn't see any, but if I do, I'll send them your way."

"This is why we're friends." She raised her hand for a high-five and I obliged. "But really, how was it?"

"It was good. I helped with lab equipment and then I assisted Dr. Pierce for the rest of the afternoon."

"Shut. Up," one of the girls on the opposite couch said. I think her name was Sandy. "He's so freaking hot. I seriously considered changing my major just for the opportunity to get close to him."

"Well, be jealous, bitch. Because Oaklyn and I have him for Astronomy this semester," Olivia taunted.

"Whore," Sandy returned with a smile.

"I've heard he's a manwhore," the other girl said. "But totally reserved."

"How would you know, Cindy?" Olivia asked.

"How could he not be? Girls throw themselves at him all the time. I'm sure he takes advantage."

"But he's a teacher. Surely, he wouldn't do anything with a student," Sandy said.

Cindy just shrugged her shoulders, letting her gossip lay wherever it fell. "The quiet ones are always the freakiest. They have the biggest secrets."

The girls moved on to another topic, but I couldn't get past what they'd said. I didn't think it was true about Dr. Pierce. Sure, I'd caught him staring at me a few times, but it hadn't felt sexual. Just intense.

My stomach fluttered thinking about it, so I shut it down. I had to work with him, and if rumors were already going around about him, I didn't want to encourage more gossip.

Chapter Seven

Callum

"I'm so happy you called again," Shannon said from across the table.

I didn't really know what to say, so I gave a noncommittal hum and smile, hoping it reassured her that I was happy I did too. Even if I wasn't sure why I'd called her again.

Liar.

Oaklyn's smiling face, her smell, the way she looked when she came and the way it filtered into my dreams—*that* was why I'd called Shannon. I wanted to try and get my mind off of Oaklyn.

"The holidays made it hard to find time, huh?" she continued. "They did for me too. Then my grandmother needed help back home after hip surgery, which made me late to start my new job. But I'll get there next week."

"I'm sorry to hear about your grandmother. I hope she's doing better."

"Much."

She continued to talk about her trip home and a tiff between her and her cousin. I took a sip of my bourbon and zoned out. She did enough talking for both of us. Shannon was beautiful with a wide smile and a joie de vivre she couldn't fake. As for me, it had taken a few drinks in the dark of my stiff sitting room before I'd finally convinced myself to call her.

I'd needed someone to help distract me from the past week at school with Oaklyn. It had been torture. She was friendly to everyone and had a bright laugh that lit her face. I'd watched her smile with such innocence, and I'd had a hard time reconciling her to the girl who fucked in front of people. The girl I wasn't going to go see this weekend. I could spend one weekend away from Voyeur.

I still hadn't called Daniel about her schedule. I was too scared to explain my predicament to someone else, and I'd just decided not to go.

But I thought about it constantly. I would find myself wondering about the guy she was with. Occasionally, I'd be able to identify the twisting in my stomach as jealousy. Wanting to do to her what he'd done to her. Knowing I couldn't.

I wondered who else had watched her. Was it anyone she was around on a daily basis? Were they keeping it from her? Or was I the only pervert lusting over my nineteen-year-old student?

But at least I was trying to change that. Which was why I was sitting across from Shannon instead of at the bar at Voyeur.

"Would you like any dessert?" our waiter asked, halting Shannon's monologue and bringing me back to the present.

"Oh, no," Shannon said with a smile, her hand on her stomach. "I shouldn't. Gosh, I can't. I'm so full."

"No dessert this time, thank you," I said to our waiter, but kept my eyes on Shannon. I'd hated that I'd zoned her out. I didn't like making my dates feel like they didn't have my full attention.

"Another bourbon for you?"

"No, thank you. I'll just take the check."

Shannon reached inside her purse and I halted that. I was old-fashioned in believing that I'd asked her out, therefore it was my treat.

My chivalry seemed to light a fire in her eyes as she took the last sip of her wine. When she set it down she dragged her finger along the wet rim, her gaze heavy and full of desire.

"Would you like to come to my place for a drink?"

I should have seen the question coming. And maybe I had, but I still had to ask myself: Could I? I knew what it entailed. I knew what she was really asking. And I wanted to. I wanted to lay down with her and feel her skin pressed to mine without a sheen of sweat covering my body as tremors shook my limbs. I wanted to follow this woman home and possess her in a way that made me forget the innocence that taunted me.

I needed to prove I could do this, and I needed to push Oaklyn from my mind.

I would focus on Shannon and her beauty and let that guide me. Let that anchor me in the moment.

"That sounds nice."

She smiled, not hearing the slight tremble I fought to mask.

I followed her out to her car, walking her to her door and got her address letting her know I'd meet her there.

When I got in my car, I did the breathing exercises I'd been doing since I was a teen. Giving myself positive affirmations. I could do this. I could go further than before. I could let her hands touch me and pleasure me without panicking.

My sweaty palms gripped the wheel tightly as I drove to her place. Once I'd pulled into the apartment complex, I waited a bit. Getting my heartbeat down to normal and thinking about Voyeur to amp up my desire and overcome the nerves. When I closed my eyes, I saw Oaklyn's head pressed back, her lips open on a moan of pleasure, and my cock began to harden.

My eyes flicked open, pushing her from my mind. I stepped out of the car, letting the cool night air wash over me.

Shannon greeted me at the door with a smile and another glass of bourbon. As soon as I entered, her fingers linked with mine, and she moved me to her couch. I took one sip, letting the spicy alcohol slide down my throat and held her eyes. I set my glass on the coffee table and brought her fingers to my lips, kissing each one.

I knew I was good at the seduction, at making a woman feel wanted, letting her know I desired her. I could even pleasure a woman repeatedly until she forgot her name. Whisper dirty words and touch her perfectly.

I just couldn't follow through and let her reciprocate before the past sunk in on me.

Shannon set her glass down before scooting close enough to press her thigh to mine and leaning in to kiss me. I watched her eyes close as her soft lips pressed to mine. Watched her lashes slip closed as she allowed me entrance to her mouth and I tasted the fruity wine on her tongue. When her hands began to skim up my thighs, I linked my fingers with hers and held them between us.

I wanted the kissing to last longer. If I had to be honest, I was lonely, and kissing was an intimacy I could gain the most from. I needed this.

My heart kicked up when her hands slipped from mine and moved to my shoulders as she threw a leg over my lap and straddled me. Her flowy skirt rode up her thighs and exposed the tops of her stockings. When she began to grind on me, I moved back to the kissing. I cupped her breasts, trying to remind myself of who was on top of me. She moaned as I flicked my thumbs across her nipples and the sound sent shockwaves down to my cock and hope floating through me.

But then her hands dropped to the crotch of my pants and I jerked, my heart beating in an uneven pattern before settling into an erratic thump. I focused on the feel of her soft breasts under my palms. I focused on her vanilla scent that screamed woman. I focused on her face and smooth lips smiling at me as she got my zipper undone.

Thankfully it was dim in the room, the only light coming from the kitchen through an open doorway. She couldn't see the sweat beading on my forehead. Or the panic fighting its way through my body. As soon as her small hand snaked under my pants and brushed the skin of my dick, I lost. I lost the battle with my past, with my ability to hide my panic. I hit a brick wall of shame and embarrassment.

I didn't want to have to explain to her how I'd gone so far and why I was jerking back now. So, I did the next best thing. I flipped her to her back and pinned her hands above her head. Her eyes widened in excitement and she rolled her hips against mine. I kissed down her neck as I worked my hand under her panties and pushed my fingers inside her. I worked her over, using all the skills I'd learned when I needed to avoid the topic of why their hands weren't on me. She moaned, and I focused on the task until she was squeezing around my fingers.

I knew what came next. That she'd want to return to touching me and I couldn't. I'd tried, and I'd failed, and now I needed to get the hell out of there.

As soon as she'd finished coming, I paused, freezing my whole body.

"Shit."

"What?" Shannon asked breathlessly.

"My phone is going off," I said, relying on her dazed state to distract her from the fact that my phone wasn't going off. "I've got to take this. I've been expecting a call from a friend. His wife is due any day now." I pressed one last kiss to her lips and pulled back, quickly refastening my pants.

"Oh. Okay." She copied my moves and adjusted her skirt as she walked me to the door. "Let's get together again soon," she said, stepping in close. Peeking up from below her lashes, she grazed her hand across my crotch and I fought to not flinch. "I want to return the favor."

I endured one last caress before I was able to escape. The touch churned my stomach and nausea burned through me.

I wasn't going to call her again. It had been a mistake to even try.

Sitting in my car, I waved and pulled off.

My jaw clenched as anger at myself replaced the nausea. Embarrassment burned my skin. At a stoplight, I considered turning the other way and going to Voyeur. Maybe she'd be there. Maybe I'd be able to replace the feeling inside me with a better one. A performance to spark my imagination into something hopeful.

Without overthinking it, I made the turn toward Voyeur, my mind conjuring which boxes I'd check when I got there. I imagined a fist lost in Oaklyn's long hair, gripping it, holding her tight as she's fucked. Picturing myself as her partner helped the nausea and embarrassment wane. A manic joy brewed inside me with each mile, and by the time I'd reached the club, I was on the edge of losing it.

There I was, in the dark of my car, an erection straining against my pants at the thought of fucking my student.

The nausea roared back. I was her teacher. She was a teenager. And to make myself feel better, I imagined fucking her. I gripped the steering wheel, like holding it tightly would help me keep a grip on my self-control. I swallowed, weighing the pros and cons.

Pro: Go into Voyeur and feel better, imagining yourself in the place of some man who fucks Oaklyn.

Con: Make a rash decision and go inside to have your nineteen-year-old student make you feel better as you imagine fucking her.

What the hell was I doing?

I put the car in reverse and made my way home. Halfway there, I spotted a liquor store, and I swerved in to grab a bottle of bourbon, ready to make myself forget the mess I'd become.

Weak. I was weak, and I hated it. Deep breaths were my best friend as I made the last turn to my street. By the time I'd pulled into the driveway, I felt halfway human again. Halfway like a functioning adult. Enough of one to put the liquor in the top cabinet and not crack the seal just yet. I only needed to find complete control again, and I'd be fine.

I'd be fine.

Chapter Eight

Oaklyn

I'd lied to myself when I'd said I'd eventually adjust. It had been one week, and I was pretty sure I was dying from lack of sleep. I'd worked all weekend, including Sunday night. I hadn't gotten home until one and still had to study for a quiz I had the next day. Who gave a quiz in the second week of classes? Then I'd had to head to the physics department. Thankfully I'd been able to leave early since Mr. Erikson didn't have much work for me and Dr. Pierce hadn't been there.

I'd fallen into a small coma early in the evening and woke up earlier than usual that morning. I tried to keep my eyes closed and fall back into dreamland but failed. So, I went ahead to campus and figured I'd get some work done. I walked into the building where my physics class was, hoping to find it empty, so I could sit in there to work for the thirty minutes before class.

I looked in the room through the window to find all the seats empty and pulled the door open to enjoy the quiet. When I'd walked through the threshold, I noticed Dr. Pierce at his desk. His head popped up at the noise and he looked me over with that intense gaze again, the thick-rimmed glasses doing nothing to lessen the stare, before clearing his throat. "Hey, Oaklyn. You're here early." He pulled the white sleeve of his shirt back to check his watch to make sure I was indeed early.

"Hey, Dr. Pierce. I hope it's okay I'm here early."

"Of course. Have a seat."

I grabbed one in the front row and began unpacking my books. "No point in going to the library for thirty minutes just to pack up and leave again."

"Smart choice. Very efficient with your time. I can appreciate that."

A moment stretched where we both smiled at each other, not saying anything. His eyes lingered on me, softening, almost melting like they were warming. Or maybe that was just me, warming under his stare, interpreting it as more, wanting it to mean more. Butterflies fluttered in my stomach sinking into my core as I imagined him staring at me with heat burning my skin. An anxious energy flooded through me as I wondered if he could read my thoughts pouring from my own eyes.

I needed to break the moment before I made a fool of myself, so I blurted out the first thing I thought of. "You have that whole Superman thing going on with your glasses," I said, pointing at my own face. He tilted his head and gave me a confused look. Shit, I was so dumb. I'd have been better off letting the staring continue. "I mean, like, because Superman wears glasses."

"You mean Clark Kent."

"Um . . . " Now it was my turn to be confused.

"Clark Kent wears the glasses and when he takes them off he's Superman."

"Duh." I said with a self-deprecating laugh. "I'm more of a Marvel girl."

"That's a good choice. Marvel is better than DC any day." He pulled his glasses off and set them directly in the center of the paper he was working on, giving them a small nudge to line up evenly. "Are you sure you're not a physics major?"

"Positive."

"Well, you'd fit in perfectly in the department. You'll have to make sure you're around for when Mr. Erikson and Dr. Fischer get into their weekly debates about DC and Marvel."

I laughed. "That sounds . . . fascinating."

"Hey, they can get pretty heated."

"I don't doubt it."

Seeming pleased that I believed him, he moved on to another topic. "You're a biology major, correct?"

"Yup. Hoping to move forward with physical therapy."

"That's a lot of school."

"No more than you did."

"That's true. Why physical therapy?"

"Oh, I love anatomy and the way the body moves. All the mechanics about it. I find it fascinating how one small tear, sprain, or fracture can cause a butterfly effect of other issues. How amazing is the human body? I also, love the idea of helping others, but didn't really want to go full force into the medical field of hospitals and such."

My words faded as I noticed how his eyes dropped to my lips as I rambled. I licked them and then bit them in response to his gaze. The movement seemed to break his concentration and he sat up straight, clearing his throat. It was his turn to change the subject now.

"And you said you were nineteen?" He coughed after asking the question before continuing. "Did you wait a year after high school to come to college?"

"I wish," I said, rolling my eyes. "My birthday is in early November, so I'm always the oldest.

"Well, if it makes you feel better, my birthday is in late August, so I'm always the youngest. Trust me, it's much worse."

"I don't know," I said, leaning my elbows on the desk. Did his eyes just drop to the V in my shirt? He was probably just looking around, and I felt dumb thinking otherwise. God, at this rate, I was going to become campus gossip—the girl who tried to seduce her teacher because she imagined false advances. Heat seeped into my cheeks and I continued talking. "Being asked if you were held back because you couldn't write your letters is pretty rough."

"Very traumatic," he agreed with a nod. "It may be worse when you're called the baby when you can't go out with all your friends to the bars because you're only seventeen. Even worse when they call you to come pick them up after they managed to score drinks."

I rolled my lips over my teeth to hold back my laughter, finding it impossible to believe anyone would call the large Dr. Pierce a "baby".

"Sure, laugh it up," he joked.

"No, no. I'm not laughing at you. I'm laughing at the idea of anyone calling you a baby. I mean, were they giants? Or did you hit a late growth spurt?"

"I guess size didn't matter to them."

"I'm sure that was their excuse to all the girls."

As soon as the words left my mouth my eyes widened. I just made a sexual joke to my professor. I opened my mouth to take it back, swallow my words, something, when his head fell back, and a laugh exploded from his mouth. His throat exposed, looking more attractive than I thought any throat would look, and his chest shook with each sound. I wanted to go to him and bury my mouth against his skin, wondered how it tasted. I shook the thought away, feeling juvenile for even letting the thought cross my mind.

"I'm sure it was," he agreed, still laughing. Once he was under control he sat up and mirrored my position, his elbows on his desk. "So, are you from Cincinnati?"

"Nope." My voice cracked over the word and I had to clear my throat. Buy myself some time to rid the fantasies clamoring for space in my head. "From Florida. I wanted to move away from all that heat, and I'm hoping to attend graduate school here."

"Your family must miss you."

Just bringing up my family was a punch to the gut. I'd been avoiding their calls and responding with short messages, the hurt still too fresh. Especially when I was exhausted from all the work I had to do to make up for their mistake. "They're just happy I made it. I'm the first of my family to go to college." Which was why they didn't understand how serious I was.

"Did you get a scholarship to help with out of state costs?"

I snorted. My scholarship was sitting in my parents' driveway. "I did. Not enough, but some to help out."

"So, you work?"

For some reason he seemed as uncomfortable to ask about my possible job as I felt to answer. His eyes dropped to his hands clasped in front of him and swallowed.

I licked my lips and swallowed to buy some time to think of an answer that would hopefully divert his attention. Instead, my genius brain only came up with, "Yeah."

"Oh, um . . . where?"

"Um . . ." I lifted my head and froze. His blue eyes were locked on me, like he was holding me in place, demanding my truth. He looked at me like he already knew what I'd done. But there was no way, because he was Dr. Pierce and no teacher, not even a professor, made the kind of money to afford Voyeur; or would risk their position as a teacher to hang out at a sex club. "Um," I said again. "I work—"

The first few students walked in, saving me from coming up with a lie. I spent too much time with him to try and remember some random lie. Not only that, but I was the *worst* liar.

We each blinked and sat back in our seats. Dr. Pierce straightened his pens and papers that were already straight and moved to stand at the front of his desk as always, greeting the students as they came in.

Olivia came in and managed to distract me enough to let my heart calm down and get myself under control enough to focus. Once everyone was seated, Dr. Pierce began class.

"Hello, my name is Callum Pierce, and I have astrophilia."

Students shuffled and murmured their confusion as to why our professor was starting the class like an AA meeting, and wondering what the hell astrophilia was.

"A rare love and obsession with planets, stars, and outer space." His explanation brought a few laughs and some groans at how cheesy he was. "It's why I love teaching. And maybe, by the end of this semester, I can impart some of that love to you."

"Doubtful," a guy in the back said.

Dr. Pierce merely gave him a squinted look and continued. "Now that it's week two, I want to go ahead and assign you your end of the semester project." A chorus of groans broke out among the class. "I know, I know. Just horrible," he said with an exaggerated sigh and pretended to collapse against the desk. That earned him a few giggles from the other girls up front. "You will be picking one of the big stars to do a presentation about. In that presentation, I'd like you to use pictures you took yourself. Therefore, you will need to meet with me one night this semester, so I can help you work the telescope. I'll put the sign-up schedule on our dashboard online."

Once he'd finished explaining the criteria, he moved on to lecturing. But my mind was still stuck on meeting with him one night. Would the meetings be individual? I knew I saw him almost every day, but the idea of a dark sky filled with stars screamed intimacy. My chest fluttered at the thought.

And I squashed it, not letting myself continue down that path. I had shit to accomplish and didn't have time to lust after Dr. Pierce.

I refused to end up being another girl who giggled in the front of his class.

Especially since I was barely a blip on his radar.

Chapter Nine

Callum

Two days.

That was how long I stayed away from Voyeur after my conversation with Oaklyn on Tuesday.

Maybe she won't be here, I thought as I entered my identification code at the door. The hope was hollow at best considering a larger part of me hoped she would be there. I'd come earlier in the week and had missed her, telling myself I was happy about it. Then I'd watched another couple perform and struggled to not picture Oaklyn the whole time.

I was a fucking mess.

When I walked through the doors, I pulled my baseball cap low. I'd gone home to put on jeans, and a baseball cap, knowing I'd be asking for trouble to show up in the suit I wore to work that day. She'd spot me instantly and I couldn't even begin to imagine the ramifications of her knowing I was there. Guilt pinched my chest, but desire burned hotter and became bigger than anything else I could feel.

I discreetly tried to keep an eye on my surroundings and headed to the bar, sitting in the corner to get a better view. But when the bartender set my beer in front of me and moved away, Oaklyn stood at the other side, laughing with another employee.

I stared, I couldn't help it. She wore a long, flowing red silk chiffon robe, barely tied at her slim waist and hinting at her curves encased in a strappy red bra. I wanted to peel it off her. Wanted to see if her panties were just as flimsy as her bra. Wanted to see her take it all off for me.

Quickly, I dropped my chin, letting my hat cover my face when she began to turn to look in my direction. I squeezed the bottle, trying to let the cold, hard glass calm me down. Maybe if I slipped it between my legs it would ease the erection straining against my pants.

I ached to request her. To make her do all the things I fantasized about her doing. And I hated it. That wasn't the point of Voyeur. It wasn't to lust after a performer and fall in love with watching them. It was about watching anyone, the person unspecific to the fantasy. I felt like I was breaking the rules, and it had to stop. I chugged the rest of my beer and set it down before heading to an iPad and blindly selecting a woman for a solo performance.

But even with an oblivious selection, fate had set me up with a girl who looked similar to Oaklyn. I was fucked.

I moved back to my spot on the bar and waited to be notified the room was ready. This time I only asked for a water.

It didn't take long for a woman maybe in her forties to approach me. I wouldn't be able to guess her age if it wasn't for the fine lines around her eyes that gave her away. Otherwise her body was sleek, encased in a tight black skirt and white blouse that was mostly left unbuttoned.

"Hey, do you need any company?" she asked, trailing her finger down my arm. "I'm Anne by the way."

"Hey, Anne. I'm Cal, and unfortunately I've just made a selection and will be leaving soon." I added a smooth, regretful smile. I didn't want to be rude.

She licked her lips. "Do you need any company in there?" she asked, nodding her head toward the back rooms.

I had to admire her boldness. Most people came to Voyeur because they knew what they wanted, and they wanted to satisfy that craving for a kink most people didn't understand. I came because if I was going to be so fucked up, I'd at least have the best kind of porn available. I'd watch what I couldn't seem to force my body to go through with. But being there didn't usually mean you came to find someone to take to a private room and do whatever as the performance went on. Sure, conversations went on and people met like at a regular bar, but what happened in the back was usually not on the table without knowing someone.

"I'm okay alone tonight, but thanks for the offer."

Thankfully I was saved from further conversation when my wristband buzzed. With a final nod, I left and headed to the back room. It was dark when I entered, and I turned the knob on the light switch just enough so I could see where I was going. A black leather couch and two armchairs filled the middle of the room. Side tables sat between them, holding lamps on each. A shelf sat along one wall that held towels, an assortment of lotions and lubes, and condoms. Also, a binder with the other selections you could request, including dildos, straps, and about any other apparatus you could think to use in a small room with a couch and two chairs.

I grabbed a bottle of warming lube and a towel before flipping the switch to let them know I was ready and sat on the couch that faced the glass wall. From my side, the glass allowed me the privacy I wanted, but still let me feel like I was in the room. I knew from their side, it was a black shiny wall they couldn't see through.

I was unzipping my jeans when the girl came in. She moved around the room like she was at home before she sat on the edge of the bed and spread her legs. Her light brown hair fell behind her as she moaned when her fingers slipped beneath her white panties.

My cock grew harder and I gripped it tightly with lube coating my fingers. I stroked slowly up and down, swirling around the head and flexed my hips. Her bra came off and her large breasts seemed to defy gravity with how perky they were for their size. I tugged my jeans down a little further, pulling my balls out and cupping them in my hand, squeezing them with each stroke of my shaft.

Her breathing increased, and her moans became louder.

And I fought to chase an orgasm.

Her panties came off and both hands were working over her wet pussy.

I saw her long red nails and struggled to stay hard.

The performer's moans were too fake. Her breasts too large. Her makeup too heavy. And her pussy was completely shaved. I knew Oaklyn had a thin landing strip that matched the color of her hair.

All of it was wrong.

While I wanted to close my eyes and picture Oaklyn as I stroked myself to orgasm, I also didn't want to. I didn't want to have to admit what she did for me. I didn't want to admit the control I'd given her. I didn't want to admit how much I craved her.

"Fuck," I said on an angry breath.

I gave up, tucking my cock away after wiping myself down. I didn't want to turn off the light to let her know I was gone just yet. It felt disrespectful to not stay for the full performance and as much as I wanted to get the fuck out of there, I didn't want to hurt her feelings because I was slowly going insane. Thankfully, it didn't take long and as soon as she had come down from her over-the-top orgasm, I flipped the switch, letting them know I was gone, and bolted.

With my head down, I rounded the corner and smacked into someone. Immediately, I started to apologize and turned to see if the person was okay, when I heard her voice apologizing first.

Oaklyn.

"I'm so sorry. I totally rounded that corner too fast without even looking."

My heart jumped in my throat and panic zipped through my body.

I didn't think she had recognized me yet, so I kept my head down and didn't turn to her fully. With a gruff apology and saying it was okay, I got the hell out of there.

I waited to hear her call my name, chase me down to see that it was me, but it never came.

The cold night air welcomed me as I pushed through the doors and only one thought filled my head as I drove home.

That was too fucking close.

ɣ

Oaklyn

That was weird.

I watched the man walk away, his wide shoulders slouched over a trim waist. I hadn't got a good look at him before he bolted, just a strong jaw with stubble and a black ball cap covering his hair.

I shrugged off the encounter and the niggling feeling that he was familiar. I'd probably just seen him around Voyeur before. Then it clicked. He was the man at the bar from earlier. Charlotte had pulled my attention to him, letting me know he was staring at me pretty intently. I'd brushed it off, blaming my outfit and thought nothing more of it. The members at Voyeur stared and I tried not to think too much about it. I tried not to think too much about anything at Voyeur. Just let my body do the work and detach as much as I could.

"Dammit," I said when I turned to walk away and bumped into another hard body. Tonight wasn't my night.

Strong, warm hands gripped my biceps, steadying me. "You okay?" Jackson asked.

"Yeah. You're just the second guy I've bumped into in the last few minutes and I'm starting to question my ability to walk."

"I'm sure you walk just fine," Jackson said, chuckling. "You're just a man magnet."

"I guess there are worse things to be."

"And I was actually looking for you." I looked up and raised my eyebrows in question. "I got another request for a sex scene and you're the only woman here who I know isn't signed up for anything intense like the BDSM rooms. Plus, we put on a really good show. So, even though you're not signed up for it tonight, I wanted to ask anyway." He gave me his best smile, trying to lure me with his looks.

The problem for him, was that I wasn't affected by Jackson's looks and he knew it. You had to give the guy credit for trying.

"I'm sorry, Jackson. I just can't tonight. I'm too tired to even think about it."

"Setting my manly pride aside at you being too tired to think of hot sex with *me*," he joked. "Are you okay? You seem off tonight."

My shoulders dropped, and I let out a deep breath. I loved Jackson for caring. We'd only known each other for a little more than a month, but we'd become fast friends. Grinding on someone naked kind of forces a fast bond. But he didn't have to care for me as much as he did, and I counted my lucky stars that he did. This job was easier having him on my side.

"I'm okay. Just getting worn down. School and work and work and work are getting to me."

"I get it. When I was in college, I was working here too, and it takes its toll on you. Mind you, I wasn't working two student worker positions at the same time, but I can relate a little."

Jackson had a degree in marketing and actually helped Daniel out part time with the finances, but I hadn't fully asked him why he still performed and didn't go get a real job. Maybe I'd have to do dinner with him some time and get to the bottom of that.

"Okay, well I won't push. Even if the money is really good and you give great head."

I slapped his chest as he wrapped his arm around me but laughed all the same.

The money usually was good when we put on a sexual performance together, but we tried to get away with faking it as much as we could. And a couple of times when the money was high enough, I'd fallen to my knees for him or let him bend me over to perform oral. I'd let him touch me in a way that allowed people to watch his fingers between my thighs.

Yet, it still never formed a romantic connection between us. When the light turned red and we left the room, we were back to two friends bantering with each other. Every time we entered together, it truly felt like entering a stage and putting on a show. Hell, I got more excited from filing papers in the same room as my professor. I also felt more shame for that than working at Voyeur.

I was sure that Jackson got more excited thinking about the guy he liked. He was tight lipped about his attraction, but I'd begun to know him well enough to pick up on his cues.

"How's your guy?" I asked, noticing his jaw clench at my question.

"Straight as an arrow."

He looked down and gave me a smile, trying to play it off as a joke, but the smile didn't reach his eyes, and I hated it for him.

"I'm sorry, Jackson."

"No worries at all, Oak. It's why I swing both ways. I'm not limited to just one."

Just as we were about to enter the bar area, he gave me a tight squeeze and leaned down to whisper in my ear. "No matter the life we have now, we'll be fine in the long run."

Standing on my toes, I softly kissed his cheek. "I hope so."

Chapter Ten

Oaklyn

"No lunch today?" Dr. Pierce asked from behind his desk, unwrapping a sub sandwich.

I looked down, embarrassed by my lack of food. Not wanting to admit how poor I was, I settled on a half-truth. "I haven't had time to go to the grocery store, and out-of-state colleges kind of suck up all my eating out money."

"That's right. Yes, I know all about out-of-state fees."

"Where did you go?"

"I actually went here."

"Oh, that's cool. Where did you come from?"

"Well, Oaklyn, when a man and a woman love each other very much—"

"Oh, stop it," I said laughing, enjoying the way his laugh blended with mine. "You know what I meant. What state did you come from?"

"California."

"Wow, that's a long way away. What brought you here to Ohio?"

I almost regretted my question when he seemed to flinch. Maybe something had happened back home to make him escape to Ohio? Guilt assailed me thinking that I'd brought up bad memories for him, but it was dashed away when his expression shifted to a smile, albeit a little forced.

"I had a friend come out here and tell me about the program they had. So, I went for it."

"Is he still here?"

"No, he actually moved back to California after graduation. But I made another friend in college, and we've remained close."

I wondered who his friend was. His smile looked happy and content, and I wondered if it was a woman. A pinch of jealousy hit me, and I had to fight from rolling my eyes at how dumb it was to be jealous of your teacher's possible girlfriend.

Hunger also hit me, and as though admitting I had no lunch wasn't embarrassing enough, my stomach rumbled. I cringed and reached for my water bottle, hoping that would help.

"Hungry?" Dr. Pierce asked.

"It's okay. I'll grab something when I'm finished here. Since I came in early, I'll have plenty of time to pick up some groceries before heading home." I tried to take discreet deep breaths to stop the blood rushing to my cheeks. "Let's just say I've learned my lesson about being lazy with my shopping," I said, trying to make a joke.

"Here," he said, handing me half of his sub. "Split my sandwich with me. Donna got me a whole one when I only wanted a half. It will just go to waste."

I cocked an eyebrow. We both knew a man his size needed a large sandwich.

"Take the sandwich, Oaklyn."

"Thank you," I said, taking it from him. The first bite was phenomenal. It was a simple club sandwich, but I was so hungry the flavor of the bacon and cheese exploded on my tongue. I closed my eyes and swallowed a moan along with the bite in my mouth.

When my eyes flicked open, he was staring at me with an unmistakable heat in his eyes. Other times I'd ignored it, pushed it under the rug, called it my own imagination. But the way he stared at me—at my lips—there was no ignoring that heat. The way his bright blue eyes darkened when I slicked my tongue across my bottom lip to collect any crumbs.

There was no hiding how much I liked it.

But even if I couldn't ignore it, I could try to keep it under wraps because he was my professor and a look meant nothing. People watched me at Voyeur all the time. If I stared at a cute boy at a coffee shop, it didn't mean I truly wanted him. It was simply finding someone attractive. Nothing more.

Besides, what would I do? Pursue him? Flirt? Make it obvious? He was too sophisticated to act on an attraction to a student. Too smart. He could easily report me for misconduct. I'd lose my scholarships or extra income. All for a silly feeling.

So, I pushed it down hard and moved on, breaking the spell.

"So, California? I bet your parents miss you," I repeated the same statement he'd made to me the other day in the classroom.

He coughed behind his hand and looked away before answering. "I'm sure they do, but they visit enough."

"Do you ever go see them?"

"No."

The answer was short and hard. No hesitation at all, like he didn't even consider it. I wondered again if something had happened to make him leave and maybe not *want* to go back.

"Oh, yeah. It's probably a long trip." I said, giving him an out.

He nodded, taking it, and finished the last bite of his sandwich. "How about you? Did you go home for Christmas?"

"No. It was too expensive, and I had to work."

The small wince that flicked across his face almost happened too fast for me to see, but he continued his questions before I could think any more about it.

"I bet your siblings and family missed you."

"I'm an only child, but my extended family is really close-knit. I definitely missed them this year." I finished off the last of my sandwich and couldn't remember a time I'd felt more satisfied. Sure, it was dramatic, but I had been really hungry. Maybe because it was from him, it had tasted that much better. "What about you? Any siblings? Cousins you're close to?"

Paper crinkled, and I looked to see his fist clenched tight around an envelope.

"I'm also an only child," he said calmly, releasing the paper, like he hadn't just had a reaction.

He played it off so cool, I began to wonder if I'd imagined it, but the crinkled paper in front of him proved it.

It wasn't my business, no matter how curious I was.

"I bet you were an all-star kid." My eyes roamed over him, taking in his large build. "Football?"

His laugh filled the room and it seemed to always hit me like it was the first time. "Hardly. More like the class president and leader of the physics club. I did play soccer for a bit though."

"Me too," I said excited to have something in common. "But I sucked."

"God, so did I. My buddy said it was the greatest gift to the team when I quit. I never understood the sport anyway."

My body shook with laughter, imagining him fumbling around. "I loved it. Sucked. But I loved it. However, I ended up joining the dance team my senior year to stay active."

His eyebrow lifted as though I surprised him with that. His expectations of my dance skills were probably too high, and he imagined someone good at dancing.

"I kind of sucked at that too. I was okay. But I can't dance. Moving to a count is a lot different than finding your rhythm."

"You paint a hell of a picture," he said, lifting his water for a drink.

"Let me guess. You're an amazing dancer. B-boy? Hip-hop? Whacking?"

He almost spit his water across the desk, a little bit slipping from his pursed lips as he fought the laugh. He ended up coughing which mixed with his choked laugh.

And I laughed with him. The room just a blend of our sound making beautiful music.

But it came to a screeching halt when someone at the door interrupted us.

"Callum?" A tall, slim blonde walked in and straight to his desk, laying a kiss on his cheek. I thought she was going for his lips, but he turned at the last minute. My whole body froze as I watched her place her hand on his shoulder. Their movements seemed to filter to me in slow motion.

"I thought I heard your laugh. I had no idea you were a teacher here. I'm the new secretary in the chemistry department."

Dr. Pierce looked at me to alert her to my presence since she seemed to talk like I wasn't even there. I didn't know how she'd missed me considering she had to walk past me to get to him.

Obviously, she didn't get the hint because she just kept talking. "I've been here all week, I don't know how I've missed you," she said, resting her butt on his desk and stroking her fingers down his arm.

I noticed his eyes flick to the stack of papers that had moved out of alignment and it gave me satisfaction to know that her disorganizing his desk irked him.

Watching her hand make its way up and down his jacket, a jealousy I had no right to feel burned through me. I didn't even know her—hadn't even seen her face yet—and I hated her.

Dr. Pierce cleared his throat, talking for the first time. "Shannon, this is my student-aide in the department, Oaklyn."

She turned, seeming surprised to see me. Of course, she was gorgeous, and I hated her all the more for it. "Oh, silly me. Hi, Oaklyn." Her head cocked to the side. "Such an unusual name."

"I like to call it unique, but I've heard weird before too," I said sarcastically, which she missed completely. I wanted to call her a rude bitch, but bit my tongue because I knew I was overreacting and needed to calm the fuck down. She just laughed and turned her attention back to Dr. Pierce.

"I'd love to get together again. Pick up where we left off." She leaned closer to him, speaking softly like I'd magically not be able to hear. "Maybe let me return the favor."

Ohmygod. Ohmygod. I didn't know what favor she was talking about, but my mind could conjure a few that made me want to knock her off the desk.

Dr. Pierce happened to look over at me as my eyes tried to bug out in panic. I was not getting trapped in there and tortured with her recount of their *activities*. I had to get the hell out of there.

"Whew, look at the time." I interrupted. The conversation was unprofessional, and it felt like a punch in the gut. "I should get going. Thanks for sharing your sandwich, Dr. Pierce."

I tossed my bag over my shoulder and bolted, not taking a moment to look back.

Being in that room caused me to have stupid feelings. Feelings I needed to walk away from and ignore. I needed to move past the stupid crush and focus on school.

Maybe if I said enough, my heart would stop trying to pound out of my chest every time I saw him.

Chapter Eleven

Callum

I forced myself to look away as Oaklyn's full lips stretched into a smile that would rival the sun and focus my attention back on lecturing the class.

The same way I'd forced myself to not visit her at Voyeur the past week. I hadn't gone at all. I didn't trust myself. Instead I'd looked up porn. I'd opened up one of the videos I liked—one of my fantasies.

I'd jerked my cock as I watched the woman run her tongue up the length of his erection. I pumped harder and faster watching his hand dig into her hair, holding her to him as he fucked her mouth. I tried to tighten my muscles in advance of my orgasm when he came down her throat and a stringy rope of cum slid down her chin. But nothing. Not a damn thing. No matter how much I watched or how much I imagined myself in the same position, I couldn't come. Like my body was punishing me for depriving it of Oaklyn. I'd slammed the lid shut and ended up feeling as hollow as before I began.

I'd discovered Voyeur when I was looking for something more than a video. Something that helped me cope with the loss of intimacy. At least I was closer to it than I was staring at a computer. Somewhere along the way, I'd discovered that I just enjoyed watching.

After my failed internet search, I'd ended up with my hand clutched around a glass of bourbon, drinking way too much as I wondered what she was doing. Wondering what kind of performances she was putting on. Who she was putting them on with.

Why the hell was I so obsessed with her?

I'd been attracted to women before. Even found myself in fulfilling relationships. But this felt different. Bigger. I think it started as a physical reaction that bordered on obsession. An attraction that made me desperate to watch more of her. Then I'd met her. I'd talked and laughed with her. I began imagining touching her. Fucking her. And when I did, it didn't fill me with the panic and dread it usually did when I tried to convince myself the next time would be different.

My thoughts of Oaklyn were more. Something about her felt different, and fuck if I knew what it was. It didn't matter though, because she was my student. My nineteen-year-old student. It didn't matter that she made me feel different than any other woman. I was older, and I should know better. So I stayed away from Voyeur as much as I could.

It hadn't stopped the lunches and conversations in my office though. It hadn't stopped my heart from beating double time when I saw her. It hadn't stopped my imagination from running wild. But at least I wasn't seeking her out. I was actively not going to watch my student strip down and finger herself as I watched her rose-tipped breasts heave in pleasure.

Sometimes, when I really missed watching her, I'd try and stay at work later, finding ways to keep her with me in the office past everyone else leaving. Meaningless tasks. I'd feed her dinner, so we had a reason to stop and talk.

But I'd had to be more careful. Shannon popped in to say goodbye every day since last week when she discovered we worked in the same building. I discouraged her attention as much as I could without being rude, but she still stopped by randomly. I only hoped she didn't notice my attraction to Oaklyn.

I felt like it was written all over my face.

"Please make sure to read the online assignment and answer the questions before the next class," I said loud enough to be heard over the rustle of students packing up to leave.

Oaklyn's eyes caught mine before I could look away. I managed to return her smile before turning away to pack my things. I couldn't help but wonder if Oaklyn's face showed more than she wanted me to see. The way she looked at me was anything other than the teenager I knew her to be. Her eyes sparked with more. With a yearning she couldn't hide behind the demure tilt of her lips no matter how hard she tried. She looked at me like she knew what desire was and imagined me giving all of it to her.

Yes, I noticed her attraction. I tried to dismiss it; convince myself she was no different than some of the other students, especially the girls with their flirting and crushes.

But it wasn't other students I dreamed of at night. It wasn't other students I imagined sliding into and whose moans I heard, waking with my hand fisted around my cock.

Most dreams like those ended much differently. They'd morph from sex with a woman I wanted, to my worst nightmare, waking me up in panic, sweat coating my body, and my hand fisting the sheet instead of my dick.

It wasn't that I didn't want to have sex. I just didn't trust myself to not freak out. One night I'd even tried. I'd gotten drunk, determined to lose my virginity and I had. But as soon as she'd touched me, I broke into a sweat, somehow still pushing on before running from the room, swearing to never let myself be so vulnerable again.

I'd been vulnerable enough in my life and I didn't want to be there again.

"Dr. Pierce." Her gentle voice pulled me out of my thoughts, and I noticed almost the whole class had cleared out while I'd been lost in a dark memory.

"Yes, Oaklyn?"

She smiled when I turned my attention to her, looking almost shy.

"I signed up for the last slot for the telescope, but I'm the only one, and I wanted to make sure that was okay. I can try and make another night, so you don't have to make the trip just for me, but I'm not sure when yet."

"No," I rushed to reassure her. "That's perfectly fine. Maybe some-one will sign up and join us later."

Honestly? I hoped not. I loved any excuse that would get me alone with her. The thought of being under the stars—just her and I—with-out any prying eyes watching us. The possibilities almost scared me,

"Awesome. I'll see you tomorrow."

I watched her walk out, my eyes dropping to the way her ass moved under her leggings. Realizing my huge mistake, checking out my student in the middle of school, had me jerking my attention away. I berated my-self as I collected my things and headed out to meet Reed for lunch.

I was almost to the restaurant when my phone rang. Seeing it was my parents, I ignored the call. I didn't have long to talk, and their con-versations usually required an hour or more. I didn't blame them for the long conversations. I knew they missed me and could only find so much time to come out and see me. One time, my mother tried to broach the subject of me coming home and I immediately shut it down. California was no longer my home. It only held the worst of my memories and things I'd rather forget.

I pocketed my phone and had the hostess show me to our table. Reed greeted me with a smile and a back slap before reclaiming his seat. It wasn't until our food came that he began harassing me.

"Hey, you never told me what happened with the girl from our last lunch. Please tell me you actually called her and went on a date."

"You'll be happy to know I went on two dates with her."

"Did you fuck her? If I remember correctly, she had a nice rack."

"You're fucking married."

"A man can notice. Karen knows I'm all hers," he said with a shrug. "So?"

"No, I didn't. And it's a good thing because she works with me and that would have been hell."

"What, you've never banged anyone you worked with?"

I glared at him as I rotated my beer bottle until the logo faced me. "The only women I work with who are single are an older receptionist and a new student aide."

"A new physics major? In the middle of the semester? I thought you weren't getting another student aide until next year."

"No. She's a bio major and does student work in their department too. She needed help paying for her tuition and is trying to pick up extra hours." My lips twitched as I considered how impressed I was with her work ethic. I'd seen better people give up easier than Oaklyn. "She's tenacious. Smart. Determined."

"Oh, fuck no," Reed said, bringing my attention back to him.

"What?" I asked. But I knew. Reed knew me too well to not pick up on the feelings I was sure were pouring out of me no matter how hard I tried to hold them in.

"You fucking like her. A *student*." His voice rose with incredulity.

My stomach dropped at just hearing it said aloud. "Would you keep it the fuck down? People I work with could be here and what would they think if they heard you?"

"Then don't like your fucking student," he shot back, eyes narrowed in concern.

"I don't like her. Okay?" I tugged at the collar of my shirt, trying to give myself more room to breathe.

"Bullshit."

"It's not bullshit," I said harder than I intended. I lifted my drink to my dry mouth to give myself a second to think of my next words. "She's a student and that's that. I would never cross that line. She's too young, and she's my student."

"Yeah, you said that already. Are you trying to convince me or yourself?"

We stared at each other, and I knew I wasn't leaving that restaurant without at least admitting something.

I finished the last half of my beer in one go and set it down before looking back at Reed.

"Fine," I admitted through a clenched jaw. "I like her. She's beautiful and funny. Fuck does she make me laugh." *And she makes me forget,* I wanted to say. My chest warmed just thinking of the ways to describe her. "She just. . . Just makes me feel good."

"Fuck, dude. I was hoping you'd tell me she had a tight ass and huge tits. I wasn't expecting you to wax poetic about how she makes you feel." He finished his beer too, probably feeling the severity of my admission. "I would have been a hell of a lot less worried if that was the case."

"I know," I said miserably.

"So, you met her in the office?"

I thought about telling him she worked at Voyeur, and I'd seen her there first, but I wanted to protect her. I didn't want Reed to judge her.

"No, she's my student. So, I saw her in class first."

"Cal, what are you going to do?"

"Nothing." My tone was hard and brokered no doubt. "She's my student. I would never exploit that. And no matter how I feel about her, I just bury it."

"Okay," he said. Simple. Which with Reed, the less he said, the more concerned he was. But no one could have been more concerned than me. I felt like I was constantly on the edge of a precipice with Oaklyn.

"Just be careful, Cal."

Be careful.

It was easier said than done.

Chapter Twelve

Oaklyn

It was a miracle.

I had a night off from work and was all caught up on my homework. Even a little ahead. Which was the only reason I'd let Olivia talk me into going out to "act like a typical college girl." She'd rattled on and on about how much fun it would be to experience a frat party even if it sucked. She explained how we at least needed to cross it off our list.

She bounced in the passenger seat as she slicked on a coat of lip stain. Her excitement both sparked my own and reminded me how tired I was. But she was right. I wanted college and everything that came with it. I was working my ass off to earn it, so why not take it.

I parked a block from the frat house, which wasn't at all what I'd expected. It was nothing like I'd seen in the movies, with people passed out on the lawn clinging to red Solo cups and beer bongs. At least not from the front. Only a few people lingered on the patio, nodding as we walked in. No questions as to who we were or if we were invited.

The real party greeted us when we walked through the door. The music that had been a mild rumble blasted outside, practically exploding when the door opened. People hung out in groups throughout the house, holding those red solo cups that had been missing outside. Music played through the speakers and the middle of the room was a dance floor.

Olivia grabbed my hand and led me down the hallway to the kitchen. More people mingled and spilled out into the fenced-in backyard. Apparently, that was where the beer bong and passed out people resided.

"Let's get a drink," Olivia shouted over the music.

We each poured a shot of tequila and downed it before sucking on a lime. When we poured another, we at least waited for a little toast this time. "To finally being able to act like normal college girls. May we have fun and flirt with all the sexy boys."

"Here, here," I said, raising my glass to clink against hers. Lime juice dribbled down Olivia's chin and we both laughed.

"Can't take me anywhere."

"Nonsense. You're the classiest bitch I know," I said with an exaggerated wink and a gun.

"God, I miss hanging out with you."

I missed hanging out with Olivia too. Between two work-study programs, Voyeur, and school, my time felt like it was vanishing before I could even realize it was there.

"Well, I'm here now." I pulled her to my side just as a voice interrupted our girl-fest reunion.

"Hey, hey, ladies."

A few of the guys from our physics class sauntered up to us.

"Hey, boys," Olivia said with a sly smile.

"Care to do another shot with us?" the tall one asked. I think his name was Connor.

"Sure," Olivia said.

And it progressed from there. We had formed our own hoard of people and we talked, joked, and laughed. I did a few more shots until I noticed Olivia doing more than a few at a much faster rate than me. Besides, although we discussed an Uber, if I was sober, it would save us the cost.

I mingled on the edge of our group, Olivia's bubbly personality claiming the guys' attention. I didn't mind observing. We moved our circle to the living room after Olivia claimed she needed to shake her ass on me. Who was I to deny the girl?

We put on a hell of a show, switching between jumping around and her bending over to twerk against me. After a few more songs, I stepped aside to grab a water and stand back. I watched her flit from one guy to the next but kept my eye on one that seemed to constantly be behind her making her uncomfortable with his roaming hands. When he shifted in front of her and turned his baseball cap backwards, moving his muscular arms to her butt and his head into her neck, I saw her jump and move her hands to his shoulders. He pulled back laughing and she seemed to laugh too, but I saw how uncomfortable she was. She looked like she was trying to brush him off as nicely as possible, but he wasn't having it.

I made my way through the crowd to get to my friend. When I reached her, I tried to play it off and get her away as discreetly as possible, not wanting to cause a scene. Especially with how drunk he seemed.

"Olivia," I whined. She turned to me with hazy eyes filled with relief. "You promised you'd dance with me." I tugged at her arm to extract her from her partner—fuck he was big up close—but he yanked her back into him out of my grasp.

"No. We're dancing."

"Dude, lay off. I just want to hang out with my girl," I say, still trying to keep calm.

"Tough shit. Go find another girl to grind on, lesbian. She doesn't want your pussy anyway. She'd rather have this." He crudely groped his crotch with a disgusting smile. His loud voice began to garner the attention of people around us.

Some of his friends cheered, "Yeah, bro. Nice catch for the night."

"Sexy fuck for later."

"Send us pics of those tits man. Or better yet, a video of them bouncing as you fuck her."

Olivia's tired eyes popped open, and she began to wriggle her arm free, but his grip tightened, and she winced in pain. These people were fucking pigs, and I was done with this shit.

"Let her the fuck go."

"No need to be jealous. I'll fuck you too."

"No way, man." My heart shot into my throat when an arm banded around my waist and hauled me back against a hard body. The stench of pungent beer burned my nostrils and churned my stomach. "Would that make you feel better, baby," he spoke softly against my neck, and I tried to curl away from him. "We can always share, too."

He stretched his arm in front of me and held up his hand. The go-liath that was holding Olivia high-fived my captor. Olivia's glazed eyes met mine and began to fill with tears.

No. No, no, no. Adrenaline shot through my body. I used all my strength and slammed my heel down on his toe. He cursed in pain and pulled back, but still held tight to my arm.

"You fucking bitch!" He tossed me behind him, and with no one there to catch me, I fell, landing against a table pushed off to the side. Pain shot up my arm as it scraped against the corner. My head thud-ded hard against the edge, and I blinked to clear the black dots before me. Why wasn't anyone doing anything? Tears burned my eyes in fear, embarrassment, and rage.

Ready to get up and fight him with an epic warrior cry, going down fighting for my friend, I was stopped when three guys stepped into the circle.

"Let her the fuck go, dickhole," Connor said, his two friends at his side. One reached back to help me up. "Or we'll report you to Coach and get you kicked off the team."

I stood next to one of our heroes, still burning with rage, when the asshole tossed Olivia at Connor, where she stumbled into his arms.

"She's not fucking worth it. Too fat."

I stepped forward, aiming for his balls, but the guy who helped me up held me back, shaking his head. "Let's just get out of here."

They walked us out to our car, helping a sniffling Olivia into the front seat.

"You okay to drive?" Connor asked me.

"Yeah. I'll be fine. Thanks for your help in there."

"Evan and James are cunts and deserve to be kicked off the football team. I'll be telling the coach anyway."

"Thank you," I said one last time before I got in and drove off.

I parked in the teacher lot outside of the science building because it was the closest to Olivia's dorm. When I walked past, I looked up at Dr. Pierce's office and saw the light on. What was he doing here so late? Looking at my phone I noticed it was only ten-thirty. Still late, but I almost laughed at how short a time we lasted at the frat party. Less than three hours and we'd already checked that off as an experience we'd never want to repeat again.

I got Olivia settled and tucked in with no protest and very little help on her part. The alcohol was hitting her. I left a bottle of water and some aspirin on her desk for the morning.

"Guys are jerks. Thanks for being my friend, Oak."

"Any time." I kissed her forehead. She was out before I even reached the door.

When I walked past the science building again, Dr. Pierce's light was off. I must have just missed him.

Walking back to my car I remained vigilant. Looking around, partly scared that someone might have followed us for revenge or something equally dramatic. The adrenaline was wearing off, and the stinging in my arm increased. I needed to get home and take care of whatever damage was caused. The pain stretched down my arm and up into my shoulder. My head ached and each throb was a reminder to how vulnerable I was. Only ten more feet to my car.

I almost swallowed my tongue when a dark figure emerged from around the corner.

"Oaklyn?" a familiar voice asked.

My whole body shook as I fought off the fight or flight that gripped me. I was sure he heard it when I said his name.

"Dr. Pierce? Hey."

He stepped into the light and his eyebrows furrowed. "You okay?"

"Yeah, yeah." I took deep breaths to get my heart rate back to a normal pace. Tonight was turning out to be hellacious on my nervous system. "You just scared me."

"Sorry about that," he said looking unconvinced. "What are you doing on campus so late. You don't live in the dorms, do you?"

"I was just dropping my friend off. Coming back from a party."

He nodded his head, but still watched me closely. "I thought those ran later than eleven."

"Maybe. I guess it just wasn't for us. Especially when it's filled with dickholes. Sorry," I finished, apologizing for swearing in front of my professor. However, he didn't seem concerned about that.

He walked a few steps closer, looking me over with obvious concern. "What do you mean? What happened? Are you okay?"

"Yeah," I answered weakly. "Some of the guys were just getting handsy with Olivia and me, threatening things. So, I tried defending us." I laughed humorlessly. "But you know, it's hard to be five-five and move a mountain. I got shoved and fell pretty hard." I gestured to my arm and watched his jaw harden. A muscle twitched in his cheek, and I rushed to explain the ending. "Some other guys stepped in to help and got us out of there."

I looked down, too ashamed to meet his eye. Ashamed that we'd fallen into the assaulted girl category. Ashamed I couldn't do more to defend myself and my friend.

"Let me see," he said, his voice hard.

My head shot up. His usually bright eyes were dark and looked to be barely restraining his rage.

"I'm fine."

"Let. Me. See."

Taking a deep breath, I shed my coat and exposed my arm. I think we were both shocked to find dried blood that had dripped down my elbow and a decent gash.

"Mother fuck," he muttered.

I almost laughed. Dr. Pierce was light and happy when he taught, and in my slightly manic state, his cursing was funny somehow.

"Follow me. We have a first aid kit in the department."

"It's okay. You don't have to do—"

"Oaklyn, please."

Despite his anger, his eyes seemed pained.

"Okay," I agreed, not hating the idea of him tending to me.

I followed him into the building. We didn't speak at all until we reached his office.

"Take your jacket off. I'll be right back." His voice seemed brusque and loud after the silence.

I did as he asked and sat in the chair in front of his desk. When he returned, he carried a first aid kit and sat in the chair next to me. While he searched for what he was looking for, I looked him over. He'd lost the tie he usually wore in classes, leaving a few buttons open, exposing a smattering of chest hair that screamed masculinity. It was crazy, but I had to fight to keep from leaning forward and touching it. His hair was more mussed than usual. Like he'd spent the evening running his frustrated fingers through it. It was a good look on him.

"Alright," he said. "Turn a bit so I can see."

When he got a good look at the injury, his eyes closed, and he swallowed hard. His concern caused a burning behind my eyes. How long had it been since someone had been upset by my pain? Maybe I missed my family more than I thought.

"It's not as bad as it looks."

"It's going to look worse tomorrow," he said through a clenched jaw. "This is going to hurt a bit."

His long fingers wrapped behind my arm, brushing against the tender skin, sending goose bumps down my arm and up my neck. It was the first time he'd touched me, and the heat from his skin seemed to burn the memory into my brain. The light pressure was more erotic than any touch I'd ever had. Was it only the forbidden aspect? The fact that I couldn't have him, made every touch all the more intense?

Suddenly, I sucked air in through my teeth as he wiped around the wound with alcohol and then poured peroxide over it. Instead of erotic tingles from his touch, the fiery burn had my own jaw clenching.

"Sorry," he whispered. Gritting my teeth, I nodded as he continued. "So, what exactly happened tonight?"

"We went to a frat party," I said, shrugging like it explained everything.

"Did anyone . . ." I could hear his deep breath before he spoke again. "Did anyone touch either of you? In any other way."

"No, not really. Olivia was dancing with this guy and he got a little more handsy than she wanted, so I came over to try and rescue her." I laughed humorlessly at how dumb I sounded. In hindsight, it was stupid to think I was going to make a difference. "Thank god for some of the guys we knew there. They stepped in after my rescue attempt failed."

I shook my head, recalling the night. Frustrated with how it all had played out. "There were so many people who did nothing. Just stood there as he threatened to-to rape her."

His hand clenched around my arm, and I jerked. "Ow."

"I'm sorry. So, sorry," Dr. Pierce said. I glanced over my shoulder at him. He was taking heavy breaths, looking like he was trying to collect himself. When he noticed me staring, he grabbed a Band-Aid. "You should report it."

Another humorless laugh. "There's no point. Nothing *actually* happened, and no one would be able to do anything." I furrowed my brows at the sad truth. "That's just the way the cookie crumbles."

I looked over my shoulder again. He looked up as he stretched the last Band-Aid on my arm. His eyes shot through me, so intense with how close we were. So blue, I felt like I could drown in them. The Band-Aids were in place, yet he hadn't moved away. My heart was beating double-time, pumping a fiery heat through me.

"If you ever find yourself in a situation like that again, you can ask me for help."

His eyes flicked my lips as I slicked my tongue across them.

"Thank you," I said on a breath, dropping my eyes to his mouth. Maybe if I leaned in a little closer, he'd meet me halfway. My eyes began to droop closed, my mouth drawn to his.

He jerked back, turning away from me to clean up the trash. He cleared his throat. "That's going to be sore tomorrow. Have a friend help change out the Band-Aids and keep it clean. Should be better soon."

"Yeah." The word barely escaped my parted lips. My eyes dropped to my lap as tears threatened.

What the fuck was I thinking? What had I been doing? Fuck, I was so dumb. So fucking dumb.

The self-ridicule kept coming, and I couldn't deny any of it because I felt like a predator, and there was no hiding my attraction now. How was I going to spend the rest of the semester with him after this? *Fuck*.

Embarrassment seared through me. When he left to go return the first aid kit, I quickly put my jacket back on and tried to leave before he came back, not wanting to face him. I got as far as the front office door before he came back in.

"Wait for me. I'll walk you to your car."

I couldn't turn and look at him. With my hand on the knob, I said, "You don't have to do—"

"I do. Please."

I kept my distance and my eyes down as we walked toward the parking lot. At my car, I muttered a quick thanks and tried to get in, but a hand pressed the door back closed. Finally, I turned to look into his eyes. I tried to read them, tried to understand what he thought of me, of what had just happened.

They looked. . . regretful?

"Here's my number, should you ever need it."

I took the card he extended to me, taking in the masculine handwriting.

"Thank you." I looked at him again, trying to find the regret again. Trying to find out if I was right or just crazy.

Maybe he *was* just as attracted to me as I was to him.

He was just so much smarter than me to not act on it.

Chapter Thirteen

Callum

Oaklyn walked into the office the following Monday and gave me a timid smile. Probably unsure of exactly how I'd act after Friday night.

That night . . . That night had split me open. Seeing her jump when I said her name. Seeing the lingering fear and frustration in her eyes. Then seeing her arm. I didn't know how I'd kept a lid on my anger. To find out it was from some asshole threatening to sexually assault her and her friend? My stomach churned remembering the wave of nausea that had hit me when she'd said it. I'd managed to hold it together enough to take her upstairs and take care of the wound. As I'd bandaged her arm, I salivated over the feel of her flesh beneath my fingertips. Even if it was just her arm.

There was nothing sexual about what I'd been doing, but the tension had crackled between us, heating up the room. She'd turned to look at me, so close, her deep golden eyes had fused onto mine. Her tongue had peeked out to slick across her lips, pulling my gaze to the soft pink flesh. I'd wanted to lean in, taste them, flick my own tongue across them. I'd been so entranced by the way she'd leaned toward me. I'd thought of nothing else but moving closer too. I'd watched her eyes drift close, and I was ready to say fuck it and give in.

Then the alcohol pad began to seep through my pants, the cold tickling at my thigh. It'd been minor, but enough to snap me back to reality. It might as well have been a bucket of cold water doused over my head.

My chest had clenched when I saw her eyes widen in confusion, when I saw the sheen of tears before she'd looked down in embarrassment. I'd given her space to collect herself, taken a walk to replace the first aid kit, calling myself every stupid name in the book. I'd resolved to apologize when I'd returned, determined to take responsibility for leading her on. Then I'd seen her trying to bolt, and I'd forgotten my whole plan. Scratched everything and instead pretended like nothing had happened.

Which is exactly what I'd continue to do today too.

"Feeling any better?" I asked when she stepped into my office.

"Yeah," she said, moving to sit in the chair in front of my desk. I fought to keep my eyes from trailing down to watch the way her skirt rode up her thighs as she sat. "A hell of a lot better than Olivia. I think she was still hungover yesterday."

"I don't miss those days," I said, cringing.

"What?" she mock-gasped, pulling her hand to her chest. "You? A rowdy boy in college?"

Laughing at her dramatics, I shook my head. "More like rowdy high school boy."

"Was this before or during the class presidency and physics club? I won't judge," she held up her hands. "Physics club would drive me to drink too."

"You're very funny, Miss Derringer."

She gave a shameless shrug, and I loved the way it made her ponytail sway. Maybe I could blame that for putting me in a trance long enough to allow the next words to pop out.

"I struggled a little as a teen. Drinking helped."

She hid her shock at my confession pretty well. Not that it was much of a confession, just probably not something a teacher talked about with his student. I could see her eyes widen a little before she nodded her head like she understood.

She had no idea how much was really behind those two sentences. I'd struggled with my anger—my loss of control—and drinking helped me numb myself enough that I didn't find the need for an outlet. But it wasn't long until my parents had had enough and got me into therapy. My therapist recommended getting involved in school and then came physics club. As lame as it sounded, it was the first thing to get me excited about something in years.

Fucking stars, man. Saved my life.

I laughed at that, then admitted, "Physics club was my jam. Gave me something else to focus on."

I didn't know why I'd shared so much of my past. Something about her, the innocence and acceptance that emanated from her made me want to confess all my secrets. I needed to change the subject before more word vomit came out.

Thankfully, Donna popped her head in. "We're getting lunch from the sub shop. You want anything?"

Oaklyn's stomach growled right on cue and her cheeks blushed.

"I'll take a large club and two bags of potato chips."

Oaklyn's head popped up at that. "Dr. Pierce, no. I packed a PB&J. I'm go—"

"Two, Donna," I interrupted Oaklyn and held up two fingers to Donna. She gave me a nod, smiling at Oaklyn's protest.

"Let us treat you every once in a while," she said before walking out.

Us. Like it was the office that wanted to gain pleasure from watching Oaklyn's lips move with every bite, and not just me.

"Oh, that reminds me," Oaklyn said, hopping up from her seat and whirling around to dig in her bookbag.

My eyes trailed to the way the soft material of her skirt swayed higher as she moved. The expanse of thigh entranced me and shot straight to my cock, making it twitch under my slacks. She stood, and I looked away before she fully turned and faced me.

"Brownies!" She held up a Tupperware container victoriously. "And I made sure to add peanuts just for you. Although I hear Mr. Erikson likes them too, so you may have to share."

"Hmmm." I pretended to think about it. "I don't think so."

Her soft laugh filled the office, and I couldn't help smiling too.

Oaklyn set some brownies on my desk before taking the rest out to the main office for everyone to share.

After lunch, I put on some music to help distract me from the soft noises she created as she filed. It seemed every swish of paper drew my eyes to her, like she was shouting at me, demanding my attention. However, the music backfired on me when I glanced her way to find her standing in front of the cabinet, swaying her hips to the beat of the song.

I wasn't even sure she was aware of what she was doing, but the motion sucked all the moisture from my mouth and I struggled to swallow the desire choking me. Fuck. I wanted to place my hands on her hips and inch the skirt up until the cheeks of her ass peeked out. Then I'd rub my hand across the soft skin and sway with her. Work my hands around the front as I pressed my cock against her soft globes and buried my fingers between her thighs.

"Dr. Pierce." Her soft voice interrupted my fantasy and I jerked, blinking away the image to find her staring at me.

My heart thundered in my chest as I realized she'd turned to find me staring at her ass. Shit. Shit, shit, shit. I took deep breaths to stop the blood rushing to my cheeks and swallowed, hoping my voice sounded normal and not at all nervous about what she'd say.

"Sorry. I zoned out a bit."

Her teeth dug into her bottom lip and she seemed to be trying to hide her own blush as she walked forward to put a paper on my desk. I scooted further under my desk, hoping she didn't notice the tent in my pants.

"I was wondering where you wanted me to file this one."

I looked over the paper she handed me, and just stared at it, trying to regain my composure. "Bottom cabinet." Giving her what I hoped was a reassuring smile, I returned to my work, berating myself the whole time.

Before I knew it, the day was over.

"Is there anything else you need before I head out?"

"No. Thank you, Oaklyn." She nodded with a smile and began to pack up her bag. "Headed home for the night?"

She let out a heavy sigh. "No. I have to work tonight, so I'm headed there and then home."

It was a struggle to keep my face neutral, but somehow, I managed. She waved goodbye, and I tried to focus on my work. Tried to not think about her performing and being surrounded by men. What if one of them took it too far? What if she was hurt again?

Rationally, I knew Daniel took the utmost care of his employees, but after seeing her Friday night, the pit in my stomach wouldn't abate.

Giving up on the papers in front of me, I shut everything down and headed home. Each mile I drove, I thought about her and wondered if she was okay. It haunted me, irrationally taking over every thought.

I walked in my house and slammed my door, carefully hung up my jacket, stomped up the stairs, and got undressed. I draped my tie onto the rack, and tugged until it perfectly lined up with the rest; placed my shoes on the floor alongside my other dress shoes, the laces carefully tucked inside; coiled my belt tightly and put it in the drawer with the buckle facing out, and dumped the rest of my clothes into the empty laundry basket.

I stood in my walk-in closet, wearing only a pair of black boxer briefs, my chest heaving, feeling no calmer than I had when I'd left school. Just feeling too much, period.

I needed a drink. I took long strides to reach my door and as soon as my hand rested on the handle, I remembered my conversation with Oaklyn and how I explained how far I'd come since needing to drink. Now look at me, ready to storm downstairs and chug straight from the bottle. I had more restraint than that.

I forced myself to breathe in for five seconds, out for five. In for five seconds, out for five. I didn't dare let go of the handle until I had regained control. By the time I did, my fingers tingled from squeezing the metal knob so hard.

I carefully walked back into my closet and grabbed a long-sleeved Henley, jeans, and my ballcap with *Cincinnati* stitched across it. Then I strolled downstairs, grabbed my keys, and headed to Voyeur. Rationalizing the whole way that if I was the one watching her, then no one else could and I'd limit the risk of someone pushing too far.

I didn't hesitate when I reached the club. I kept my head down, hat shadowing my face as I stuck to the edges of the room, keeping my eye out for her. Of course, I saw her as soon as I entered. Her magnetism had me stopping and staring. She had a tray of drinks and was laughing with a couple at a table. She had on the same swishy skirt from earlier, except now, she only wore a lacy bustier that showcased her breasts to perfection.

Control. I needed control. I'd gone to Voyeur for a reason and I needed to focus on that.

I went back to the iPads and made my selection, not bothering to sit in a booth in case she came to take my order.

Maybe thirty minutes later of watching her flit around the lounge, smiling, flirting, talking with all the customers, my wristband finally buzzed. I darted down the back hallway and entered the private room. I flicked on one of the lamps, casting a dim light across the two leather club chairs. I didn't even acknowledge the wall of toys and lube, knowing I wouldn't need them tonight.

The leather creaked in the silent room as I looked through the glass at the setup waiting for Oaklyn. A simple scene of a girl on the couch watching something sexy and then getting herself off to it. No nudity. Nothing graphic.

She walked in like it was her own home, natural as could be. She moved to the couch, slightly slanted so, I could see more than just her profile, and turned on the TV. Some soft core porn filled the screen and she looked on enraptured by the couple on the screen. I wondered what she was thinking. What she was imagining.

My fists squeezed the armchair, my heartbeat echoing in my ears, as her hands coasted up her legs, dragging the skirt up her thighs, but still not exposing anything as the material fell at her core. Her hands continued their ascent, cupping her breasts. Her eyes slipped closed and her lips opened, a moan reaching through the glass and stroking at my cock.

The semi-erection I'd had since walking in hardened to my full length, pressing against the confines of my pants. One hand kept working her breast and the other moved back down to between her thighs. Moving the skirt aside, but still not showing anything, she began her show.

Her legs spread. The muscles in her arms strained. A flush began in her cheeks and spread down below her heaving breasts.

I adjusted myself in my seat, shifting my hips, rocking my erection against nothing, my hips just desperate to move on their own in time with hers. I waited for the glass to begin fogging as my heavy pants filled the room.

My head swam as all the blood rushed to my cock. I kept my hands glued to the leather. I would not move. I would not pull my cock out and stoke it to the movement of her fingers under her skirt.

There might be indents from my fingers burrowing into the leather, but I wouldn't move.

She whimpered, her face scrunching up, her whole body contracting as her arms moved faster. Her back arched and I almost lost it when one of her nipples popped free of the confines of her top.

I groaned, flexed my ass, thrusting my hips up off the chair.

Fuck she was beautiful.

When I expected her to tug the top back up, she instead began rolling the bud between her fingers. If she didn't come soon, I was going to come in my pants.

The tight rosy bud held my attention as I imagined latching on to it, sucking it into my mouth as I fucked her with my fingers.

I clenched my jaw, ground my teeth and tried to swallow past my dry mouth, and finally—fucking finally—she came. Her hips thrust off the couch and her thighs shook. Her cries rang out louder than the couple on the screen and I had to squeeze my eyes closed. It was too much.

Breathe in for five seconds, out for five. In for five, out for five.

More moans and whimpers.

In for five, out for five.

One last satisfied sigh, and I opened my eyes to find her breast safely tucked away and her sagging against the couch. I counted to twenty, then stood with jerky movements, adjusting my cock to make it less obvious, flicked the light to red, and stormed out of the room, heading straight to the iPads to make a second request.

If I bought her time, then no one else could. It wasn't for me. It was for her.

God was going to kill me by striking me down with lightning, or I was going to die from blue balls.

At that moment, a lightning bolt was far more preferable.

Chapter Fourteen

Callum

I walked into Voyeur for the fourth time in two weeks. I knew I shouldn't be there, yet I couldn't stop. I had to make sure she was okay.

I'd kept a close eye on her, taking advantage of all the time we were around each other. Walking her to her car when I could. Something inside of me pleaded with me to keep her safe. To protect her from the horrors of the world. The horrors of boys too amped up on power to consider they were wrong.

I shuddered and focused instead on keeping my head down under my hat as I made my way to my usual corner of the bar. The blonde, Charlotte, saw me and gave a nod, letting me know she'd bring me the beer she knew I ordered every time I came in.

Scanning the crowd, I found Oaklyn almost immediately, my attention always drawn to her. Being so in-tune with her made the days difficult. I did my best to pretend the almost kiss had never happened, to pretend I didn't know how soft her skin was, but it was all a lie.

Every day my desire seemed to be pulling at a leash as it tried to break free and announce to everyone that I wanted her. I stared more when I knew I shouldn't. I tried to make her stay later, just for the chance that we could be alone.

And on the nights I came to Voyeur, I watched her with a new level of feeling. When I watched her fingers skim her thighs, the tops of her breasts, any part of her body, I remembered what it felt like. Something so small and so minor, but it resonated through me, latching on like a leech to my memory.

I continued to select innocuous things each time, refusing to jack off. No matter how much my hard cock pressed against the zipper of my pants, begging to be let free, I refused.

Like the rationalization made it any better that I was there, watching my student come.

My eyes found Oaklyn again and I finished my beer. I moved to the edge of the room, never looking away from her pert nose and smiling lips. Tonight, she wore a white lace body suit, like she was a virginal bride on her wedding night. Except there was nothing virginal about the shorts that just reached the bottom of her cheeks and the deep V in the front and back. The lace only heavy around her breasts and core.

I reached the iPad to make my selection and scrolled until I found the typical under the sheets with no nudity. Then I looked over at her. She leaned on the bar to talk to Charlotte and it put her ass perfectly on display, her breasts seeming so much larger pressed between her arms as they tried to spill out from the lacy V.

The sexiest part? She wasn't even doing it to lure people in. She didn't realize that half the men in the bar were drooling over her. A look of innocence shined through and made her seem all the more untouchable to them, probably making them want her even more. Making *me* want her more.

Moving my hand to tap the screen and check the box I knew I should check, I changed my mind. My finger checked a few boxes I knew I'd regret later, but standing there, watching her, I didn't give a shit.

I lurked in the corners, my eyes never leaving her. She pulled her arm up when her bracelet went off to notify her of a request. My request.

Less than ten minutes later, my arm band was going off to let me know I was all set to head to the room. My heart pounded as I walked down the hall. A roaring sound in my head only being broken by the click of the switch flipping up to let her know the room was occupied. I took deep breaths as the leather creaked beneath me as I sat. The oils and lubes on the table begging me to use them on my cock.

I remained seated, closing my eyes, fighting to ignore my erection, already rock hard with thoughts about what was to come. I'd never requested something so direct and, before it even began, a part of me regretted it. It would be a punishment to watch her so exposed and open to me.

Then she came in. Like there wasn't someone watching her, she carried a water bottle and then set it on her nightstand. With her back to me, she tugged one sleeve down her shoulder and repeated the process with the other, baring her back to me. My hands clenched around my thighs as I watched her thumbs hook into the fabric and push it down. All the way down, keeping her legs straight, exposing everything she had to me before standing up and stepping out of the fabric.

I watched her reach in the bedside drawer and extract a thick, flesh colored dildo. A moan rushed out of my chest when she finally turned, and I saw her perfect tits. I took in her slim stomach and thin landing strip over the most perfect pussy. It'd been so long since I'd seen her naked, and I felt like a man in a desert finding an oasis.

But she'd only just begun.

Oaklyn crawled on the bed, prowling across the sheets until she found a spot in the middle. She rolled to her back and bent her knees, spreading her legs wide. Her fingers toyed with her nipples, making them ruby red before trailing down and cresting her mound, finally delving between her lips.

She spread her wetness all around her opening, rocking her hips against her probing fingers until her other hand grabbed the dildo and eased it between her thighs. Slow pushes, a little at a time, getting deeper on each pass. The deeper it went, the louder her breathing became.

When she resumed plucking at her nipples, I groaned again, pressing my palm against my aching length. Fuck, I couldn't do this. I couldn't breathe from my desire. I needed more. I needed relief. Just some space I thought. Just something to help ease the pressure threatening to explode inside me.

The sound of my zipper reverberated in the quiet room, making music with her increasing moans. I panted with her as I watched the dildo slowly slip in and out of her wet cunt. My fist gripped my shaft and began moving with the rhythm of her hips as she fucked the toy. I watched it appear shiny from her juices and disappear deep inside her. I stroked harder, feeling the pressure build in my balls as I imagined it was me pressing deep.

My heavy breaths were so loud as I fisted my cock faster, almost at a punishing pace, racing toward an orgasm I knew was wrong, and I didn't deserve. But I couldn't fucking stop.

Her hips pressed up, lifting her ass off the bed as she let out whimpering moans, her fingers quickly moving over her clit as she came. And I came with her. Long white ropes of cum shot out of me into my waiting palm.

We seemed to breathe in unison and as much as I hated myself for what I'd just done, I couldn't reject the euphoria of feeling so close to her. Of feeling like I'd gone farther with a woman than I had in a long time. Most of the time, I watched and came much earlier than the performers, cleaning up and staying until the show was over. It had never felt so personal or so connected before.

I wanted to hate myself, hate the situation I'd put us both in, and I did. But at the same time, I didn't.

Finally getting my breathing under control, I grabbed tissues from the nearby box and started cleaning up. With my penis still out, but soft, I stood and washed my hands before walking to the door and turning off the light, letting her know the room was vacant.

When she noticed the light, she seemed to sag against the bed and in those moments when I watched her—when she thought she was alone, I didn't see the sexual woman who worked at Voyeur. I saw a tired college student. For the first time I noticed the dark circles under her eyes that not even makeup could cover.

It hit me like a punch to the gut. How tired she must be working three jobs and going to college. I watched her lay there, staring at the ceiling, sinking into the blankets before closing her eyes for a long blink. What was she thinking? Did she hate it? Did she hate the idea of someone in here gaining satisfaction as she shared parts of herself— gave parts of herself to others?

The questions churned in my stomach, and I quickly tucked my cock back in my pants, pulled my hat low and got the fuck out of there.

Chapter Fifteen

Oaklyn

"Are you heading out, Oaklyn?" Mr. Erikson asked me.

"Not quite yet. I'm going to swing by Dr. Pierce's office and see if he needs anything from me before I go."

"Okay. Thanks for all your help today."

"No problem. I'm just lucky I'm not the one doing the lab this week. Looks brutal."

We'd spent the afternoon setting up the physics lab for an advanced class this week. Just in case I wasn't sure before that I was in the right program, writing up all the equations with weird symbols and prepping the materials, I was sure now. Physics was bananas.

"I'm sure you'd knock it out of the park," Mr. Erikson said with a chuckle.

"I appreciate your confidence."

"Any time. Have a good night, Oaklyn."

I walked down the hall toward the main office and found Donna's seat empty. Then I looked at the clock and saw it was already after six. I hadn't realized it was so late. Hopefully Dr. Pierce hadn't left either, otherwise I'd stayed for nothing. I headed toward his office and saw the light shining out from the half-open door.

I peeked in and found his dark head bent over his desk. He was writing on a paper with red pen, and I could only assume he was grading. Beside the paper he was working on, there was a perfectly placed stack of papers and another red pen sitting lined up with a blue one. I'd never known someone to be so anal about lining objects up. Sometimes I'd find him straightening Donna's desk or moving an office supply less than a quarter of an inch to perfect it.

I rapped my knuckles on the door before entering. His head popped up, and I was met with his Clark Kent glasses. When he saw it was me, he smiled, and I felt my cheeks stretching in return. I couldn't help it.

"Hey, Oaklyn. Come on in."

"I was just stopping by to see if there was anything you needed help with," I said, walking in and leaning on the back of a chair.

"Did Mr. Erikson finally let you free?"

"Yes, after torturing me for hours with the thought of being a physics major." I placed my hand over my heart.

"Hey, now. It's not too bad."

"That lab looks like hell."

"It is," he agreed easily. "But it weeds out anyone not serious in the second year. Every program has a class or lesson that thins the herd."

"Weaklings," I said dramatically, making him laugh.

"Well, I'm about to finish up grading these papers and then I have to scan in the assignment for the next class. Then I should be done."

"Can I help?" I offered, not quite wanting to leave. I liked his laugh, and I didn't want to miss an opportunity to hear it. Besides, we'd formed a friendship over the last month. More than occasionally we'd eat lunch together, discussing our favorite superheroes and other silly topics. When I could afford it, I'd bake brownies for the office, but made sure to add nuts to at least half because I knew it was his favorite.

We were friends. I was a friend who probably watched his lips move too closely, but still a friend.

"Actually, yes, you can help. The papers I need to scan are on top of that bookshelf. If you get the ladder from down the hall, could you grab them for me?"

"I don't need a ladder," I said with exaggerated confidence. "I may only be five-five, but I make it work for me." I scooted the chair over to the shelf and looked back before climbing on. "Besides, I'm way too lazy to have to go get a ladder and then take it back."

"Alright, Mighty Mouse. Just be careful."

I stepped up on to the cushion and tried to reach the folder. I couldn't see on top, so I reached blindly.

"No, not that one," Dr. Pierce said when my hand landed on a stack of papers. "It's the one further back."

My face was pressed to the spines of the books, my feet cramping from trying to push up higher and my T-shirt riding up past my jeans exposing my skin.

"Here, I'll get it," he said, beginning to stand.

"Nope." I gave him a hard stare. "You grade papers. I will conquer this reach." He didn't come running around the desk, but he did remain standing.

I looked at my options and put my foot on the thin arm of the chair. Getting a good balance, I held on to the shelf and moved my other foot to the other side. I only wobbled a little bit, which brought him out from behind the desk.

"Please don't fall, Oaklyn." He stepped closer.

"I'm not going to fall," I said, laughing.

I fully extended my legs and could finally see the folder at the top of the shelf. "Who put these up here?" I asked reaching for them. "Whoever files for you, really needs to get better at their job."

"I'll fire her in the morning."

"Good plan." I lowered my arm to hand the papers down and the angle threw me off. My foot slipped and the next thing I knew, I was doing exactly what I said I wouldn't.

Falling.

My heart pounded and in that split second, all I could think was how dumb I must look after I made a big deal of getting the papers. *Idiot.*

Strong arms wrapped around me. One behind my back, fingers firmly pressed to my arm and the other over the top of my thighs, his hand gripping close to the crease of my ass. I rolled in toward his hard chest, hands pressed to his sculpted pecs, and my face buried against his crisp, white shirt.

"I've got you." The vibration of his words rumbled against my palms and shot straight toward my core.

My body came to life, acknowledging every part of me in contact with him. My heart thumped painfully against my chest, either from adrenaline or excitement—excitement that moments had passed, and he still hadn't let me go.

Swallowing hard, I raised my head and looked up into his eyes, watching them darken right before me. "Thank you."

The arm across my legs, slowly lowered them back to the ground, but the arm around my back, kept me close. Could he feel my heart beating against his chest? Or the speed at which my lungs were trying to expand?

Solid ground hit my feet, yet I still floated above the ground, my hands holding tight to him.

I licked my lips and his eyes followed the movement before his own tongue repeated the process against his.

And I acted. Without thought. Without a care beyond what my body urged me to do.

Lifting up on to my toes, I recklessly pressed my lips to his.

A wave of chills washed over me. Excitement at the feel of his soft lips spread across my skin. His hand on my back contracted, but it was the only part of him that moved. It took me less than a moment to realize he wasn't kissing me back. He wasn't shoving me away, but he wasn't reciprocating either.

I'd made a mistake. I slowly eased back, breaking the connection between our lips, and opened my eyes, wanting to lose myself in the flecks of gray in his open eyes, and realizing that while I'd been lost in a moment I'd probably regret forever, he'd stood frozen, with his eyes open.

"I'm. . . " I tried to say the words, but they barely fell out in a whisper. They were hollow anyway, since I still clung to him. Was still pressed solidly against him. "I'm sor—"

I never got to finish before he leaned down and attacked my lips. For as frozen and inactive as he'd been a second before, he was giving it ten times more. He was devouring me, like a desperate man trying to push past all the reasons this was wrong. To drown in the pleasure of feeling our bodies close.

He stared at me as he licked at my lips, my eyes opened in shock with the complete one-eighty. But then I opened my mouth, meeting his tongue halfway, tasting him, and on a moan I tried to swallow, his lids slid closed.

I dug my hands in his hair and lost myself to the moment. Closed my eyes and focused solely on the taste of coffee on his tongue, the feel of his hands pressed against my back, holding me tight against the erection I could feel against my stomach.

He trailed his lips across my cheek and down my neck before working their way up again. This was happening. I couldn't believe it.

His hands dropped to my ass and squeezed the soft flesh, groaning at the feel of me in his palms. Fuck. Had a man ever sounded so satisfied at just grabbing my butt? Confident in his desire for me, I threw everything I had into the kiss. Nipped at his lips, sucked on them the way I wanted to suck on his cock.

One hand continued to grip me and hold me close, moving to the center of my bottom where his long fingers reached around the curve of my ass, barely touching the edges of my core. I wanted to rock my hips back to give him better access, encourage him to go further. But I was distracted by his other hand moving around my front, skimming my sides before cupping my breasts. My nipple hardened even more, almost reaching for his thumb as it circled and flicked across the tip. Each swipe sent shocks to my pussy and I was almost desperate to rub against him.

When was the last time I'd been touched from pure desire and not because someone paid me? I'd forgotten how good it felt, how exciting. Adrenaline coursed through my body, making every sensation stronger.

I needed more.

"Dr. Pierce," I moaned when he'd begun making his way down my neck again.

And he froze. His lips halted their descent and the hands that had been pushing me to the edge of exploding, pulled back and curled tight into fists.

"Shit," he whispered, the word brushing against my cheek. "Shit. Shit. Shit." He stepped back and looked at his hands clenching and un-clenching by his side before finally meeting my eyes. "I'm sorry. That was—"

"It's okay." I rushed to interrupt.

The guilt and regret in his eyes was too much, and I needed this gone. The past few minutes of my fantasies coming to life faded as fast as they'd come. Despite the feeling of my heart closing in on itself, beg-ging me to hold on a little longer, I knew it needed to end. I shouldn't have kissed him. I'd fucked up, and the struggling indecision in his eyes weighed me down.

I needed to not drag him down in my mistake. I couldn't listen to his apologies about how much of a mistake it was to have kissed me back, to touch me like he'd die if he didn't. I didn't want to hear his regret over something that had filled me with euphoria. "It's okay. It was nothing. A moment. And all my fault. I'm so sorry. It was dumb."

My apology was light, brushing what had just happened under the rug like it was no big deal. Like I couldn't still feel my lips tingling and my stomach dropping. A part of me wanted to demand he continue, to make him not give in to my escape. But the rational part of me knew I had three more months with him. I didn't want this moment to color everything. I didn't want it to change everything we'd been.

"Oaklyn, this is not your fault."

"It is. I kissed you like a silly girl. Like all the other girls that hit on you."

"You're anything but a silly girl." He ran a large palm across his face. "You are smart, sexy, and alluring and so beautiful. And god . . . " He paused, looking me over before sinking his teeth into his bottom lip. I wanted to get lost in those words, but I saw the *but* coming before he'd even said it. "You're nineteen—my student—and I should've known better."

I dug my nails into my palm to help center myself. To focus on that instead of the pain his rejection caused.

I wanted it to be over, and I never wanted it to be brought up again.

"It's okay. Let's forget it." I reached down and collected the folder I'd dropped and handed it to him. "Here you go. I should get going."

He took it from me but tossed it on the desk. "I can scan them in tomorrow. Let me grab my things so we can walk out together. It's late."

"Sure," I said with a forced smile and nod. I watched him close his laptop and lifted my backpack to my shoulder, hating the awkwardness. Desperate, I tried breaking it with a joke. "You should probably straighten that folder on your desk before it gives you nightmares tonight."

He moved the folder and smiled, not acknowledging that I was right.

While he did that, I went ahead and grabbed his jacket from the rack in the corner. As I held it out to him, something fell from under it.

"Whoops," I said, leaning down to pick it up.

"No. That's okay," he almost shouted, lunging for the hat.

But I got to it first and picked it up, brows furrowed as I studied it. I'd seen that hat before, the word *Cincinnati* stitched across the top. But where?

"Thank you," he said, snatching it out of my hand and shoving it in a desk drawer.

Where had I seen that hat before?

Then it hit me.

All the blood drained from my face as I turned to look at Dr. Pierce. His gaze was cautious, and I took in his jaw, clenched and familiar. How had I not noticed it when I saw it?

He'd watched me. *He'd watched me.* The words ran on repeat over and over, curling around my chest, swirling into my stomach until I thought I'd heave.

"You . . . " I tried to get it out, but I didn't have enough air in my lungs. "You—"

"Oaklyn." My name crested his lips softly, almost a plea because he knew I knew.

"Voyeur." I said it. I threw it out there and there was no going back. "You're at Voyeur. You *watched* me at Voyeur."

"Oaklyn." He stepped toward me, his hands out. "I'm so sorry. It's not wha—"

"Stop," I shouted. "Just stop." I looked him over, trying to read his face. What he thought. How long he knew. What he saw. What he wanted. Why he did it. Each question hitting at my core, spreading like ice water through my veins. "Just stop," I whispered, a plea I was embarrassed to let escape.

"Please."

I clenched my eyes shut trying to think. Trying to block him out and understand. Trying to figure out what to do next.

"I sat here beating myself up for being attracted to you. For luring you into kissing me. I beat myself up thinking I was just a child and not good enough. I—I was embarrassed for lusting after my professor, thinking about how *wrong* it was." A humorless laugh escaped my pinched lips. "But why bother with kissing me—touching me or facing me, when you can just sit behind a glass and watch me play with myself with no limits or expectations."

His hand rubbed at the back of his neck before they reached out to me again. I stumbled back a few steps, not wanting him to touch me. Not now. "That's not what it was. I didn't seek you out. It just happened. You were there. So perfect and I'm so sorry."

I heard him, but none of it penetrated the fog of embarrassment and hurt of being betrayed. "I felt crazy thinking I had imagined the attraction. That you would look at me a certain way, but you sure did look at me a certain way. You looked at me and saw me naked. Of course, you looked at me."

Tears burned the backs of my eyes as I thought over the friendship we had built and how dumb I must have been to be the only one enjoying it. He was just keeping me around because I turned him on. I'd been a fool.

"That is *not—*"

"What was your favorite scene?" I asked, disdain dripping from my words. "What did you see when you watched me in class? Did you remember the way I moaned as I fucked myself? How about when Jackson fucked me?" Each scenario was said louder than the last. "Or was it your favorite when you could make me suck his cock per your request. Did you imagine it was you?"

Dr. Pierce took another step forward, I held my ground this time. He stood over me, his nostrils flared as he breathed heavy and a muscle ticked in his jaw. "Oaklyn," he ground out.

"Do you want to see me strip now?" I whispered, dropping my backpack. I ripped my jacket off and began working on the buttons along my shirt baring my white lace bra. "Do you want me to get naked for you right here and do whatever you want?"

His hands latched on to my biceps and halted my progress. "Enough," he shouted, his voice cracking over the words. When he spoke again, it was softer, tinged with desperation. "That's enough."

This close with his hands on me felt dirtier after the way he'd touched me a moment before. The way he'd kissed me and made me feel cherished. Made me feel wanted in a way that didn't require me to perform. I hadn't realized how cold the performances felt at Voyeur until I had Callum's lips pressed to mine. Tears glossed over my eyes as I thought about how he'd called me beautiful. Had he meant it? Had he meant any of it?

His brows furrowed in pain and for a moment, I wanted to believe him. Believe that it was all happanstance and not at all what it seemed. Believe that what we shared in this office was what was real.

But I couldn't, because it hurt too much.

I jerked out of his hold. "You're not allowed to touch the perform-ers."

Not even bothering to button my shirt, I snatched my jacket up to my chest, grabbed my bag and got the hell out of there.

Chapter Sixteen

Callum

I shouldn't have been there, but she'd been avoiding me since she'd found out and I needed to talk to her.

It had been painful to watch her in class. I tried to focus, but the pain in her eyes was too hard to ignore. And behind that pain was heat. A fiery tension so strong, I could feel it. It was as if we'd been bound together by honesty and now that we'd seen it, we couldn't hide it away anymore. I didn't think I wanted to.

Our friendship shifted to a different path in the office that night. The hurt had thrown us off course, but the truth of our feelings set us on a different one, still together. At least I hoped. Once the possibility of losing her friendship hit me, I realized how much I'd come to need her. It hadn't just been Voyeur and watching her. It had been her laugh and bright presence in my office. Her smile from across the desk as we shared a sandwich.

I didn't want to lose that, and I wanted to explain, but she'd bolt from class as soon as it was over.

I had another opportunity when I walked in to find her in the copier room. I'd closed the door and stared at her back. She didn't react, didn't turn to look at me, or make any eye contact as she brushed past me to open the door. I turned to follow, and the palm of my hand pressed to the wood and held it closed.

She didn't immediately jerk away, so I stepped in close. Not pressing into her but letting her feel my heat. With my heart thundering in my ears, I tried to get her to listen to me.

"I'm so sorry, Oaklyn," I whispered down close, my words moving her hair. It felt like a punch to the gut when her breathing hiccupped, choking me, but she needed to know. "I meant what I said in the office. You are beautiful and smart and funny. The kiss we shared? That was us. Not Voyeur."

Her body sagged, slightly leaning back into me, and for the first time, I felt like I could take a deep breath again. Leaning down, I grazed my nose along her hair. "Please forgive me."

A moment later, she'd stiffened again. "Let me out."

And with that, the breath left my body again. But I'd stepped back and let her leave. When I came back into the main office she was gone. Donna told me that Oaklyn had left because she was feeling sick.

I knew it was a lie. I also knew, from my obsession over the last two months, that she worked almost every Friday night. That admission alone should have had me turning the other way. It should have been the big flashing sign that I'd gone too far. But every time I thought of her, my heart hurt a little less. My anxiety slipped further away. For the first time in nineteen years, I'd felt hope, and I wasn't letting it go so easily.

As soon as I walked into the main area, I spotted her by the bar.

There was a direct line of sight to her standing off to the side gathering drinks on a tray. She wore tall black boots that went over her knee. A patch of her thigh was left bare before a short purple skirt swayed around her legs with each movement. Above that was another patch of skin baring her belly button before black lace covered the top half of her abdomen and barely encased her breasts.

She was beautiful.

My heart thundered in my ears as I weaved my way in and out of people, ready to make her listen to me. Scared that she wouldn't. She could easily call security, say that I was stalking her and have my membership revoked. I doubted her success if she went that route, but it would at least buy her more time.

As I approached, I watched her push her long wavy hair behind her ear and I wanted to lean down and suck on the stud secured on her lobe.

"Oaklyn."

She froze at my gravelly voice, but eventually turned. She didn't say anything, just stared me down, and I did my best to decipher the swirl of emotions I saw in her eyes. Hurt, mixed with nerves and heat. So much heat. Out of my periphery I could see her breasts rising and falling as her breathing sped up. Somehow, I fought from staring and held her gaze, opening my emotions for her to see as much as I could.

I wanted her to feel my own hurt, my own desire, my own nerves, because, fuck me, I was nervous. Nervous that she would slap me and walk away. Nervous that she would stay, and I'd have to face every-thing after that.

My brows furrowed, and I had to look away because I hadn't thought of what was next. I just thought about how I couldn't lose her. But what happened next?

"Are you done hiding the fact that you watch me now?" Her voice was still soft but filled with sarcasm. "Why even bother going through the selection process? Just tell me to my face what you want me to do."

"I wanted to talk."

She ignored me and kept pushing, and I let her because she had every right to be pissed and take it out on me. "Do you want me naked or partially covered? Under the blankets? Alone? With a dildo or a vibrator? Or do you want me to get Jackson?" My jaw clenched. The more I got to know her, the more I hated watching her with him. "Do you want to see his head buried between my thighs? Do you want to watch me gag on his cock? How about watch as my breasts sway and he fucks me from behind."

"Stop," I choked out. "Please."

She swallowed and dropped her eyes, but not before I saw the regret. Oaklyn wasn't mean by nature. I could see she wasn't happy at my pain. Same as I wasn't happy with hers.

"Do you think I'm a whore?"

I reeled back at her whispered question. I almost didn't hear it over the music with her face looking down.

I reached my hand out and linked my fingers with hers, needing to touch her. To connect with her so she could feel me. Feel my sincerity.

"You're not supposed to touch us," she said, but didn't pull away. In fact, her fingers tightened, afraid I'd let go.

"Oaklyn. Look at me." She looked up and barely met my eyes from under her lashes. "You are beautiful. Smart. You are tenacious and determined. I respect your drive and need to succeed. Not everyone is born with money, and I'm impressed with your ability to find a way to get what you need."

"I have sex with people for money."

"No. That's not what Voyeur is, and you know it. You know, I know it. You're not getting paid to fuck people. To let them use your body. You are *not* a whore."

She nodded and dropped her eyes again. "Thank you."

The soft skin at her wrist pulsed under my thumb. I had an idea to prove to her I didn't think less of her. As much as I didn't want to see her with Jackson, if she wanted to see what she did to me when I watched people, then I would bite the bullet.

"Do you trust me?" I asked.

"I shouldn't after how much you've lied to me."

"I know. I don't have enough words to make you understand how sorry I am. And it's not fair of me to ask if you can trust me again after keeping everything from you, but I am. I want you to trust me, so I can prove to you how sexy I find you." I watched her throat move over a swallow and risked asking again. "Will you give me another chance and trust me?"

Her golden eyes assessed mine. It was one of the longest moments of my life, but she finally said, "Yes."

The word swelled in my chest, expanding it to almost bursting. I didn't deserve her trust after the way I'd kept watching her a secret, but it didn't stop me from holding on with both hands. "Accept the request from client four-seven-two."

She hesitated but nodded.

I brushed my body against hers when I walked past, heading to fill out my form.

Once I was done, I didn't look to see if she was watching me. I went to the restroom to splash cold water on my face, calming the rush of adrenaline burning through me. I stared up at the blue eyes meeting mine in the mirror and almost didn't recognize them. Almost didn't recognize the flash of excitement I saw there. Voyeur satisfied a need inside me, but I'd never felt so much that I was on the edge of something more. That feeling was stolen from me before I'd even had a chance to know what it was. Now, it made me feel like a teenager going on my first date.

The band on my wrist vibrated, and I inhaled as deep as I could before heading down the hall to the room indicated, except this time I didn't enter the private room. I walked into the main room and made my way to the overstuffed chair sitting in shadow in the alcove. It hid most of me, but she could still see parts of me in the shadows, and I wanted her to know how turned on I was by what she did.

The door clicked open and in came Oaklyn and Jackson, fumbling their hands over each other. Jackson kissed all down her neck walking her backwards. He kissed down her chest, back up to her cheeks, but never her lips. Per my request. Her lips were mine.

I unzipped my pants and eased them down my hips. Enough to pull my aching dick and balls out.

Jackson pushed Oaklyn back on the bed and her eyes flicked to me in the corner for just a moment and widened as she took in my fist wrapped around my cock. Jackson pulled her back into the moment when he fell to his knees, flipped her skirt up, and pulled down her panties. He spread her thighs wide and ran a palm down her pussy, making her jump. He kissed his way down to her core before burying his head between her thighs.

Oaklyn gasped, arched, clung to the sheets as Jackson ate her out, her eyes constantly flicking in my direction.

A primal part of me hated that another man was tasting her. I had to swallow down the urge to growl "mine" and rip him back, so I could finish the job. So, I could lean down and slick my tongue through her wet folds. But the way she kept looking for me as her hands clenched in pleasure, I knew she was with me. And as her breasts heaved from her moans, I remembered why I loved watching so much. I'd never had a connection to the women I watched before, and it added a whole new layer to the experience.

My cock twitched, and I pumped my fist harder. I imagined it was my head buried between her thighs. My tongue lapping up her taste. My mouth making her come. I had to squeeze my dick to hold off my own orgasm once Oaklyn finished.

Jackson placed one soft kiss to her slit and then got up to leave.

It was just Oaklyn and I in the room, finally, but the show wasn't over. No, the fun had just begun.

She rolled over on the bed and crawled up to reach in the nightstand, pulling out the same dildo I'd watched her fuck herself with before. She resituated herself and spread her trembling thighs open for me. I could see how glistening wet she was and I wanted to taste her. With a shaking hand she pressed the thick head of the cock against her opening and slid it in. Our groans mixed, making the most beautiful sound.

She slipped it out and pushed it back in, slowly fucking herself with it. I pulled my hand away from my cock and began talking.

"I've been coming to Voyeur for five years." Her eyes shot to mine and paused. "Keep fucking yourself." She obeyed, and I continued. "Voyeur provided an intimate scene that I could feel a part of. It wasn't as cold as porn on the internet. It was graphic and beautiful, and it turned me the fuck on. I saw you right before Christmas. You came walking out of a room and stole my breath. Innocence and sexiness. I'd thought about you over the holidays. I didn't even know what it was, but just a glimpse and you stuck with me. Then I saw you perform for the first time after the new year. And when I watched you, I'd never felt so connected with anyone. I became addicted. Then you walked in to my class and my world tilted."

I squeezed my cock again when she moaned and the dildo moved faster. I wanted to get up. Go to her. It hadn't been a part of my initial plan, but I needed to touch her. The desire burned in my chest and ignited my body, making my dick twitch in my palm. If I stood, I'd be putting us both at risk. My job, her schooling, her future and mine. All of it.

But staring at Oaklyn, her eyes glazed and looking just as desperate as I felt, I knew I couldn't leave this room without finally giving in.

I stood up, my cock still hanging out. Still hard.

"Wha—What are you doing?"

She hadn't stopped, but slowed down and as I stood before her, I watched the glistening piece of silicone, coated with her juices, moving in and out. "Are you going to press your panic button?" I asked. I lifted my hand to hers, pausing to make sure she was okay with me touching her. Making sure *I* was okay with touching her. One last chance for us both to stop.

Looking down at her swollen lips wrapped around the end of the toy sent a resounding yes through me. I was done waiting and pulling back. Her head shook, and I dropped my hand to hers, pushing the toy back in.

"Good." I pushed her hand away and began to control the motions. "I couldn't believe I'd become so infatuated with my student. A nineteen-year-old student. It didn't stop me though. Especially when I got to know you. The infatuation turned to truly liking who you were as a person. Forming a friendship with you. And as much as I hated myself, you still gave me something no one else ever had, and I couldn't turn away."

I pushed all the way in and lifted my thumb to brush against her clit, making her hips pop off the bed. She was so warm. So wet. I watched my digit roll across the swollen rosy flesh and pictured myself pulling the toy out and pushing myself deep inside her. My cock jumped at the thought tapping her thigh. However, no matter how she made me want, the panic still hid inside me, lingering less, but still there.

"Please," she begged me.

I removed the toy and lifted her to stand. Her body trembling before me, I unzipped her skirt and let it fall to the floor. Then I stepped into her, pinning my cock between our stomachs. I groaned at the contact and she lifted her hands to my shoulders holding herself to me as she rested her head on my chest.

I fought impossibly hard to control my breathing, my skin prickling as a dizziness swarmed my head. Her skin against my length was the closest I'd been to fucking a woman and wanting to.

But I couldn't. The warmth and pressure surged behind my closed lids and I had to pull back before it triggered something other than excitement. Pinching my eyes shut, I pushed the memories down, not ready to stop.

I turned her around to face the bed, too quickly for her to look at my face. I flicked my fingers against the clasp at the back of her top and watched as it fell to the floor. She stood before me completely naked, completely on display. Leaning down I bit her shoulder and stared at her breasts from over her shoulder that I'd seen so often before. My palms engulfed them as I held them gently, letting my thumbs roll across the tip. She gasped and jerked, her butt pressing against my dick, and I pushed her to bend over the bed. My fingers trailed down her back, across the crack of her ass and played at her wet opening before shoving inside.

I needed to feel her. I needed to be as close as I could to her heat. I couldn't handle it on my cock yet, the memories still clinging, but I could still feel her.

"Dr. Pierce," she moaned.

"Cal." Pressing against her, pinning my hand, I bent over and kissed up her spine to her neck and whispered. "Call me Callum or Cal while I'm inside you."

And she came. Her legs trembled as my fingers worked in and out of her and my thumb rolled over her clit. We both moaned when her tight cunt clenched tight around me as she rocked her hips back, fucking herself on my hand. The sounds mixed together like music to my ears as her cum slid down my fingers.

It wasn't until that moment that I realized I was rocking my own hips against her soft skin. Dry humping her like a teenager as I buried my fingers deep inside her, wringing her orgasm from her body.

I almost laughed at how euphoric something so juvenile could feel. A twenty-nine-year-old man, giddy over being able to dry hump a thigh. Skin-to-skin. Not breaking out in a sweat. Not having any tremors. Not having my heart beat out of my chest in panic as the past crept in. The breath whooshed out of my lungs under the emotional weight of feeling my dick press to her soft skin, amazed and awed by the feel of it.

She collapsed onto the mattress when I removed my hand and turned her head to look at me. Could she see the excitement, the desire, the heat boiling inside me? I wanted her to see it all. I wanted her to know how much I honored the gift she was giving me. I held her eyes as I licked every ounce of her cum off my fingers.

"Callum." It was the first time she'd said my name and it shot through me, straight to my balls and I had to come. I almost felt bad taking advantage of the freedom of not being shackled by my demons, but I couldn't find it in me.

I wiped my palm over her pussy to gather her juices and fisted myself. Hard and fast, I jerked my cock against her ass, holding her eyes and letting her see my desire, focusing on her to keep me in the moment. Her golden eyes locked on mine, her full lips parted and panting. She was my anchor as fire licked down my skin pulling my orgasm from me. I shot long ropes of white cum all across her ass as she arched up accepting it all. My whole body clenched as my orgasm tore through me. All the more intense with a woman—this woman—in front of me.

I had never touched myself—bared myself in front of a woman before and the significant moment washed over me. I collapsed on top of her, pressing grateful kisses across her shoulders, fighting back tears. I'd never been this way with a woman. I'd never been able to.

"Thank you, Oaklyn. Thank you." I barely croaked the words past the lump in my throat.

"Of course, it's my job."

Her words were a bucket of cold water over me, and I froze. "Don't cheapen this," I pleaded. I couldn't diminish the enormity of what I'd just done. Because of her.

"I'm just stating the truth."

Another bucket of ice and I couldn't stand there as she made one of the biggest moments of my life nothing but a job. Nothing but something she felt she had to do. I couldn't listen to it. I wouldn't. I pulled back and began fastening my pants. "This isn't your job and you know it. This was me and you."

"What does *me and you* even mean anymore? Now that all of this is out in the open, you don't have to hide anymore. You can waltz right in and know I'm available for whatever you want." The hurt bled through the cold tone she tried to use. I hated that I'd put it there. I hated that she had to work here and even wonder. "You don't have to hide anything at school anymore and be my friend."

"That's not at all—"

"I can't right now, Callum. Just . . . not right now." Her tired admission pierced my heart.

She hadn't moved from her spot yet by the time I'd finished dressing. She still lay flat on the bed, her head in the blanket and my cum on her back. I had to try and talk to her one more time. Make her understand how wrong she was.

"Oaklyn, please."

"Just go, Callum."

I closed my eyes tight and tried to gather myself, tried to fight back the ball of emotion working its way up my throat.

"Please," she whispered.

So I did as she asked. I left. I didn't want to, and I didn't think it was the end of it all, but I left because in that moment, I knew she needed time to process.

But I wasn't letting go. I wasn't done trying with her yet. Not by a long shot.

Chapter Seventeen

Oaklyn

I pressed ignore on another phone call from my parents. It was too windy on my walk across campus, and I just didn't have it in me to talk to them. They sent me messages with their apologies and let me know how proud they were of me, but I just couldn't hear it and respond the way they were expecting. I didn't feel like I was doing anything to make them proud, and while I'd forgiven them, I was still bitter and angry about the situation I was in.

Especially after last night.

A shiver shook my body as I remembered what Dr. Pierce had done to me. A mixture of emotions twisted inside my body.

Heat from the way he'd watched me, the way he'd touched me, the way he'd stroked himself, the way he came.

Shame from letting him touch me and letting my anger go so easily. From admitting my deepest fear that he would think I was a whore, that maybe *I* thought I was a whore.

I shook off the feeling and focused on getting to my appointment. Dr. Denly, my department advisor, had emailed me yesterday asking me to come see him this morning before classes. He hadn't said what it was about, and all the possibilities had my nerves firing off on high alert.

If I was nervous for my meeting with Dr. Denly, then I was petrified of Dr. Pierce's class. Maybe my meeting would run late, and I'd have an excuse not to go.

I knocked on the open door. "Hi, Dr. Denly. You wanted to see me?"

"Yes, yes. Come in." He pulled his wire-framed glasses off and leaned back in his chair, indicating I take a seat. "Bit chilly this morning, isn't it?"

"Sure is," I agreed, shedding my jacket. "I'm looking forward to the spring."

"Me too." He clapped his hands together and smiled. "But I didn't ask you to come so we could chit-chat about the weather. I wanted to discuss an opportunity with you. It came across my desk yesterday and you're one of the first people I thought of."

"Okay," I said.

"I know we talked about your money situation earlier this semester, and I wanted to let you know about an internship that is opening up with the athletic department. You'd be helping out the physical therapist."

"Um, wow. Thank you. Are there any certain criteria they're looking for?" I asked, all of this sounding too good to be true.

"They usually want someone who is a sophomore or higher and has anatomy and physiology under their belt." My heart plummeted since I checked none of those boxes. "But you're a good student, Oaklyn. The program will start over the summer with some training and officially kick off next fall. And you have advanced A&P from high school. Pair that with my recommendation, and I'm sure they will overlook a few things. We'll also get you signed up for the right courses to show them your initiative. I think you're a good fit."

"I—I'm so honored you thought of me," I said, a wide smile splitting my face. "Thank you so much."

"Of course." He stood from his desk and walked over to me with a paper. "Here's the application. Look it over and fill it out. Deadline is in two weeks, so don't waste time getting it back to me."

"I won't," I said, stuffing the paper in my bag and standing to leave. "Thank you so much for this. I won't let you down."

I walked toward physics, practically bouncing with excitement at the possibility of a paid internship. It wasn't much, but with all new scholarships and loans, my work study programs, and maybe finding another job, I could quit working at Voyeur. Not that I hated working there, but the reality of Dr. Pierce having seen me brought a whole new issue into play that I hadn't really considered.

What if I ran into other people who'd seen me? What if it was someone I knew, and they used it against me? Judged me?

I needed that internship.

Walking into class, I kept my head down and avoided eye contact with Dr. Pierce. I'd entered close to class starting, which prevented me from sitting in the back like I'd planned. Olivia waved at me from our usual spot in the front where she'd saved a seat. Damnit.

"Where were you?" she whispered.

"I had a meeting with Dr. Denly about a paid internship."

Her jaw dropped open and her eyes widened with excitement. She was about to ask another question when Dr. Pierce started the lecture.

"I'll tell you later."

Despite spending most of the time avoiding his gaze, his voice drew me in, and I lifted my head. He'd been staring right at me and now that I'd looked, I couldn't turn away. It was like he controlled my ability to move. I was frozen under his gaze.

Electricity was a living breathing thing between us. Did everyone see it? The more I stared, the more I saw. Yes, the heat was there, but something else. Some other emotion I couldn't decipher. I tried desperately though, needing to understand what he thought. He'd left me lying there on the bed after I almost begged him to leave, but I couldn't help but remember his soft kisses and his thank yous, as though I'd given him some gift. I'd been scared of what happened next. Scared that he would think that I could be bought for sex, worried that now that he'd had me, he would let me know what he really thought of me.

The thoughts had run through my head, and I'd panicked. Would I have turned around and seen regret lining his eyes? Would I have seen disgust? Any of the emotions I'd imagined seeing on his face had scared me. I wasn't even sure of what I'd *wanted* to see. Was I hoping for desire, happiness, caring? Was I hoping to find that he'd want more than just sex? Was I hoping he'd have a blank stare ready to ignore any of it?

My body and heart had wanted to shout how right it felt to have his body over mine. How perfectly we aligned, and how his lips felt on my skin. My mind had wanted me to run, tried to convince me that I'd made a huge mistake letting my professor touch me. So, I'd been a coward and demanded he leave, taking control of the moment before any other emotions could. However, watching him now, what I was feeling took my breath away. The heat was there, but so was desire and . . . Hope?

A book fell with a loud smack onto the floor, and it broke the lock between us. We blinked, and finally I was free.

I still watched him too closely, trying to avoid his eyes when he'd glimpse my way. I watched his long fingers grip the marker as he scribbled across the board and all I could think about was how they'd been inside me. How they'd felt when they'd wrung an orgasm from my body. I remembered the way he'd licked my cum off of them as he held my stare.

"Dr. Pierce."

"Call me Callum or Cal while I'm inside you."

I heard it over and over in my head. My breathy moans and his rough voice that still sent shivers skittered over my skin just remembering it.

His moan haunted me last night when he came all over my ass and back. I woke to a bruise on my shoulder from the way he bit me as he touched my breasts for the first time. I lifted my hand and rubbed against it over my sweater, loving the soreness and the constant reminder of it.

His eyes locking on the motion, causing him to stutter over his words. His gaze seared me with heat. He was remembering too, and it made the ache that much sweeter.

"Class is over, sister," Olivia said, pulling me from my trance.

I looked around and sure enough, Dr. Pierce—Callum—was sitting at his desk, stealing subtle glances my way as the rest of class began to pack up.

"Sorry," I said, shaking my head. "Had a late night, and I'm pretty tired now."

"How's it going, by the way?"

"How's what going?"

"You know," Olivia said, bobbing her eyebrows. "*Work.*"

"Oh, yeah." A blush heated my cheeks, and I looked down to stuff my papers in my bag, not wanting her to see. "It's good. Fine."

I kept my answer vague, not wanting to talk about it. I wasn't necessarily ashamed, but it wasn't your typical job either. Certainly not one you talked about in public, even to your friend who'd helped you get the job. But mostly, I was worried that once I opened my mouth, I'd confess my exploit with Callum.

"Fine, don't spill all the details. At least tell me hot guys work there. Maybe you could pass my number along to one of them."

"Sure," I agreed laughing. Unconvincingly, it seemed.

"Are you doing too much?" she asked, placing a hand on my shoulder. "You sound more than just a little tired."

"It's just one semester. It's a lot, but there's a light at the end of the tunnel."

"You know, the offer still stands about me loaning you the rest of what you owe," she said, fiddling with her bag.

"Olivia," I sighed. "Thank you, but I can't."

"Why?" she asked, her irritation making her sound snappish. "Why are you being so stubborn?" She took a deep breath to collect herself. "I'm sorry. I just miss you and I don't get it. You'll take loans from all the banks and work yourself to the bone, but you won't let me help."

I'd explained to her before, but not in all its painful details. "My parents always struggled with money, but they never took loans. They worked more jobs and cut expenses, but they never took loans. Then one time—one freaking time—their best friends offered them a loan when my parents had nowhere else to turn, and it ruined them. Their *close* friends lorded it over them, asking for favors and extras. They never signed anything because they were friends, and they abused it by changing the payments, asking for more on different months without notice. Or changing the dates and getting pissed when my parents didn't have the money."

For the first time Olivia looked at me with understanding.

"My parents always made the payments, no matter the circumstances. Which usually meant we went without. And my friendship with their daughter deteriorated right along with everything else. She became snobby and made fun of my family for not having enough."

"I'm sorry. I didn't know."

"It's okay. I never told you," I said packing up my bag. "Money changes people, Olivia. It changes situations and relationships, and I can't have anything change between us."

"Aw." She put her hand over her heart and pouted dramatically. "You'd rather suffer than lose me. It's true love."

"Like I said, there's a light at the end of the tunnel. In the new school year, I'll have more scholarships and *bank* loans. It will be great," I finished with a forced smile, looking up to see Callum's eyes jerk away again.

Standing, I tossed my bag over my shoulder and kept my eyes glued to the door. I just had to get out of there, and I'd buy myself one more day of avoidance.

"Miss Derringer," Dr. Pierce called.

Shit. I'd been so close to freedom. I should've explained to Olivia outside the classroom, taken my opportunity to get the hell out of there.

It was too late now.

Cautiously, I turned with raised eyebrows and hoped I hid the panic rushing through me.

"May I have a word? It's about the sign-up for the project."

How did he keep his face so calm and collected when I was trembling from the inside out? I needed to get out of there.

"Umm, I can't, sorry. I actually have to get to my next class. Emailing me might work best." I gave a forced smile, turned and grabbed Olivia's arm, and got us the hell out of there.

"Wow, that was awfully brave to turn down Dr. Pierce's request. He seemed serious. I would have stayed with you. You know, just friendly support. Not at all so I could drool over him more." She laughed and bumped me with her shoulder. "You know what? Be less brave next time."

I laughed too, but mine was tinged with a little desperation.

I felt anything but brave anymore.

Chapter Eighteen

Callum

I waited all of Friday for her to show up. I canceled meetings, put off phone calls, declined a lunch invitation. Until I finally got up the nerve to ask Donna if she'd seen Oaklyn.

"Miss Derringer called in this morning to let me know she wouldn't be in."

"Oh." I nodded "Okay."

"Sorry, I didn't tell you sooner, the Post-it note I wrote it on got lost under all this craziness. Do you need me to find you another student aide for something?"

"No, no. Thank you."

I'd returned to my office and tried to focus on anything but Oaklyn. Once the clock struck four o'clock and people started going home, I still sat there. Rationalizing that if she thought I went home and wasn't there, that she may show up for something. It didn't happen.

The sun had lowered over two hours ago and I needed to admit defeat. I closed down my computer and tossed my glasses to the side carelessly. Oaklyn flooded my mind as I wiped my hands down my face. How had I gotten here? An adult lurking in his own office waiting for his student to *possibly* show up. I should've been home, but my desires were urging me to do all I could to see her.

I stared at the black frames haphazardly laying in the middle of papers, having knocked the stack out of alignment. Immediately, I re-situated the papers until the edges evened up, grabbed the glasses and folded the arms in before resting the eyewear at the top center of my desk.

Shaking my head at my inability to just toss something on a desk, I stood from my desk and packed up my bag.

I had just stepped off the elevator on the bottom floor when I heard my name.

"Callum?"

Taking a deep breath, I closed my eyes and forced a smile on my face when I turned. "Hey, Shannon. What are you doing here so late?"

"Ugh." She dropped her head back with an eye-roll. "Staff meeting. It didn't start until almost six, so we're just getting done."

"That's disappointing for a Friday."

"Tell me about it." A bright smile stretched across her lips as she stood a little taller. "Good news is that I got to run into you."

"I'm not sure I'm good enough to make a late staff meeting worth it," I said, laughing and looking away.

She bit her lip as her heavy eyes looked up to mine. She wasn't done with me yet. "I think you are. Hey, you want to get a drink?"

Taking her in, I considered it. I considered saying yes and finding a distraction in Shannon's company. She was beautiful, my age, and more importantly, not my student. She checked a lot of boxes, but it wouldn't have worked out, no matter how much I should have wanted to try, and I didn't want to lead her on.

"Thank you for the offer, but it's been a hell of a day, and I'm just going to head home for an early night."

"Okay," she said, disappointed. I hated that I did that, but I would have hated myself more if I'd gone when I knew it wasn't where I wanted to be. "Maybe some other time."

Evading an answer, I nodded once, letting her take from that what she wanted. "Well, I'm parked over here. You have a good night."

"Thanks, Cal," she said to my back. I'd already turned toward my car.

By the time I got into the driver's seat, I was at a new low. Feeling like I was never going to find a relationship, that maybe I didn't deserve one. Didn't deserve intimacy like a normal twenty-nine-year-old man. I hated these waves of emotions that hit me. Fifteen fucking years and I still let my demons rule me. Would they forever keep me from a future with a companion? There was a beautiful woman—sweet, kind—standing in front of me, and I'd turned her down. Why? Because all I could remember was a racing heart and sweating when she touched me?

I sat in my car, gripping my keys too tightly waiting to hear the crack of the plastic fob.

Maybe I could go to Voyeur. It always calmed me when I was down about my bleak future. Maybe Oaklyn would be there. And what? Maybe I could pin her to the bed again and feel her squeeze around my fingers? Maybe so I could feel her soft skin on mine?

So *she* could calm my mind?

Fuck, when was the last time I'd been around a woman intimately and not had my mind racing, preparing for the panic to set in? The last time I came with someone so close and didn't end up shaking with old nightmares consuming me?

She was an enigma. I couldn't even think of what it was about her that was different. It made no sense. If it had, then I would have happily tried to recreate that magic with almost anyone who wasn't off-limits.

Yesterday had been hell. Watching Oaklyn sit there and try not to look at me as much as I was trying to not look at her. When our eyes had collided, she'd touched her shoulder and I knew she was remembering the way I'd bit into the soft flesh. Was there a mark to remind her of me? My dick twitched at the thought even now. I'd had to stand behind the lectern for a solid five minutes to get myself under control as I lectured.

As they'd packed up, I'd scrambled for a reason to get her to talk to me after class, making it appear anything other than my need to reassure myself and her that the night at Voyeur hadn't been just a figment of my imagination. Ask her what it meant?

Instead, she'd brushed me off and bolted.

Now, as I backed out of my spot, my body urged me go, go, go.

I pulled up to the stop sign to leave the school campus and my hands gripped the wheel, pulsing tight around the leather.

Right to Voyeur?

Left to home?

Right?

Or left?

Taking a deep breath, I began to turn the wheel to the right, when my phone rang. No one was behind me, so I waited at the sign and answered.

"Hello?"

"Callum," Reed greeted me. "What are you doing?"

"I'm just leaving work, man."

"Work? At seven-thirty on a Friday? Damn, your life is boring."

"You have a point or just calling to criticize?"

"I do love to give you shit, but no. Come over for dinner, and we can watch the game. We ordered way too much food and Karen has her sister over. I need some help to balance out the testosterone."

I didn't even hesitate. "Yeah, man. I'm on my way."

I turned the wheel left and headed to Reed's house.

* * *

"So," Reed started, which should have been my first warning. "How's the student? You cave and fuck her yet?"

I choked on the beer I'd just tried to swallow. Cupping my hand beneath my chin, trying to catch any liquid before it spilled on their couch. Karen would kill me if she walked in and saw me making a mess on her new couch. We'd had dinner and then Karen and her sister sat at the table drinking wine, while Reed and I had gone to the bonus room to watch the game. At that moment, sipping wine and talking shoes sounded preferable to answering Reed.

Had I fucked her? Not really.

"No. Jesus." I settled on complete denial. "Things are fine, why would you say that?"

"I think thou doth protest too much." Reed knew me too well.

"Everything is . . . fine."

"So, you're thinking about fucking her," he said with a smirk, trying to rile me up.

"Fuck you."

"What? If she's interested, why not?" he responded with a shrug.

"I'm her teacher. She's nineteen. She's my student. She works in the department." I held my fingers up as I listed off each reason.

"Will you have her again in class?"

"No, she's a different major."

"Is she underage?"

"No. Where are you going with this?"

"Is she hot? Interested? Willing?"

"Reed," I growled. He'd obviously had too much to drink. I didn't need him listing off reasons why I should rather than reasons why it wouldn't be insane.

"Come on, man. Live a little."

"She's a child."

He tossed his head back and laughed out loud. I looked toward the door, waiting for Karen to pop in to see what was so funny. That was all I needed, Reed telling his wife about my predicament. God, the look she'd give me would probably wither my balls, and I wouldn't have to worry about sex ever again.

"She's an adult," Reed said once he'd recovered enough. "And even hearing you say she's a child, I know you don't believe it." He stared at me with knowing eyes. "I haven't seen you this riled up about a woman in a long time. It's good to see, man. Even if there is the issue of her being your student. She won't be forever." Another pause. "Tell me about her."

I finished off my bottle of beer, wondering if it was a good idea to talk to my friend about my student, whom I liked and had already been sexual with.

Fuck it.

"Oaklyn is . . . " Closing my eyes, I pictured her laughing on the other side of my desk. Of her smiling and calling me Clark Kent. "She's smart. Determined. Beautiful. She's kind and god, the way she looks when she laughs." Nothing could stop the smile stretching across my lips. She did that. Just the thought of her.

"She sounds hot." Reed broke the moment, and I gave him an irritated side-eye. He only bobbed his eyebrows and took another pull of beer.

"You're a pig. Karen deserves better."

"You're damn right I do," Karen said from the doorway. My heart thudded hard, and I wondered how much she'd overheard. If she heard anything, she didn't let on. "But I love him anyway," she said, walking over to perch on the arm of the couch. She leaned down to kiss Reed. "Aubrey left and it's late, so I'm heading to bed."

"Okay. You feeling okay?" Reed asked Karen and a look passed between them.

"I'm fine, babe."

"Should we tell him?"

"Tell me what?" I asked, trying to keep up with the conversation.

"I'm sure you're dying to gossip with your boyfriend."

"I really am," Reed agreed before turning to me. "Well, friend. It's happened. Hell has frozen over, and fate has decided I'm fit to be a father. We're pregnant."

The first feeling hit me in the chest like a sledgehammer. All the more intense because I wasn't expecting it. I should have been happy and elated for my friend. Instead, my heart closed in on itself with jealousy.

My mouth moved somehow, trying to force something out. "Congratulations, you guys," I finally managed. "That's amazing. Karen, if he ever gets out of line, I'll whip him into shape. I'm serious. Ice cream any time of the night. If he doesn't deliver, I'll make sure he pays."

She laughed as I'd intended. "Thanks, Callum." She was too entranced with her husband, the father of her future child, to see the pain I was sure marred my face.

"All right. I'm off to bed," Karen said pulling me out of my revelry. "You two girls don't stay up too late gabbing."

"Okay, honey. I'll kick him out soon," Reed agreed, winking my way to let me know he was joking.

"Good. You know I hate sleeping alone." She leaned down with a smile before gently kissing him, his hand on her still-flat stomach. I felt more like a voyeur now than I ever had at the club.

I wanted what was in front of me. I wanted a wife. A family. A woman to carry my child. My chest ached with a strong desire for those things; my limbs were heavy from wanting to reach out and take them for my own. I just didn't know how to get to them, waiting on the other side of the dark cloud holding me back. But I wanted them. And when I looked closely and imagined what I wanted, the faceless woman who set me at ease in my future began to take shape.

And all I could see was Oaklyn smiling up at me.

The image knocked the wind out of me. As Reed stared after his wife, I took a moment to collect myself. What the hell was I doing? Oaklyn was avoiding me, and I couldn't stop imagining her in my future.

What was I doing?

I wanted to pull out my hair, distract myself from the flood of emotions she brought out in me. Pleasure, desire, want, happiness, panic, stress, hope. All of them at war within me. And the more they fought each other, the less control I felt.

I'd just finished my third deep breath as Reed turned back around. We didn't talk much the rest of the night, just finished watching the game. Him with a contented smile on his face, and me staring blankly at the screen trying to come up with a plan to screw a tight lid back on my emotions.

By the time I pulled into my driveway, I knew what I had to do. I didn't want to, but indifference was a safe emotion.

At least it had to be better than everything Oaklyn sparked inside of me.

Chapter Nineteen

Oaklyn

Slamming another drawer closed, I looked toward Dr. Pierce's office, hoping he had heard, and it annoyed him. I refused to think of him as Callum. He'd made it clear this week that he was officially Dr. Pierce.

Abusing his power as my superior, if you asked me. It was the second night he'd kept me later than necessary. The whole office was deserted except for me and him. Every time we spoke, it was Miss Derringer with a distant voice. Lacking all emotion. What the hell had changed from the heated looks in class last week? Was he pissed that I'd refused to stay to talk to him? That I'd called out on Friday?

I'd just needed time to process, the whole situation clouding my mind. Then the entire time I'd worked at Voyeur over the weekend, I'd been looking for him. Constantly waiting for him to walk through the door, come to me and demand I take his request for another repeat.

My heart had been erratic every minute I was there, worried that he'd come, more worried that he wouldn't.

And he hadn't.

Feeling that desire for him to come to me had cracked open a door to clarity. I wanted him to. For the first time I had a solid feeling of want. Not fear or indecisiveness but *want*. Want for him to walk through the door and stare at me the same way he had in class.

But he never came and clocking out on Sunday night had been depressing.

I hoped I'd have time to talk to him on Monday, that we would sit and have our lunch and figure it out. But he'd shut his door and told me I should go grab some lunch and be back in an hour. I'd stared at the wood between us with my jaw hanging open. When he finally opened the door again, it was to request I type up meeting notes.

"If you would, Miss. Derringer," he'd said, gesturing to the papers on the corner of the desk without even bothering to look up from his work. As though those same fingers hadn't been buried inside me, hadn't made me come.

That had been the beginning of the benign requests and menial tasks.

Reorganize the beakers.

Rewash the beakers.

File these papers alphabetically. File these numerically.

Make these copies and organize the packets.

Go to the chemistry department and help them move the centrifuge up to our floor.

I was waiting for him to ask me to get on the floor and spit-shine his shoes. I ground my jaw at each request. I hadn't hoped today would've been any better after his completely ignoring my existence in class, but I hadn't expected him to keep me late. *Again.*

It made me want to regret having let anything happen between us, but I didn't. Not really. I missed the friendship we'd formed. I missed sharing lunches with him and laughing over our easy banter. That was the most painful part of all of this.

Even though staying late on a night I had off from Voyeur and could catch up on homework was a close second.

I walked to his office and stared at his head bent over some papers. I knew he knew I was there, but he refused to look up and acknowledge me. Why bother?

"I'm done with everything, *Dr. Pierce*." I made sure to stress his name, so he had no doubt I felt his cold shoulder.

"Another thirty minutes and I'll be ready to lock up. You can help me," he said, not even bothering to look up.

That was enough. It was after seven and even if we hadn't shared our experience, I wouldn't stand for this disrespect. I was sick and tired of him acting like an asshole. I had more than two months left with him, and I wasn't going to let him think he could walk all over me.

"You can't keep me here."

That got his attention. Finally, his head lifted, and he stared at me with blank eyes.

"Excuse me, Miss Derringer?"

I scowled at the *Miss Derringer*. A small flicker of something crossed his eyes. Too fast for me to see. I stomped, like a child throwing a temper tantrum, further into the room and slammed the door. No one was around, and the heavy wood banging shut made me feel better.

"I may only be a teenager and you're my professor, but you can't take advantage of me like this."

He laughed. Actually *laughed*. My eyebrows rose high on my forehead. His head fell back, and mouth opened around the deep rumble escaping into the room to taunt me. I took a deep breath and furrowed my brows. His chest shook with humor he couldn't seem to contain.

"This is not fucking funny," I growled.

Getting himself under control, his eyes were no longer blank when he looked at me. The blue almost glowed in the dimly lit room. I took an involuntary step back as his gaze raked over me, each inch of my body igniting with his stare.

"Oaklyn, trust me when I tell you I see you as anything but a teenager. Anything but my student."

The way he said my name after refusing to all week, felt like a gift.

"Then what?" I asked with less fire and anger than had fueled me a moment before, but no less frustration.

He stared, his eyes dropping to my mouth as my tongue slicked across my lips. Then they dropped even further to his desk. He nudged a pen that was already in line with the one next to it, then a stack of papers that was already straight. His hand seemed to float across the desk, looking for a distraction rearranging anything they came across.

My irritation grew with every item that he moved just a fraction of an inch. It bloomed in my chest, squeezing my lungs. Each second I waited for an answer, it spread until I was ready to explode. I stomped the last two steps to his desk, snatched the pens up, and tossed them down on the ground.

His head jerked to the floor where the three pens lay scattered, then it slowly turned toward me. His brows furrowed, his jaw clamped shut, the muscle clenching in his cheek, his breathing growing heavy. He looked like a bull ready to charge.

Well I was fucking ready.

I threw my arms wide. "Huh?" I shouted. "What do you see when you look at me?" I had wanted the question to come out strong and demanding. Instead it slipped out as a desperate plea.

Dr. Pierce pushed his chair back and stood, not taking his eyes off me as he moved to stand directly in front of me, towering over me. My neck arched so I could hold his gaze and I had to fight from taking the last step to close the gap between our bodies. He looked over my face, and I almost whimpered when I watched his tongue roll across his lips.

I thought I knew his answer, but nothing prepared me for what he said next.

"I see you sprawled out on a bed. Naked. Your body flushed as you roll your rosy nipples between your fingers. Tugging at them. Making them hard." Heat washed over my body as I sucked in a gasp, but I refused to look away as he continued. "I see your head thrown back as you laugh at a joke I shared over lunch." He took the last step toward me, and I swayed closer. Pulled in by his confession.

"I see you in class, your lips stretched in the most beautiful smile, and I remember the taste of them." He leaned down closer, so I could feel his words against my skin. "I'm desperate to taste them again," he growled.

Fire zipped down my spine to my core and I was sure I was going to combust from the pressure of desire—of need—bubbling up inside me.

His breath caressed against my mouth, urging it open, and I pressed up to my toes to close the gap. Groaning, our lips locked together, melding as one, glued together by his words of desire, by the memory of the last time we kissed. This time there was no hesitation as we wrapped our arms around each other, holding tight like we were trying to become one. His tongue pushed past my lips, demanding I let him in and taste what he wanted.

I opened willingly, moaning when his tongue brushed mine. I tasted him in return, the taste of mint and him, the man. My fingers dug in his hair as he leaned down to reach more of me, his hands skimming over my hips to grip the cheeks of my ass, bunching up the material of my dress.

We each pulled back to breathe, and when I opened my eyes, his were still closed as he rubbed circles, massaging my bottom.

"What else, Dr. Pierce? What else do you see?" I whispered against his lips.

He exhaled a heavy breath from his nose before he gripped me tight, and growled, "Callum. Call me Callum," against my lips. He hoisted me up and I wrapped my legs around his waist. His mouth began devouring mine as the room spun, and he turned to sit me on his desk. He pulled back only to trail kisses down and back up my neck where he nipped at the lobe of my ear.

"I see you bent over my desk, my fingers disappearing inside you."

I inhaled sharply at the imagery and tried to lower my hands down his chest, needing to touch him. He stopped me, gripping my wrists tight and pulling them down to the desk behind me. I wanted to protest but then his kisses moved past my neck, going as far as the V of my dress would allow.

Stopping at my breasts he looked up at me and bit at my nipple through the cotton, causing me to jerk in pleasure.

"I imagine your perfect ass covered in my cum. I imagine rubbing it in, soaking it into your skin. Maybe then you would know what it feels like to have me be a part of you."

I didn't know what to say. That was so much more than sexual. It was much deeper than what I'd hoped he felt for me. I opened my mouth to ask more, but a groan escaped instead as he bit my other nipple and began dragging his hands up my thighs and under my skirt.

"Dr. Pier—"

"Callum. Callum when I'm inside you," he said, falling into his chair and rolling between my spread legs.

"But you're not—ohhh."

"What was that?" he asked with a smirk, his fingers pushing in and out of me.

They moved so quickly under my panties. I was so wet, there was no resistance as he shoved two fingers inside me and rotated them.

"Callum," I said on a breath.

He groaned against the skin of my inner thigh. "I see you naked on a bed, legs spread wide with a dark head buried between them." His eyes locked on my core as his hand twisted.

I couldn't help but wonder what he saw, my dress still pulled down enough to block my view. However, it rode up when he used his free hand to lift my leg and place my foot on one arm of his chair.

He pulled his fingers out and I whimpered at the loss, but then he lifted my other leg to the other arm of his chair. There I sat, my legs spread wide on my professor's desk. My pussy exposed from my panties being pulled to the side, so he could see what he did to me.

"I imagine it's me. I imagine how soft the folds of your pussy will feel against my tongue. If you're sweeter directly from the source rather than licking you off my fingers."

And then his head was between my thighs, his tongue digging into my opening before trailing up to circle my clit. His moan vibrated through my core and I thrust up against his seeking mouth. He sucked and bit and laved at every part of me as my whimpers filled the room. My thighs shook with the effort to hold them open and let him have his way. He ate at me like a starving man, and I couldn't ever remember anything feeling so good.

Maybe it was because he was older with more experience, but that moment when he thrust his tongue inside me over and over, I didn't care. He moved back up to flick across my clit and I was close. I needed him to stay there. I moved my hand and dug my fingers in his hair to hold him and he grunted, his whole body jerking before his hand shackled my wrist and moved it back to the desk. He held it there as he put all he had into making me come.

I wanted to ask what had just happened, but his mouth sucking at the lips of my cunt distracted me. The more he worked, the more lost I got, falling into an abyss of pleasure until finally I was exploding. Long moans slipped from my lips as my whole body contracted, my hips pushing up hard against his mouth, my fingers clenching around nothing as they dug into the wood of the desk.

His licks got softer and eventually turned to gentle kisses before he worked his way back down my thigh, ending at my knee.

Panting, I watched him sit back and wipe his chin with the back of his hand and I knew I needed more. I wanted to taste him like he had tasted me. I wanted him to be a part of me like I was a part of him.

I dropped my feet from the arms of the chair and slid off the desk before he could object and began working on his belt.

"Oaklyn," he panted, his breaths coming heavy.

"I want to taste you. I want to hear you moan as I suck you."

His breathing picked up faster once the button on his pants was undone, his loud exhales fighting with the sound of his zipper sliding down.

Looking up, I bit my lip and took him in. Sweat had broken out on his brow and his eyes were pinched shut in what looked to be concentration. I reached my hand inside his boxers, just grazing the soft flesh covering his hard length when the chair jerked back, and he stood. The force knocked me back on my butt and I stared up at him in confusion.

His eyes were wide and frantic as his chest heaved up and down in what I was beginning to think wasn't restrained desire.

"Callum," I whispered.

He dropped his eyes to me, and they looked pained. "I'm sorry, Oaklyn." Then he stepped around me and began fastening his pants. I scrambled up from the floor.

"What?" I asked. I was so confused, my mind scrambling to keep up. But my body knew. My chest squeezed tight, a piercing pain in my heart. My face flushing in embarrassment of rejection.

"I can't. I'm sorry. I just can't."

I stared at his back as he paced to the door. When he reached it, he didn't turn around to look at me and it hit me like a slap to the face. It was a far bigger rejection that he couldn't even look at me as he turned me away.

"What the hell?" I asked, hating the tremble in my voice.

Finally, he turned, but kept staring at the floor. "It's late. We should get going."

The piercing in my heart spread, causing a fire to burn in my chest. The burn reached my eyes and I blinked, not wanting to cry in front of him, but confused and hurt by his rejection. He wouldn't even look at me. Was he so ashamed of what we'd done? Why? Why had he gone so far only to turn me away?

I didn't understand and the more I tried, the more questions bombarded my thoughts and I couldn't get any of them out past the painful lump in my throat. It choked me, and I hated it. I hated it even more when a tear broke free.

I refused to stand there and listen to any possible reason he may have had to pull back so suddenly. I couldn't bring myself to do it. Brushing the tear away, I turned to begin gathering my things.

It was pointless as more tears fell, my sniff giving away my weakness.

"Oaklyn, I'm so—"

"No!" I spun around to face him. "Fuck you, Callum. I get it, I'm young and your student, and you probably regret it, but maybe you should've figured your shit out before eating me out."

His eyes looked pained as he took in the tracks of my tears. He took a step forward with his hands out, but I would completely crumble if he touched me now.

"No," I said again, swerving around him and heading toward the door. I stopped at the entrance but didn't turn around. "I'll see you in class, *Dr. Pierce.*"

And with that, I walked out with my head held as high as I could, choking on as many tears as I could hold back.

When I got home, I fell to my bed and cried. Hating how mad I was at him for rejecting me.

Hating that he was ashamed of what we'd done.

Hating that he was the one to stop it.

Hating *him* because he'd made me feel so good.

Hating *him* for saying everything he'd said.

Hating *him* because I didn't really hate him at all.

And that made me feel as immature and naive as he probably saw me.

Chapter Twenty

Callum

Oaklyn barely made eye contact with me the entire time in class the next day, and I'd know if she had considering I stared at her the whole time. At least as much as I could without sending alarm bells to everyone in the class. I couldn't even blame her. She had every right to never acknowledge my existence ever again.

What the hell had I been thinking? After talking to Reed, I was too close to seeing reason in his suggestions that I give in, so I'd taken a huge step back, not wanting to tempt myself. I'd probably been colder than I should have been, but I hadn't wanted to not have her around. So, as I remained indifferent, I gave her menial tasks to keep her late, making her stay until I was ready to walk out way past everyone else leaving. I liked listening to her putter around when the rest of the office was silent. I could've almost imagined that she wanted to be there.

Except for last night when she'd had enough and stormed in, a ball of fire. She'd stomped in refusing to take my shit, and she'd lit a match inside me. I'd had such a short fuse, that the smallest spark was going to detonate it. The explosion had burned bright and consumed us both. When she'd thrown her temper tantrum and asked me what I saw when I looked at her, I saw the vulnerability. I saw the hurt, and it had pulled the honesty right out of me. It had tugged and tugged until my body was being honest right along with my words.

Too bad my body had lied to me thinking it could follow through with what I'd started. I'd believed that as long as I focused, I'd be fine. Then she'd fallen to her knees and the sweating began. Then the tremors. I'd tried to relax, tried to think of anything else, but when her small hand had brushed against my dick, I'd panicked. My body reacted on instinct, jerking back, and she'd looked at me with so much confusion that I hadn't been able to hold her pained gaze.

I'd hated seeing her cry. Hated that I'd hurt her.

As much as I knew she deserved to shut me out, I couldn't let her. I needed to find a way to make it right. Maybe if I said the right words, I could buy myself time. Like I had with the other women I'd been with when I hadn't been ready to be alone again.

With Oaklyn though, it wasn't about being alone. I wasn't ready to let go of *her* or the picture of a normal future she conjured so easily in my head. The feeling in my chest at her laugh and sense of humor. The sheer need that consumed me when she looked at me. Yes, she was beautiful and sexy, and I desired her more than any other woman, but I'd never *wanted* like I did when I thought of her. I'd never felt like I could actually achieve my desires as much as I did when I was near her. I wasn't ready to let go.

I needed to talk to her. Explain to her. Something. Anything.

Maybe she'd understand if I told her. If I admitted my demons.

No. It wasn't possible. I'd find another way.

But that chance didn't come as she bolted out of class. It didn't come when I missed her on Friday. Meetings consumed my day, one right after the next. I barely got a glimpse of her as I walked into the office to see her saying goodbye to Donna. I did, however, hear her say she had to work tonight when Donna asked her about her plans.

I'd become desperate enough to track her down anywhere. I couldn't wait for the whole weekend to pass before I got another chance. Which was how I ended up outside Voyeur close to midnight. I'd gone home and attempted to try and talk myself out of coming, but I'd failed.

Oaklyn stood at the bar when I walked in. Not hesitating, I made my way over to her.

"Beer and a water?" Charlotte asked me when I leaned against the bar next to Oaklyn.

"Just the water, thanks."

Oaklyn rolled her lips between her teeth. I remembered what they tasted like, the way they felt pressed against mine, and I knew, despite how wrong it was, that I was in the right place, doing the right thing with her. My body came more alive just looking at her than it had in years.

"What are you doing here, Dr. Pierce?" she asked, still staring at the counter.

"You can't keep avoiding me."

"I've done pretty well so far." Her head tipped, and her eyes flashed in my direction. I took in the hurt before she looked away again.

"Please, let me talk to you."

"Well, *Dr. Pierce,* looks like I'll continue to keep avoiding you, because I'm off. You'll have to find another girl to watch tonight."

"I don't want anyone else."

"Could've fooled me."

Fuck. There it was again, the hurt. I opened my mouth to tell her how much I wanted her when Charlotte placed the water in front of me and looked between the two of us. "Everything okay?"

Holding my breath, I waited for Oaklyn to say something to have me removed. It would have been easy for her considering it was common knowledge that Daniel only protected one thing more than the club members, and that was his employees. She could say I was harassing her, and I'd probably be escorted out. Depending on how much she divulged or exaggerated, she could have my membership revoked.

Relief washed over me when she nodded her head just slightly. "Everything's fine."

I had to take it as a sign that maybe she didn't want me gone as much as she claimed. I had to try.

"Oaklyn," I began when Charlotte walked away. "Please, talk to me."

"Callum," she sighed. My name coming from her lips soothed me, and some of the tension in my shoulders relaxed. She opened her mouth to say more but was interrupted.

"You're off, Oak," Jackson said walking up to her other side. "See you later this week?"

She turned her back to me and hugged Jackson. "Yeah, I'll see you next time."

I faced the bar, not wanting to see her in his arms. A primal part of me, one that had never existed before, wanted to scream that she was mine. Drinking my water, I watched her walk toward the back room without even a goodbye, and I was left facing the shirtless boy who was able to touch Oaklyn whenever he wanted. He gave me a narrow-eyed stare, but I didn't waste time giving one in return. I threw a twenty down on the bar and went to wait outside the employee lounge. I wasn't ready to give up so easily.

It wasn't long before she was coming out, bundled up and ready to go. Her eyes were on her phone, so she missed me standing there.

"Oaklyn," I said, getting her attention.

She looked up and rolled her eyes before returning them to her phone. "I'm tired, Callum. Can we not do this?"

Instead of answering, I looked down at her phone at the Uber app she had open. "What are you doing?"

"Ordering an Uber," she answered like it was obvious. Which it was. I just didn't understand.

"Why? Where's your car?"

"It needed some work and it's taking longer than they expected."

Checking the time, I saw it was almost one in the morning, and I hated the idea of her taking an Uber. What if something happened?

Placing my hand over her phone, I stopped her. "Let me drive you home."

Her skin was soft and her pulse along her wrist jumped at my touch, lighting a fuse in my fingers that shot through my arm to my chest.

"Callum—"

"Come on," I interrupted, halting her rejection. "I'll feed you on the way."

"It's after midnight. Nothing is open."

"Just . . . please."

No one was near us as we lingered near the entryway of the club, and I waited for her decision. She finally looked up and locked her eyes on mine for what seemed like the first time since Wednesday night. We were in our own bubble. The world no longer a part of the energy surrounding us.

"Fine."

I barely held my smile back as I led her to the car. Oaklyn had a lot of pride, and I didn't want to gloat in fear of her backing out.

I'd ended up taking her to Waffle House with the intention of sitting down so we could talk, but when we got there Oaklyn, hesitated to get out.

"What's wrong?"

"Maybe it wouldn't be the best idea for me to stroll in with my professor in the middle of the night."

"Shit. I didn't even think." I was so damn focused on just spending time with her that I didn't even consider our positions. I forgot she was my student. I just saw her as the woman I needed to be around. "Okay. Tell me what you want, and I'll order and bring it back out. We can eat in the car."

"Just a waffle and some bacon."

When our orders were ready, I grabbed them and rushed back out to the car. Oaklyn watched me fumble with the bags, a hesitant look on her face as though she still wasn't sure how the night would end. "Smart thinking about people seeing us. It was packed in there."

"Olivia talks about it a lot. Says it's the hot spot most nights."

"Yes, I remember the wonders of Waffle House. Best between the hours of ten at night and four in the morning." She laughed and shifted in her seat, waiting for her food container. "Your waffle, my lady."

"Such a gentleman." She set the food on her lap and tried to balance the fork and knife, but it ended up dropping when she moved to grab a napkin. She tried again, but the same thing happened when she moved the slightest bit. "Ugh. This is ridiculous."

"Don't let the plasticware defeat you," I joked as I struggled with my own utensils.

She glared at me out of the side of her eye before sighing dramatically. "Listen, if you want, we can just eat at my place. It's close by."

I hope the dim lights in the car hid my shock, but I didn't think twice about accepting her offer. Being alone with her tonight was more than I thought I'd get. "Yes."

She pinched her lips and looked down trying to hide her reaction but laughed at my fast answer. "Just don't expect anything fancy. I'm just a poor college girl."

I'd kept my expectations low, and while the location wasn't the greatest, her apartment was clean and had enough decorations to keep it from looking bare. Which wasn't hard to do considering the space was so limited. To call it an apartment was a stretch.

Either way, it was nice. Organized. And I got to watch her no matter where she moved in the small space. She took my coat and hung it on the coat rack and suggested we eat on her couch at her coffee table.

"A coffee table is cheaper than an actual dining room table," she explained. "And I never expected to have a dinner party to worry about."

"I'd hardly call me and Waffle House a dinner party." I laughed.

"It's dinner and you're company. I think it's as close to a dinner party as I'll ever get."

"Fair enough."

She bounced the cushion when she sat down beside me. It was more of a love seat, but it matched the chair sitting catty-corner, and I took it as a good thing that she shared the couch with me rather than sitting by herself.

"How are classes?"

We needed to talk, but we'd somehow pushed aside the tension, and I wanted to enjoy it for now.

"Okay," she answered around a big bite of waffle. I had to fight from leaning forward to lick the syrup sitting on the corner of her lips. Then I'd trail my lips down her neck across her exposed shoulder.

The girl had to own stock in oversized sweaters. Not that I blamed her, she looked gorgeous in them.

"Although, one class, there was this test," she said, pulling my attention back. "It was unfairly brutal. The teacher's a complete asshole to make a test that hard."

"I remember exams like that. They always took me down a peg."

"Right? I mean, who the heck expects us to know every constellation?"

I almost choked on my bite of waffle when I realized she was talking about me. Looking up in shock, I was met with shining eyes and lips pressed together to stop from smiling.

"Hardy-har-har. You're hilarious," I deadpanned after I managed to swallow. "Which one tripped you up the most? The Big Dipper or the little one?"

"Definitely the little one," she said, all serious. "How little? A lot little? Or is it really big and called little. Like Little John."

"That's a good question. You should become a physics major and discover it. I'm sure it hasn't been discovered before."

She tossed her head back and laughed, sucking the air right from my lungs. Fuck, she was beautiful.

"I miss eating lunch with you. My work-study just hasn't been the same the past two weeks."

"Me too. Your sense of humor definitely gets me through the afternoon."

A silence fell between us letting me know our time for avoiding the real topic was up.

"Why are you here, Dr. Pierce?" I winced at her return to using my professor name. "You've shown repeatedly that you don't want me. So, what is this?"

A laugh rumbled up my throat. "God, Oaklyn. I *do* want you."

Her eyebrows raised expectantly, waiting for an explanation.

My heart hammered in my chest as I thought of my options. Cut it off here and leave. Let it go. Try and stutter through a half truth and hope it satisfied her need to understand.

My eyes traced the skin of her shoulder, remembering how it felt beneath my fingertips. My mind flashed with memories of how she tasted. The sight of Reed and Karen before me, his hand on her stomach hit me. The way I imagined Oaklyn when I tried to see my future.

She filled me with a hope that maybe there was more past my fear. She made me believe, and I needed to try. I could do this. I could do this with her.

Setting my container aside, I scooted toward her and grabbed her container, moving it to the table too.

She tracked my movements with wide eyes and swallowed.

Brushing her hair behind her ear, I pressed my forehead to hers, taking in her fine features, full lips, the dips and shadows under her sweater. Her tongue slicked out, preparing for my kiss.

"Callum."

Watching her lips form my name pushed me the final inch across the precipice.

Chapter Twenty-One

Callum

Her lips were just as soft as the other night. Maybe even softer, more plush, more perfect. Something about her always seemed better each time I had her.

Oaklyn hesitated only a moment before she moaned, and her lips began to move against mine. Her tongue flicked against the seam of my lips, and I obediently opened, needing to taste her. I held my eyes open and focused on her face when her hands moved to my neck and then into my hair. I stared at the way her lashes cast shadows on her soft cheeks. I moved my hands to her waist to remind myself of the petite female in my arms and to not let the memory of another's hands pull me back.

I watched her features shift with each move of her mouth against mine. The sweet taste of syrup mixed with her own unique taste intoxicated me. I became so lost in her kiss that I hadn't even realized when my eyes slid closed and every feeling became amplified. But not the feeling of panic that had been lingering on the edge since her hands had become buried in my hair. No, I felt the sting of her teeth nipping at my lips. I felt the rush of air against my cheek when she breathed without removing her mouth from mine. I felt the fine bones of her ribcage expand and contract beneath my fingers.

She consumed me, and before I knew it, my fingers were bunching up her sweater to pull it over her head. My hands molded to her soft breasts as my thumbs stroked back and forth across her nipples. I tugged the flimsy lace out of the way and trailed my lips down her neck to latch and suck at the tight bud. I'd been so enthralled with the feel of her in my mouth, I hadn't even had a chance to think of how the way she held me made me feel anything but excitement.

The absence of panic left an opening I became desperate to fill with her. I needed to feel more. More of her against me.

I pulled back just enough to tug my shirt overhead and then went back to kissing her. Her bare chest pressed to mine sent shockwaves of lust rocketing through me. Had I ever been skin to skin with a woman? Had I ever been so lost in the now, that the past couldn't touch me?

At least I thought it couldn't. I thought I'd been so buried in Oaklyn, nothing could break through.

Then her hands were on my shoulders pushing me back on the small couch, and I fell. Fell back into my nightmare. Her hands pressed hard against my shoulders and *he* began climbing on top of me. Lost from reality, my legs were being pressed back to my chest and—

"No," I shouted, gripping her biceps and shoving back.

My eyes popped open when I heard my voice in the quiet room, bouncing around the tiny space, mocking me. Oaklyn stared at me with wide eyes, her mouth open in shock.

"I'm sorry," I managed to whisper on a heavy breath. My chest was unable to take a deep enough breath and panic began to tickle at my skin. Not just from the flashback, but at wondering how I was going to explain myself out of this situation.

"Are you kidding me right now?" Her brows dipped, and she pressed off my arms, so I would let her go. She jerked her sweater up and covered her breasts as she stared at me, trying to figure me out. "Are you serious?" she asked slower, angrier.

"Fuck," I swore, standing from the couch. I paced to the wall a few feet away and dug my hands in my hair before turning and pacing back. My fingers tightened to a fist, hoping the sting of pain would center me, help me get some control that seemed to be spiraling out of my grasp. "Fuck," I said again.

"You need to leave."

Her low but harsh command stopped my pacing. When I turned to look at her, my heart sank to my stomach like a lead weight was pulling it down. The hurt in her eyes was so strong, not even the thin veil of anger could mask it.

"Oaklyn, please." I stepped toward her with my hands out.

"No." She looked down and shook her head. "No. You can either explain what the fuck is going on, or you can leave."

In the middle of the turmoil raging through me, I wondered what she saw when she stared at me then. A man housing a scared boy? A caged animal who had been abused too many times to recover from? A grown man terrified of losing the first flicker of hope? A desperate man trying to hold on to her *and* his secrets?

I held her golden gaze as I imagined the outcomes. I could run and hate myself every day for not trying? I could confess and see the disgust cross her face and have her push me away because she didn't know how to handle such a damaged product. Would she judge me for still being chained to my past?

Or, I could confess, and she would share the weight of the burden with me. I could confess, and she would ease the haunting pain. Oaklyn was the first person I'd even considered telling. Not a single woman had tempted me to share. I'd only made enough excuses to hold off another stint of being alone. But with her? I felt safe. I felt comforted, and I didn't want to give up so easily. Could I live with myself if I didn't try to take hold of this opportunity?

With jerky movements, I put my shirt back on, needing all the armor I could get. Then I moved toward her and helped her put her sweater back on too.

"Cal," she whispered, pushing her arms into the sleeves, watching me with concern and confusion.

I sat with my back against the arm of the other side of the couch and swallowed before taking a deep breath. "Just," I started. "Just give me a minute."

"Okay." She breathed the word so softly I almost didn't hear it, but it made its way across the space between us and sunk in to me as though she'd shouted her support.

I couldn't look up as I began. Instead I focused on the way my thumb rubbed back and forth across the leg of my jeans. "I had a cousin," I started. So simple. So innocuous to the nightmare that would follow those four words. But once I began, it all came out without pause, sticking to the basics. "He was three years older than me, and I idolized him. Looked up to everything he did. Thought he knew all." I laughed a dry, humorless chuckle that hurt my chest. "So, when he put on a porn video, I didn't say anything because I didn't want him to think I was dumb. I was only eleven and he was the much cooler teenager."

Rolling my lips between my teeth, I prepared to say aloud what I hadn't in more than ten years. "I didn't say anything when he was touching my penis, saying he was doing me a favor by teaching me how to masturbate. Or that since he'd done it to me, I needed to do it back. After that, it continued, and I began to feel stuck when I really wanted it to stop and tell someone to make it stop. I was scared of what to say or how to say it. Then it slowly progressed to oral sex, then just sex. And I wanted it to stop. I didn't want to *learn* anymore. But he threatened me. He told me no one would believe I didn't want it when he was able to make me orgasm. He held my fear and shame over me, trapping me. After two and a half years, my parents really began to notice my panic attacks and how I acted out. You see, if I got in trouble, he couldn't come over for sleepovers. It was how I could keep him away. After a while, my parents put me in therapy, and I guess one day the therapist finally asked the right questions, said the right thing to get me to open up. It ended after that."

My whole body seemed to be shaking inside with tremors, but when I lifted my hands they barely moved. Inside, I crumbled, but somehow, everything still stayed intact.

I held off looking up, she hadn't spoken yet and the loft screamed with the silence. Fear had frozen my muscles, making it feel impossible to lift my head, but I did. Slowly, I lifted my eyes to hers, preparing myself for the worst.

Her slim fingers were pressed to her lips as tears fell down her cheeks in a continuous flow.

"Callum." My name came out broken past her tears.

"I don't need your pity." Fuck, I couldn't handle her pity. Somehow that hadn't factored into the scenarios I'd imagined. I hadn't thought about what would happen if she felt pity for me.

"I don't pity you," she said, bringing my focus back to her. I watched her throat bob over a swallow before clearing it. "I'd be a monster to not feel pain for you and what you went through. That's not pity. It's compassion."

The fire behind her words, the depth of feeling sinking into me caused my eyes to burn, and I looked away, swallowing hard past the lump threatening to choke me before my final confession. "I've never really been able to be touched after that. I've touched women, kissed them, dated them, but they tend to want more. Who wouldn't when they're trying to build a future? But they eventually got fed up when I continued to put them off without an explanation and refused to let them touch me intimately."

"Have you ever been . . ." Her words trailed off, but I knew what she was asking.

"Once." I cringed remembering the night. "I was in college and got very drunk to help me follow through. I was shaking and sweating the whole time and she was too drunk to notice. I left immediately after. Never tried again."

"What a horrible bitch."

My lips somehow twitched at her anger on my behalf. I hadn't thought I'd smile at all after I confessed my past.

A silence hung between us, and I didn't know what else to say. I didn't want to pressure her to say anything she wasn't ready to discuss, so I decided to give her an out. Give her some space to think about it and an opportunity to have me leave without asking.

"Do you want me to go?"

"What? Callum, God no." Her vehement denial made me jerk my head up to see her shocked expression. "If nothing else, you're at least my friend. I would never . . ." She shook her head, not finishing the thought. "I care about you. I want you to stay."

Wanted me to stay. She cared about me and wanted me to stay. The words were so simple and yet, they seeped in through my skin and began to fill some of the damaged holes inside of me. I'd told her about my past and she hadn't doubted me, questioned me, or looked at me differently. I felt . . . Lighter. Oaklyn somehow filled me up, like I could possibly be whole someday. It was like she'd helped me set down some of the load I'd been carrying for so long. How could one girl do that?

I didn't know, but I didn't want it to stop either.

"Okay."

"Okay."

We stared at each other from either side of the couch, both unsure of what to do next. I missed the heat from earlier, and I wanted to put away my confession. It was said, it was out there, now I wanted to move on. "You can come closer, give me another chance to kiss you. I won't break, Oaklyn."

She smiled, and her eyes scanned me up and down with one eyebrow cocked. "I never thought I'd break you. There's too much of you to even put a dent in."

I exaggerated puffing my chest out and flexing, succeeding in making her laugh.

Still smiling, the wheels turned behind her eyes as she worked her lips between her teeth. I held her stare, watching a decision form across her face and her look to shift, to become heated. Making a point to keep her hands by her side or behind her, she inched her way across the space between us until she sat right in front of me.

"Will you tell me if I do something that bothers you? Anything at all."

"Oaklyn—"

"Yes, or I'm going back to that side of the couch."

"Yes," I answered, my cheek twitching at her warning.

"Good." Slowly, as she held my stare, she leaned in and pressed her lips to the corner of my mouth.

It didn't take long for the kiss to become heated. I licked at her mouth, wanting to taste her again, and she almost fell forward when she leaned closer to get more of me. Not stopping the kiss, I reached for her hands and put them on my shoulders, pulling my mouth back just enough to say against her lips, "I'm fine with being touched, especially by you. Just nothing too aggressive."

"But you can touch me that way, right?" she asked breathlessly.

"Oh, fuck yes. I plan on touching you any way I can." I pressed my lips to hers and pulled back enough to say, "Gently." Then I nipped at her lips. "Or roughly. Any." Kiss. "Way." Kiss. "I can."

Then my hands trailed down her arms, over her breasts, and moved to grip the edge of her sweater, tugging it back over her head. She gripped the edge of my shirt and hesitated. I hated that she needed to hesitate, but also appreciated the fact that she did. With a slight nod from me, she tugged it off and moved back to kissing me.

And something I'd only managed to do with Oaklyn, I closed my eyes and savored the taste of her as I tugged her closer, pulling her into my chest. Her soft skin pressed to mine, and I had to pull back to breathe through the excitement of the sensation.

"Callum," she breathed nipping at my lips. "Can you . . ."

"It's okay. Ask me." I wasn't sure what she planned to ask, but I wanted to try.

"Can we start slow? Can I, can I watch you while you watch me? No touching, yet."

I tried and lost the fight to hide my wince.

"Okay. That's okay," she rushed to reassure me. "I'm just selfish to see you. More than in a dark corner or out of sight behind me."

"It would only be fair since I've watched you," I joked, but it was empty. I looked down, ashamed to have my weaknesses laid out in front of her.

After a pause, her eyebrows shot up. "I have an idea."

Oaklyn stood and began moving the overstuffed chair back into the corner. She then came back and pulled me to stand before leading me to the chair. Once I was seated, she turned off all the lights until only the kitchen light barely illuminated the couch and almost hid me completely. Then she perched herself on the cushions, facing me.

"Pretend you're at Voyeur," she whispered.

I didn't deserve her, but I watched her anyway. I watched her shimmy her leggings down and part her thighs. I watched her tug the lace of her bra aside and pluck at her nipples before dropping a hand to between her legs. She teased, rolling her head back on her shoulders before, pushing the material aside and exposing her wet pussy to me.

My hips flexed, and I groaned, dragging my hand down the erection straining against my pants. Her breaths urged me on and I unzipped my jeans, the rasp seeming to scream my intentions. Her eyes flickered in my direction but immediately went back to the ceiling. Her fingers circled her opening, and I pulled my cock out of my pants, stroking the hard flesh, not once taking my eyes from her.

"Callum," she breathed, sinking her fingers inside herself, fucking her core. I mimicked her movements, groaning at the intimacy of the moment. The way I was completely consumed by watching her, consumed by the sounds of our breathing happening in sync as though we were actually fucking.

The emotions raged through me and sunk straight to my balls. Swelling inside me, making me feel bigger than my bones, like I could conquer anything. Like an addict, I craved more. I wanted more from her.

"Oaklyn," I moaned. "Look at me." Without hesitation her eyes dropped to mine, holding my gaze, somehow not sinking lower to watch my fist on my cock. "Watch me."

She did, and my dick twitched, jumping at attention under her stare. Her fingers matched the movement of my strokes and her whole body seemed to undulate under the pressure. Her whimpers growing louder and coming faster.

"Come with me. Callum, come with me."

Her thumb snaked out to rub at her clit and her body tightened, her thighs flexing and spreading as her core tightened around her fingers. And I came. With her eyes on me, I stroked my cock until white ropes of cum shot across my chest.

"Fuck, Oaklyn," I breathed.

"Not yet," she panted out of breath. "But maybe someday."

She smiled, and my chest shook with laughter. My body felt light like it would float away. My chest expanded on each breath, each one a little easier. And she was laughing and smiling with me. Ten feet stood between us, but right then, I felt more tied to her than I did when my tongue was buried between her legs.

Oaklyn was either going to make me or destroy me. I just hoped it was the former, because I didn't have much more left to destroy.

She tugged her underwear back over herself and walked to the kitchen before coming back with a wet washcloth.

"Thank you," I said, holding her stare.

She understood that I was thanking her for so much more than the washcloth. "Anything, Callum."

By the time I'd cleaned up and tucked myself back in my pants, she'd pulled her sweater back on, but left her legs bare.

"Do you want to stay?" she asked, tipping her head to the bed off to the side.

"I don't know if I can," I answered honestly.

"Will you try?"

Could I?

For her, I'd try anything.

Nodding, I got up and moved with her to bed. I had no idea how it would go. I sometimes had nightmares and woke up shaking and sweating, but everything in me urged me to lay out on the bed and hold her as close as I could, never letting her go.

I still wanted to warn her.

"I've never done this before."

She rolled to face me and smiled. "Neither have I."

"Yeah, but you're nineteen."

"There's no required age for experiences. I'm sure there are men out there who have never shared a bed with anyone who are much older than you."

"I guess you're right."

"Of course I am," she gloated.

I brushed a strand of hair behind her ear before stroking my thumb along her lips. Electricity shot to my chest when she pressed a kiss to the pad of my finger.

"There are a lot of things I haven't done," I said, hating to admit it, but needing her to know.

"It's okay, Callum."

"I know. I just . . . You make me want to be honest. You make me feel like I *can* be honest. I'm not sure why, but it's there, just the feeling I have when I'm with you."

"Is it wrong that I feel honored at being that for you?" she asked on a whisper.

"No. I want to try with you, Oaklyn. I care about you and over the past few months you've become more than a friend. Something about you clicked with me. As wrong as all of this is," I took a deep breath before saying it again. "I want to try with you."

"There is nothing wrong with this." At her fierce tone, I cocked my eyebrow. She smiled at my reaction. "Other than me being your student, but I won't be forever, and I don't want to keep fighting this. I care about you too, and I want you."

Shifting forward, I pressed a soft kiss to her lips before moving back to my pillow. Her hand snaked out between us and touched mine, asking for permission. I opened my palm and watched her slim fingers link with mine.

Somehow, by some miracle, my breathing evened out and I fell asleep, my hand gripping hers like a lifeline.

Chapter Twenty-Two

Oaklyn

I didn't know what time it was when I first opened my eyes, but there was a glow coming out from behind my blackout curtains. I was mid-stretch when I saw my overstuffed chair pulled into the corner and remembered last night. Reaching out, expecting to find Callum, I instead met cold sheets.

A glance around showed no signs of him, unless he was hiding in the bathroom with the lights turned off, but the sheets were cold. He'd been gone for a while. I tried to ignore the doubt filling my mind as to why he had left in the middle of the night without waking me. Splashing cold water on my face at the bathroom sink, I remember how he'd said he would try, and I had to be grateful for that.

The pinch in my chest eased when I flicked on an overhead light and saw a piece of paper taped to my front door.

Oaklyn,

I had an early breakfast meeting and had to leave. You looked too beautiful sleeping and I didn't want to wake you. I can't thank you enough for last night.

C

I dragged my finger along the C, liking the sharp curve. His handwriting fit him. Perfectly in line, clean without any messy strokes between. I turned my back and leaned against the door and held the piece of paper to my chest like a love-sick fool. It was a reminder that last night had happened and hadn't just been a crazy figment of my imagination.

Although, maybe his confession would have been better if it hadn't been real. The breath left my body in a pained exhale as I remembered his story. I'd been in shock. My body had tingled with adrenaline as I hurt for the man in front of me. My mind had scrambled to process that Callum, six-foot-four, two-hundred-plus-pound Callum had been taken advantage of in the worst possible way. I couldn't imagine the lasting effects that it must have had on him, but a lot of his actions made sense after his explanation.

A part of me had hated pushing him to tell me. I would have rather him have told me he was ashamed of himself for wanting a student. I would have rather heard almost anything other than that he'd been sexually abused.

My eyes burned all over again.

He was a more beautiful and amazing man than I'd already thought him to be.

And he'd pleasured himself for me. He'd wanted me to watch. He'd wanted to share that moment with *me*. He'd felt safe enough with *me*.

The emotions had washed over me on a wave and exhausted me by the time my orgasm had subsided, that I'd selfishly asked him to stay. Needing the comfort as much as he did.

What was I going to do with all of these feelings over the long weekend? Left to my own thoughts until we went back to school on Tuesday. I had no way of reaching him. I even flipped the note over in hopes that maybe he'd left me his number, but it was blank. I kicked myself for throwing away his card in a moment of anger.

I could email him, but that felt on the edge of desperation, and I only had his school email. God forbid someone had access and opened it. What would it say?

Thanks for picking me up from the sex club I work at and taking me home. Also, for masturbating with me and holding my hand as we fell asleep. P.S. here's my number because I'd love to do it again. See you in class this week.

That would go over great.

Accepting the next few days without communication, I decided to do my research and form a plan. The next time I was with Callum, I wanted to be more prepared and maybe try for something much more than just watching.

* * *

Tuesday morning, I walked across campus with confidence. I'd come prepared, in a baggy sweater that hung off my shoulder and a lace bralette underneath. It was skimpy and bright red to match my bold lipstick and nail polish. I'd left my hair down and slightly curled, taking time to appear ultra-feminine.

I just hoped Callum thought so too.

I could tell my plan worked when I watched him do a double take as I walked in class. He stood in his normal spot leaning against the desk, greeting students with a quick glance. But when I waltzed though the door, he'd said hello to me and began to move on to the next person when he'd turned back to watch my progress across the classroom.

"Dayum, girl," Olivia said when I sat. "You got a date later today, because you look hot as fuck."

"Just needed a little confidence boost," I said, shrugging as I pulled out my notebooks.

"Well, I think you're *boosting* all the guys, if you know what I mean," she said, her eyebrows waggling. "Hell, even Dr. Pierce had to pick his jaw off the ground."

"Oh, he did not." I didn't want Olivia noticing Callum staring at me. I didn't want that kind of scrutiny on me or him. "You're hilarious, Liv."

She pretend-flipped her hair and then focused her attention up front as class began.

I was pretty sure it was just me since everyone else seemed to be focused on the lecture, but the tension seemed higher than usual. Each time his eyes landed on me felt like he was shouting to everyone who would listen that we'd come in front of each other. The seconds he stared felt like minutes, and I was sure by the end of class my heart was going to explode in excitement. Somehow, I made it through the entire hour without combusting.

Olivia waited for me, removing any chance I had to try and talk to Callum. I'd hoped to at least exchange numbers, but I couldn't do that with her by my side. Frustrated, but accepting having to wait another day, I packed my things and stood to go.

"Miss Derringer."

His smooth voice stroked across my skin, and I had to fight the heat rising from my chest, trying to seep into my cheeks. Cool, calm, and collected. I needed to remain cool, calm, and collected.

"Yes, Dr. Pierce."

"Can you please come by my office later to discuss your appointment time?" When he didn't look up from packing away his stuff, my lungs deflated under the pressure of what it could mean for him to avoid looking at me. Had I read it all wrong? Was he going to have me come up to his office and tell me what a mistake all of it was? Was he mad I'd come to class like this? Were we right back to where it all began with the back and forth? Him running hot and then cold?

All of it rushed through my head and created a dull buzz in my ear.

"Sure. I should be able to stop by this afternoon." My words sounded hollow, lacking any excitement that I'd had earlier. I almost wanted to cry as I turned to head out the door. When I looked back one more time over my shoulder, he was watching me.

And he gave me a wink.

No, he wasn't regretting anything. He was just better at hiding his emotions and needs than I was.

I wanted to give a sexy smirk back, but I was too giddy that he wasn't going to brush me off. Rolling my lips between my teeth, I fought my smile, trying to hide my excitement from Olivia. The last thing I needed was for anyone to know what was going on between me and Dr. Pierce.

My time in the biology department dragged, the minute hand taking twice as long to make its rounds around the clock. But soon, it was lunch and I had to fight from running through the halls to get to his office. I made myself walk at a normal pace when I reached the hallway and forced a neutral smile for Donna when I walked in, but she wasn't there. No one was.

Except Dr. Pierce.

I snuck into his office and shut the door, locking it, ready to set my plan in place. I knew what I'd wanted to do, but I hadn't known how it would be executed. Being able to sneak into his office undetected was perfect.

"Oaklyn, what are you doing?" Callum asked with wide eyes. He'd been looking at papers and didn't notice my presence until the click of the door. "I think people will be concerned to know a student went into a teacher's office and locked the door."

"No one saw me come in, and it's not so uncommon to lock your door during lunch."

Biting my lip, I fought to contain my smile and still take deep enough breaths to keep my heart rate under control. It beat so hard, I was sure he could see it from his seat. He slid his glasses off and cocked his head to the side as he watched me approach. I held his stare until I'd rounded his desk and worked my way between him and the desk, leaning back against the hard wood, then I let my eyes drop to his lips.

The silence screamed across my skin, bringing it to life. Nerves sparked through my body, and I almost began to talk myself out of it, but I needed to try. For him. I wanted it for him.

He groaned when I slicked my tongue across my lips.

"Kiss me, Dr. Pierce," I said on a whisper.

He stood and framed my face in his hands. Every touch was gentle and soft, so I was surprised when his lips touched mine how rough he was, how desperate his kiss tasted. His tongue pushed past my lips and I met him half way, eager to have every part of his desire. When we needed to catch our breaths, we barely separated sharing the air between us.

"I missed you when I woke up and you were gone," I admitted, hating the insecurity that tinged my words.

"I'm sorry," he answered, avoiding eye contact by shifting his head to the side, as though he was hiding.

His reaction worried me. Had something more than his meeting pulled him away? "What happened?" He shifted a step back, but I held on to his arms, keeping him close. "Talk to me. Please."

"I . . ." He paused, the muscles in his jaw ticking, and I smoothed my hand up and down his arm, giving him time to process his words. "I overreacted when I woke up."

"Callum." I hated that something bad had happened, and I hadn't woken up with him. Guilt hit me at asking him to stay and causing whatever pulled him from my bed that morning.

"I'm sorry. I didn't want to drag you into it."

I hated how ashamed he sounded. Hated everything about the situation.

"Cal," I said, my tone hard to pull his attention to me. "Don't apologize. I want to be here for you."

Those were apparently the words he needed to hear because his light blue eyes darkened with desire and he attacked my mouth, kissing me harder than before. His hands gripping my hips to put me on the edge of the desk where he could step between my legs. Dragging his palms up my sides under my sweater, he cupped my breasts, massaging them, flicking his thumbs across my sensitive nipples. I groaned at the sensation and he pulled back to drag open-mouthed kisses down my neck and across my collarbone. I became lost in him, letting my hands travel up his thick arms encased in the soft material of his dress shirt, loving the way they flexed as his hands moved over me. One hand slowly worked its way up his neck and into his hair, giving him plenty of time to pull back or stop me. His movements paused for only a split second before he continued his assault on my body.

But I needed to remind myself of what I came there to do. I needed to try to put all my research to work.

"Callum. Callum," I said to get his attention. He only grunted against my neck until I tugged his hair, and he finally pulled back to look at me. "Do you trust me?"

His hazy eyes became focused as he considered my question. I held my breath, hoping he'd say yes, but preparing myself to bounce back if he said no.

"More than anyone else."

His words formed a ball in my throat, and I had to swallow hard to work past it. I had to focus and not melt in his arms in a ball of mush. I hopped down off the desk and pushed him back until he sat. "I've been doing some research." His brows furrowed in confusion. "For purely selfish reasons," I said with a small smile.

Leaning back against the desk, I made it a point to keep my hands resting behind me. I watched his hands flex against the arm rests and I took a deep breath, beginning.

"If at any point you want to stop, talk, or do nothing, just say so. You are one-hundred percent in control. Okay?" He hesitated, scanning my face trying to figure out what my next move was—what my final goal was, but eventually nodded his head. "Unfasten your pants and pull yourself out."

"Oaklyn." My name escaped on an exhale, but when I glanced down to his crotch, his erection twitched. He may have been hesitant, but he was still excited.

"You are in control, but don't look away from me." He nodded again. "Who's in front of you, Cal?"

"You." His voice was deep with excitement and nerves. I hoped it paid off.

"Say my name."

"Oaklyn."

I nodded my head toward his pants and he began to work his buckle open with only a slight tremble in his hands. Matching his movements, I began undoing the buttons on my sweater. By the time it hung completely open, my red lace bra exposed, his cock was out of his pants and his hand wrapped around the thick length, his eyes on me.

"Just a little visual to keep you in the moment."

He only grunted and stroked his hand up to the top before dragging it back down. My mouth salivated at just the idea of tasting him. I couldn't wait to have him in my mouth. Slowly, still holding his eyes, I slid to my knees. I watched his Adam's apple bob as I worked my way between his legs and gently placed my hands on his knees.

I slid my hands up his thighs, but didn't reach for him, continuing to let him stroke himself. "Remember, you're in control. Don't look away from me."

I inched closer until my lips brushed the underside of his cock where I placed a gentle kiss. His chest heaved, but his eyes still blazed with desire as I opened my mouth and dragged my tongue from his base, over his fingers, and to the tip. His flavor exploded on my tongue when he directed his head into my mouth and I latched on. I desperately wanted to close my eyes and get lost in the taste of him, but I forced my eyes open and sucked on him.

His groan rewarded me, and his hand loosened its hold on his shaft. I took his free hand and moved it to my breast under my bra. Coming off him with a pop of my lips, I moved his other hand to my head, burying it in my long hair.

"You're in charge, Cal. You move me how you want." His hips flexed and bumped his cock against my chin. "Say my name, Callum. Who's sucking your cock?"

"You. Oaklyn," he moaned.

"Good. Now feel me to keep you in the moment." I pressed my breast harder into his palm and he squeezed. "I won't look away."

With a groan that ripped from his chest, he thrust into my mouth. I couldn't go deep because of the angle I needed to keep to hold his gaze, but I hollowed my cheeks on each suck as he pulled out. I rolled my tongue along his shaft, loving his hand in my hair, moving me how he wanted. When he pinched at my nipple, I gasped around him and almost closed my eyes, but managed to hold them open.

"Oh, god. Oaklyn," he said my name like a prayer. When I opened my mouth to let him watch me flick my tongue along his slit, tasting his pre-cum, he lost it. His head fell back against the chair and he pushed my head down further. I closed my eyes and began sucking him like I was starving. I opened my throat and breathed through my nose when he thrust up hard, pushing past my gag reflex. Not once did I give him any resistance when his hand cradled the back of my skull hard and used me. I didn't want to. Every time I choked on his head, I loved it, because he was trusting me. He was losing control with me.

Short thrusts followed the long pushes, and I focused my attention on sucking harder.

"Gonna come, Oak. Gonna come."

I latched on tight enough to let him know I wanted to swallow him, but loose enough that he'd be able to pull me off. I didn't have to worry because an instant later, he was shooting warm, salty cum down my throat, and I worked to swallow every ounce of him. He came so much, I struggled to swallow it all and some slipped down my chin. His groans were music to my ears as he fought to hold them back behind a clenched jaw. Finally, his hold on my hair loosened and I pulled back, leaving soft licks, sucks, and kisses all over his softening cock, making sure he saw me wipe any excess cum and lick it off my fingers.

With another groan, he reached for me, placing me atop his desk and went to fall to his knees, but I stopped him, pulling him into me. He looked at me with wild eyes, questioning why I'd stopped him.

"Not me. Just you today. Just you." I dragged my hand down his cheek and smiled, loving to see him so out of control. So relaxed and lost in the aftermath of pleasure.

His head dropped to my shoulder and his panting breaths brushed against my chest. When his shoulders began to shake, concern sent a chill through me, making my head light and my fingers numb. Fuck. I'd messed up. I'd fucked up. I choked on my breath, panicking, as ideas of what to do next ran through my head.

But then I heard a laugh. And another one. Until he was full out laughing. I held him to me and let him laugh, letting the sound fill me up, knowing I gave this to him. My fingers dug into his hair, and I laid kisses on the crown of his head until he began trailing his own kisses up my neck to my lips.

"Thank you. Thank you," he murmured between kisses.

"Thank you, Callum. Thank you for trusting me."

His hand slid into my hair and held my cheek. "What did I do to deserve you?"

"I don't know, but I'm glad you did it." I gave him one last kiss and pulled back. I dropped my eyes and stared at his soft cock resting above his open pants, smiling at the smear of red lipstick along the base and head. He was impressive even after coming, and I was the lucky woman who got to enjoy it—the one who got to leave her mark all over it. "As much as I could stare at you all day, I need to head to another class."

Callum tucked himself into his pants and I buttoned my sweater up.

"How are we going to get you out of here? If someone is out there, they'll hear the lock click and we can't exactly come strolling out together. Especially with your sexy red lipstick smeared like it is."

I covered my mouth only able to imagine what I looked like. He laughed at my reaction and reached in his desk, pulling out wet wipes.

"Of course, you have wet wipes on hand."

"I have to be able to clean up any messes."

I hid my smile, loving how much of a perfectionist he was. He unlocked the door and peeked out as I wiped at my mouth.

He left the door open and then walked down the hall. Not wanting to go another whole weekend without talking to him again, I jotted down my number under the baby wipes. He'd find it when he put them away, which I knew he would.

He walked back in, and I snagged a kiss before he sat in his seat. I was just grabbing my bag when Donna popped in.

"Hey Dr. Pierce. Just wanted to let you know I'm back from lunch if you need anything. Oh hey, Oaklyn."

"Hey, Donna."

"What are you doing here today? I figured you probably get enough of this place."

I looked over at Callum and held in my smirk at seeing him blush.

"I just needed to ask Dr. Pierce some questions about class, but I'm leaving now." Putting on my most innocent look, I backed out of the doorway past Donna. "Bye, Dr. Pierce."

Chapter Twenty-Three

Callum

"Oh, fuck yes, Oaklyn." I groaned softly, fisting her hair. "Suck me harder."

She moaned just enough to let me feel the vibrations down my cock and shot to my balls, currently cradled in the palm of her hand.

I couldn't believe I was getting another blow job. A *real* blow job.

God. The first one had been everything. Staring into her eyes, feeling her soft breasts, her long hair in my fist, as she dragged her tongue up my shaft had been euphoric. She'd been overtly feminine and had done everything to keep me in the moment. Not once had she looked away until I had lost my ability to hold my eyes open anymore. She'd managed to give me something I never thought I'd have. Something I'd given up on.

Hell, she'd done *research*. For me.

Looking down now, I stared as her red lips circled my cock. How they stretched to accommodate my girth as I pushed her head down and thrust up, bumping the back of her throat. It squeezed tight around my head, and when she looked up at me with her eyes watering, I knew I was done.

"Gonna come, Oaklyn. Can I come down your throat? Will you swallow it all?"

She pulled off my cock with a pop and dragged her tongue along the back, never breaking eye contact. "Every last drop, Dr. Pierce," she said deviously before diving back down and sucking me harder than before.

She squeezed my balls and I had to clench my jaw to hold back the groans that I wanted to shout into the small office as my cock pulsed, filling her mouth with my come. Despite how fast she tried to swallow, some still slipped out past her lips and it had to be the most erotic thing I'd ever seen.

She was true to her word and licked up every last drop, even swiping at the bit around her lips and sucking it off her fingers.

I jerked her up and leaned forward, meeting her half way to smash my lips against hers, tasting myself on her tongue. Each time she fell to her knees for me, my heart damn near exploded at her gift. Not the blow job itself, but the intimacy, the future, the freedom, the room to breathe without my past constantly taking up space inside me. I wondered if she saw it. Saw the gratitude and . . . Not necessarily love, but it was something I'd never felt before. I couldn't help but feel like it poured from my expression, and I wondered if she noticed.

I wondered if, maybe, she felt it too.

"I told you to call me Cal when I'm inside you," I murmured against her mouth.

She nipped playfully at mine. "I'm feeling extra naughty today. I wanted to be a student at her teacher's feet sucking his cock."

"God," I growled, my heart thumping harder. "I should be worried by how much that turns me on."

"It's just me, so it's okay," she said before blowing me a kiss.

Oaklyn sat back on her heels and began buttoning her shirt, her red lipstick smeared. I had no doubt that it coated my own lips, and when I looked down to my softening cock, there were red streaks there too.

Knowing our time left was limited, I ignored my twitching dick and tucked it back in my pants. Lunch was almost over.

"Aren't you going to wipe yourself off?" she asked.

"I'll save it for later in the shower. I can rub it off with my fist as I think of you and how the lipstick got there."

Her lids slid closed over her golden eyes, like she was imagining the scene I'd described. Then she stood with her hand out. "Can I have my panties, please?"

When she first walked in, I'd locked the door and sat her up on my desk, slipping the material down her legs and burying my tongue between her thighs. Leaning back in my chair, I smirked, not moving to retrieve the lace from my pocket.

"I think I'll hold on to these today."

"Callum," she admonished.

"You can always come by tonight and pick them up," I offered hopefully. The smirk slipped from my face when she didn't answer and looked away. "Let me guess, work?"

"I'm sorry. I would much rather be with you tonight."

I knew she would, and I hated the way I couldn't control the disappointment in my tone. I just missed her. It was midterms week, so she didn't have to come in for her work study programs, and if she wasn't studying, then she was working at Voyeur.

It was selfish of me to even have these emotions. She had formed circles under her eyes in the last week and still managed to see me whenever she had time. She was working harder than I could imagine, and I was pouting like a damn child. I had more control than this.

"I know you would." I gave her a reassuring smile and stood to wrap her in my arms.

She pressed up on her toes and kissed the dimple in my chin. "I have to go. I have one more midterm before the day is over."

"Okay. Let me make sure no one is outside."

I reluctantly let go and made sure the coast was clear. Then with one last kiss, Oaklyn left.

I spent the afternoon struggling to grade exams as my mind kept wandering to her working tonight. The more my focus slipped away, the more irritated I got. I had to stop marking papers when my irritation slipped through my work, and I began making snarky comments on them. This wasn't me. I loved teaching and I was always calm and cool, no matter what.

When someone knocked on the door, I snapped, "What?"

Donna peeked her head in with raised eyebrows. "Rough day?"

Taking a deep breath, I ran my hands across my face. "Sorry, Donna. Just a long day."

"It's okay," she said with a reassuring smile. "I just wanted to let you know I'm heading out."

"Okay. Thank you. Have a great night."

"You too. Get some rest."

I took another deep breath, taking in the neat piles alphabetized and evenly aligned on my desk. Looking at the clock and seeing it was already five-thirty, I decided to call it a day and head home.

Once I'd arrived home, I stuck my hand in my pocket when my fingers collided with a piece of fabric. Pulling it out, I stared at the black lacy material before curling my fists tight around it, imagining her naked at Voyeur now as someone looked on. I shoved the lace back in my pocket and stomped over to the wet bar and poured until the glass was over half-full. I downed it in one go and filled it up again, gabbing the bottle and heading toward the living room. Maybe some television would distract me.

It didn't work and after only a few shows, it became harder to focus. My hand dug into my pocket again and lifted out Oaklyn's panties. God, I wanted to see her. I wanted to feast on her cunt, stuffing her panties in her mouth to muffle her cries of pleasure.

So, why didn't I? Why didn't I just go to Voyeur and see her?

Just because I knew what her mouth felt like around my cock, and I had more access to her now, didn't mean I couldn't go there and watch her anymore. Voyeur was my home away from home. I had friends there I'd known since I'd begun going five years ago. So, maybe she was working, it didn't mean I couldn't go have a drink. Maybe claim an hour with her. Maybe just claim her period so no one else could have her.

Decision made, I pulled out my phone and had to squint my eyes to focus on the Uber app. Only seven minutes away. I stood and had to wait a second before walking, letting the room stop spinning first. Then I finished the last of my drink and dropped it in the sink, ignoring the sound of glass breaking. Instead, I focused on grabbing my things and making it out the door.

Thankfully, the drive went quick and I was at the club before I knew it. Standing outside the door, I took a deep breath. I needed to look a hell of a lot more sober than I felt if I was going in. They had a strict two drink minimum and I was about five beyond that. I ended up making it past the entrance and all the way to the bar, but Charlotte was giving me knowing looks, so I asked for just a water.

Oaklyn wasn't in the room. It didn't stop me from scanning the crowd like she'd magically pop up somewhere. Maybe she was in the back grabbing some stock. Maybe she was in the employee lounge. Maybe she was in a room with Jackson as he fucked her from behind.

I squeezed my fist so hard around the glass, I was surprised it didn't break. Blood pumped harder through me, pounding in my ears. With a shaking hand, I lifted the glass to take a sip, severely regretting not getting more alcohol.

I didn't understand what was going on. How I still felt like I was on the edge of snapping when I'd had so much to drink. When I was at Voyeur. Those were two safeties to help me gain my control back, and there I sat, scanning the crowd like a lunatic as angry adrenaline flooded my veins.

I was a fucking mess.

Oaklyn

"Hello?" I answered my phone. I'd heard it ring just as I was about to head back out on the floor.

"Miss Derringer?" a man asked.

"This is a she."

"Hi, this is Kyle from Tires, Tires, Tires. I was just calling you about your car."

I wanted to scream *finally*, but settled on, "Yes?"

"It looks like your tie rod ends are going bad and will need to be replaced with a new rack and pinion," he rattled off.

"I—I don't know what that means? How much is that?" I tried to control my breathing, preparing for the cost, but a looming dread hung over me.

"It has to do with your steering and tires. Between parts and labor, it's going to run you about a thousand dollars."

I don't know how I didn't drop the phone as my whole body went numb, my heart dropping to the floor at the cost. Tears burned the backs of my eyes and I closed them, focusing on slowing down my heaving chest.

"Um—" my voice cracked, and I swallowed and tried again. "Okay. Okay." My mind scrambled trying to think of dates my last school payment was due and how much money I already had set aside. "I guess just let me know when it will be ready for pick-up."

"Sure thing. Sorry about your car."

I wanted to snap at how aloof he sounded about something so devastating, but somehow I stayed as calm as possible and got off the phone.

"You okay, Oak?" Jackson asked when he came in, seeing me hunched over on the bench,

"No." I wiped the tears that managed to leak free and explained my situation.

"Damn. That sucks. What are you going to do?"

"Save up more money and hope I can get it before my payment is due to the school. Possibly just not eat for the rest of the year," I tried to joke.

Once I collected myself, I stood. I needed more money and that meant I needed to get back to work. Sitting in the back crying wasn't going to get me anywhere.

"You can always do more partner work," Jackson suggested, walking out with me.

"Yeah," I said with no commitment. "I'll figure something out."

Just as we were exiting, he threw his arm around my shoulder. "I'd even let you suck me off again if you needed to, because I'm a good friend like that."

I laughed at him, slapping his chest. "Oh, fuck off, Jackson."

"Hey, I'm trying," he said laughing with me.

We had just reached the bar when I lifted my eyes and they clashed with a familiar pair of blue ones. I immediately started to smile, excited to see Callum when I took in how his eyes were harder than I'd ever seen them. He held my stare as he lifted the glass filled with amber liquid and drank until it was empty. I flinched when he dropped it harder than necessary. My skin prickled with foreboding nerves when he stood and had to hold onto the bar top to steady himself.

He was drunk.

I slipped between patrons and moved quickly to meet Callum in the middle. I needed to get him out of here as fast as possible. You weren't allowed to be in Voyeur drunk. He could be kicked out if anyone noticed.

As soon as I reached him, he leaned down, the alcohol on his breath burning my nose, and said, "Have fun fucking Jackson?"

I reeled back like he'd slapped me. "Excuse me?"

He immediately looked away, and shrugged, the muscle in his cheek twitching.

"You just came strolling out of the back with his arm around you and it's hard to watch."

"Then don't watch," I said, my tone hard.

"I came here for you." His hand wiped down his face and his shoulders rose and fell over a sigh. "You're impossible not to watch."

I didn't know what was going on with him or why he showed up here drunk, but I needed to get him off the floor. Grabbing his hand, I turned and pulled him behind me, entering one of the empty rooms in the back.

"Is it my turn now," he mumbled once we entered.

I didn't even think before my hand snapped out and connected with his cheek. His eyes pinched closed but didn't move a muscle, the red handprint blooming on his cheek. Tears burned the backs of my eyes, and I blinked to fight them off.

When he finally looked at me, his eyes glossed over with his own pain, but I didn't understand.

"What's going on, Callum?"

"Fuck," he said, burrowing both hands in his hair. "I'm drunk. I'm sorry. I'm jealous." The words were slurred as they tripped over each other off his tongue.

"That's no excuse to say that to me."

"I know. I'm sorry," he said again. "It's just—it's just . . ." He trailed off, burying his hands in his hair and tugging, growling in frustration.

"It's just what, Cal?"

His shoulders dropped as he leaned against a dresser. He looked tired, completely different from the confident man from earlier. When he still didn't speak, I asked again. "What is it?"

"I'm struggling here, Oaklyn. Voyeur was my place. I had control and now, look at me, being a complete asshole, saying shit I don't even mean." His hands moved around, gesturing to the room. "I'm in my comfort zone, and I feel like I'm going out of my mind."

"What does that mean?"

"I don't fucking know," he exploded, throwing his arms wide, making him stumble away from the desk and lose his balance.

Watching him struggle to stand and get words out, made it clear that tonight was not the night to talk about this. I didn't understand what was going on, but, honestly, it didn't seem like he understood it much either.

Not knowing what to say, I stepped forward and linked my fingers with his, moving until barely any space was between us. He dropped his chin to the top of my head before shifting to press his lips to my forehead.

"I'm sorry I came here drunk. I wasn't thinking."

"Okay." I wasn't going to say it was fine, because we both knew it wasn't.

"I should go."

I dropped my head to his chest and nodded. Neither of us moved, standing there with each other's arms wrapped loosely around the other.

"I didn't fuck him," I confessed. Because whether he was too drunk to rationalize anything, I needed him to know that. "I've never fucked Jackson."

His hands gripped my cheeks and he made me look at him, his brows furrowed. "But I watched you."

"It was pretend. We faked the whole thing. He's never actually gone down on me either."

He blinked a few times, taking in my confession, and ended up only nodding. However, his eyes seemed to be less tortured than a moment before, and as mad as I was at him, I didn't want him to hurt.

"I should go," he said.

"Okay. Get some sleep. And water. Lots of water."

Cal gave me a small smile, and I lifted up to press a kiss to the dimple on his chin.

And then he left. When I walked out of the room, he was already gone. I spent the rest of the night serving drinks and trying to process Cal's words.

Between that and the issues with my car, I was emotionally done by the end of the night. I tossed everything on the floor when I walked into my apartment, stripped down and collapsed on my bed, laughing at how it would have driven Cal nuts to see everything strewn about.

Even after the mess that tonight was, he was the last thing on my mind before I finally fell asleep. I worried if he was okay and had drank enough water. I worried how he would feel tomorrow.

And I worried I'd never really find out what made him drink and come to Voyeur.

Chapter Twenty-Four

Oaklyn

Once the pounding in my head stopped Saturday morning, I grabbed my phone and messaged Oaklyn, worried she'd be too mad for a phone call. Not that I blamed her.

Me: I'm sorry about last night. I was wrong.

Almost immediately the bouncing dots appeared.

O: You were wrong.
O: But I'd be willing to let it slide if you explain to me why it happened.

Fuck. Fuck, fuck, fuck. I didn't want to explain to her that I lost control of my emotions. That I tried to numb myself with alcohol. So, I gave her a half-truth and hope it was enough for her forgiveness.

Me: I just started drinking last night and didn't realize how many I had. When I found your panties in my pocket, I remember thinking how I wanted to return them to you. How much I wanted to see you.

O: Okay. As much as I would've loved my panties back, I could've done without the insults.

Me: Fuck. I'm sorry, O. I can't say it enough. I saw you with Jackson and I just

I swallowed hard, taking a moment to think over my words, deciding to just be honest with her.

Me: I just let my jealousy control me. I didn't even think.

The dots floated for a while and each time they bounced, my chest squeezed tighter and tighter, preparing myself for what she could be typing.

O: Okay.

Me: Okay? Does that mean you forgive me?

O: Yes. I just need time to think about it. I just need to process everything.

Me: Okay. I understand.

O: I have to go. I have a star paper to work on and it's taking all my time.

Me: What horrible person would make you write a paper on a star?

O: A real asshole. A nerdy one.

Me: Sounds amazing to me.

O: Ha. Ha. I'll call you later. 😊

I was irrationally happy with a smiley face at the end of her message. Her sarcastic messages also lifted a weight off my chest.

Oaklyn had given me so much patience. More than I'd ever expected from someone just starting out on their future. And I went and
shoved it back in her face, by acting like a jealous, unappreciative dick.
The least I could do was give her some in return.

I'd been with women before and some had been more understanding than others. Some had been easier to distract than others. Some
hadn't bothered to stick around when I pushed them away on the first
date. And maybe the ones who had been more patient would have giv-
en me more if I'd explained, but not one had ever evoked the need to.

Not once, when faced with them leaving, had I considered sharing
my secret. Not one had seemed important enough to fight for. Until
Oaklyn. When she'd told me to leave or explain that night, it was like
my muscles had seized up and refused to move from the spot. There
was something about her that called to me, that begged me to stay and
not give up. That shouted at me that she was the one. So, I'd decided
and never regretted my decision at any moment.

We'd become closer, but still stayed the same. Laughter still filled
our conversations, but now there were openly heated glances between
us that usually ended up with kissing when we could. I couldn't get
enough of her.

With a smile on my face, and hope I hadn't fucked everything up,
I showered and went to my office to catch up on some work. At times
my mind would wander to the previous night, but I tried to push it
from my mind.

Each time Voyeur would creep into my thoughts, it led to whole
new string of emotions I didn't want. Instead of my chest expanding,
it caved in and made it hard to breathe. My skin burned, but not with
desire. My heart thumped in my chest and my breaths came a little
faster, but not because I was turned on.

No, if I gave in to those emotions, it would be a repeat of last night.

I'd worked hard over the years to get a grip on the control I'd lost.
After all the court cases had been finished and sealed shut, everyone
else was able to move on. Yet, I was left spiraling. Fifteen and six-
teen had been scary years for me as I learned how alcohol could make

me forget, how pot would make the pain easier. How taking my anger out on someone else lessened the pinch in my chest. I'd crashed and burned until my parents had had enough and pushed me back into therapy where I spent the next two years gaining control.

Yet, there I was slipping back again. Letting the visuals of possibilities as she worked torture me.

I knew it was illogical. I'd seen her sheet every night I'd been there before and not once had there been an extreme performance. Rarely anything outside of a solo performance. But maybe those had just been the nights I'd seen it. I rubbed a hand over my face and shook my head, trying to clear it.

I was pulled from my musings when my phone rang. I jumped in my chair, excited at the possibility of hearing Oaklyn on the other line.

"Hello?"

"Hey, Cal." My excitement ebbed at hearing my mom greet me on the other end of the line. "How are you? I hope I'm not interrupting any exciting plans."

"Sorry, Mom. Just a fun Saturday grading papers."

"You need to get out more. Travel."

"Over a two-day weekend? That's a bit much," I said laughing, but my laughter died off when she cleared her throat and hesitated.

"You could," she paused, probably swallowing like she always did when she was nervous to say something. "You could maybe plan a trip home."

A buzzing rang in my ear at hearing the word *home*.

"Why?" I asked so low I wondered if she could hear me.

More pausing, but I couldn't find any words to fill it.

"Sarah is getting married. They wanted you to come."

"No." The word came out without thought. Just fell from my lips wrapped in the immediate reaction I had to the thought of going anywhere near them.

Sarah was *his* sister and I'd distanced myself as much as possible from that family. They'd felt horrible. Had no idea any of it was going on and apologized profusely rambling on about family and other nonsense I'd been too angry to hear. Even after he'd died, I still couldn't bring myself to reconnect with them.

After it had all happened, there had been too much tension for my father to keep as close a relationship with his sister. Somehow, they kept in enough contact to eventually bridge the gap. Just not around me. By that point, my shame and pain had morphed into rage and anger, taking on a life of its own. I may have still been a mess now, but I was better than I was thirteen years ago.

"I'm sorry, Mom. I just can't."

"Don't you ever apologize to me. You don't owe them anything. I think Sarah is just reaching a point in her life where she is trying to reconnect. Growing up and falling in love will do that to you."

"I'll send a card."

"Okay, Callum. I'm sure she'll appreciate it." She exhaled heavily. "Well, I just wanted to call and see how you were doing and pass the news on. I won't keep you from your wild life."

"Very funny, Mom. Tell Dad I said hello."

"Will do. We're about to do a couple's cooking class tonight. He's *so* excited."

My chest rumbled with laughter. My dad hated cooking but would do anything for my mom. He was close to retiring and my mom had taken full advantage to go on as many dates as she could with him. He grumbled about it most of the time, but he enjoyed it because she enjoyed it. They were a love anyone would aspire to.

"Well you two have fun tonight. Love you."

"Love you too, baby."

I tapped the end button and set my phone in line with my stapler.

Closing my eyes, I took a deep breath in through my nose, holding it for five seconds, then slowly letting it out through pursed lips. And then I did it again until I felt like I was in control of my body. I hated that I still needed the breathing exercises this long after everything. Hated that the mention of a family member could cause me to need them.

Then I began to take stock of my body, the way my heart beat at a normal pace and didn't hurt with each thump. I wasn't rubbing at my skin, in desperate need of a shower after the phone call. I wasn't pacing away from my desk, taking long pulls of bourbon straight from the bottle.

I closed my eyes and breathed again, feeling more centered when I pictured Oaklyn's face behind my eyelids.

She was the only thing different than my last birthday, when I'd received a card from his family and I'd spent the week locked in my bedroom drinking until I passed out and then repeat. She'd shifted something inside me. Like maybe where there was only darkness and doubt, a bit of light shone through, reminding me I wasn't done yet. To not give up just yet. She gave me hope and made me want to try harder for that promise of a future.

I laughed at the juxtaposition of the feelings she gave me. She calmed me and centered me, but also pushed my limits of control. The two emotions twisted inside me and I didn't know what to do with them. All I knew, was that I wasn't ready to give up on anything. Not my control and definitely not her.

Maybe I'd take the step and go to the wedding. If I kept making improvements, maybe it wouldn't seem like such a mountain to climb. And if I had Oaklyn by my side, I could conquer the world.

My phone buzzed, and my eyes shot open to see who it was.

O: Want to see me tonight?

I barked out a laugh and immediately responded. My cheeks hurt from smiling so hard, happy to hear from her so soon. I sent a quick message back, inviting her over, into my space, promising dinner and then got to work.

"This is delicious," Oaklyn said around a bite of pasta.

She had been tense when I opened the door, but I'd pulled her into my arms and whispered my apologies up and down her neck until she'd laughed and demanded I put her down. Just like that, she smiled up at me with her golden eyes and no lingering hurt or questions. Looking just as excited to see me as I was to have her there.

"Thank you. I slaved over it all afternoon."

She raised an eyebrow and smirked at me. "And do you always serve your freshly made meals in aluminum containers with *Lucia's Italian Kitchen* on them?"

"All the time," I answered with a straight face, before finally laughing. "What can I say, I'm not the greatest cook, and it's just me. No need to be good at making elaborate dinners."

"Callum, this is spaghetti. It may not be the elaborate meal you think it is."

"Hey, there's some asparagus."

"Okay," she agreed laughing. "It's just disappointing to see such a large beautiful kitchen go to waste."

"Yeah, the house is a lot."

"Why did you buy a house this huge just for you?"

I looked down, watching the tines of my fork twirl the noodles, avoiding looking at her. "I'd hoped it wouldn't always be just for me. I wanted—want—a family. I'm just not sure it's possible for me. I thought maybe if I bought the house, I'd feel more pressure to get over everything and start one."

She didn't say anything for so long that I looked up cautiously. Her chin rested in her palm as she studied me.

"I think you'll make a great dad."

"What?" I barely breathed the word. It wasn't what I thought she would say. I figured she'd make a comment about how I would never fill this house if I didn't start filling a woman. But this was Oaklyn. She never judged me, she never made a snarky comment diminishing my issues.

"You're so passionate in class, how could you not be passionate about everything else? I bet you'd take the kids to a planetarium and force astronomy on them." She smiled. "Probably have them reciting constellations before their ABCs."

A lump at the base of my throat threatened to choke me. I smiled with her, imagining the picture she described.

"But it will totally play in your favor when you make your wife fall in love with you by taking her stargazing. A romantic nighttime picnic."

Taking a deep breath, I closed my eyes and saw it. Saw myself curled up with a woman with light brown hair and golden eyes. I saw myself making love to her under the stars. Swallowing past the lump in my throat, I somehow managed to speak. "What about you? What does your future look like?"

"A stable family. A home we feel secure in. One that I can provide because I have my degree and make a shit-ton of money."

"A shit-ton? Is that more or less than a fuck-ton of money?"

"Less. I don't want to be greedy. Especially since I want more. I want a house full of kids. I mean not an army, but definitely more than three. I hated being an only child."

"Did your parents not dote on you since you were the only one?"

"They did. They tried to be the best they could. They just worked a lot. We seemed to always just be on the edge of making it. So, I was alone as they worked two jobs each. I would have loved to have a sibling to share that time with."

"Well, I think you'll make your dreams come true. You're too determined to not have them happen."

"True," she agreed with a hard nod. "Now, let's clean these dishes up and go make-out on your over-sized couch."

"We could always just toss them in the sink."

She cocked an eyebrow at me. "I want your full attention, and if we leave a mess, you won't be able to focus. I know you, Callum."

In awe of how well she *did* know me, I sat as she grabbed both plates and took them to the sink. She followed behind me with the cups and grabbed a towel as I started washing. Her hips swayed to the music I had playing in the background and I was about to say fuck all these damn dishes and attack her. Instead, I settled on flicking soapy water at her.

"Hey," she screeched, dodging more splashes of water. "What was that for?"

"If you don't stop shaking your ass, I'm going to end up putting you up on the counter and eating you for dessert."

She slicked her tongue across her lips and tugged the bottom with her teeth. Too tempting to pass up, I leaned down and sucked it in my mouth, loving her moan.

"Now hurry up and dry so we can get to dessert."

She gave a mock salute and grabbed the dish from my hands to dry, but continued to shake her hips, peeking over at me to make sure I was watching.

"Fucking tease."

She giggled and tapped my hip with her own.

Once I handed over the last dish for her to dry, I wrapped my arms around her, pulling her back to my front. I brushed her hair to the side and began working my lips down her neck.

"Callum," she groaned.

"Better focus. Wouldn't want to drop that dish."

She swiped the towel across the glass and then set them both on the counter, not bothering to try and put it away, and turned in my arms. Her hands slid over my shoulders and burrowed in my hair, pulling me down so she could feast on my lips.

I seriously considered hoisting her up on the counter, but decided I wanted to have her laid out for me and instead gripped her ass and lifted. Her legs wrapped around my waist and I turned, not taking my mouth from hers, and headed to the living room.

I wasn't ready to have her mouth off of mine just yet, so I sat back and we made out like a couple of teenagers. I cringed a little when I remembered she actually was a teenager, but when I looked at her, I didn't see her age. I saw comfort and caring and a future. I made sure to never pressure her or feel like she owed me anything because of my position in her life. She was there because she wanted to be, and she was an adult able to make her own decisions.

Oaklyn tugged off her top and then mine. She wore another one of those lacy bra things that barely covered her, and I kissed my way down her breasts, sucking on her nipples, loving the way the soft bud felt against my tongue. Loving the gasp and moans she made when I pinched them between my teeth.

Desperate to taste her, I flipped her to her back and worked her leggings and underwear down her legs as I kissed across her flat stomach. Her legs parted easily for me to fit my shoulders between and I made myself comfortable. I kissed across the crevice of one thigh before cresting her mound and repeating the process on the other.

"Callum," she pleaded.

"Is there something you want?" I asked innocently before slipping my tongue between her folds and letting the sweet and tangy flavor of her burst on my tongue.

"Yes," she hissed.

I sucked on one of her folds, letting it go with a pop. "What is it you want, Oaklyn? Tell me."

"Lick me."

I twisted my head and dragged my tongue up her thigh, barely holding back my laugh at her growl. "Not happy with that?"

"You know it's not what I meant." She stared down at me past her perfect breasts, one nipple on edge of escaping its lacy confines.

"Show me," I said, reaching up to tug the lace aside and roll her tip between my fingers. Her hand dropped, and she pointed at her slit. "No, Oaklyn. Show me exactly where. Open up for me. Show me your clit."

Her hips twisted under me, but she moved both hands between her thighs and used her fingers to part her lips, exposing every part of her wet cunt to me. I didn't hesitate, I dove in, starting at her opening and licking all the way up to swirl around her clit. Her hand clenched, releasing its hold. It didn't matter, I was ready to feel her squeeze around me and I gave it everything I had.

I sucked on her bundle of nerves and thrust my tongue as deep inside her as I could. Palmed her breasts with one and used the other to slip my fingers inside her. I looked up the expanse of her body as she rode against my face. Coated my chin with her juices. I only froze a little when her finger dug into my hair holding me in place but pushed it back easily. All of this came more easily, and it was thanks to her.

When her cries came louder and the movement of her hips faster, I focused all my attention on her clit until she came. Each time she pulsed around my fingers, I imagined what it would feel like around my cock and I found myself humping the couch I was so turned on.

Once she'd come down from her orgasm, I kissed my way back up her body and bit at the sensitive tip of her breast. She gasped and pushed her nails down my back.

Bile rose up my throat as I remembered a deeper groan and harder fingers dragging down my skin. I jerked back and moved to the other side of the couch, burying my head in my hands. I couldn't look at her as I tried to catch my breath, tried to wipe the memory from my mind.

"Callum?" she said, but I shook my head. "Callum, it's okay."

It wasn't fucking okay. I had just had a fantastic moment of burying my head between her thighs. A moment of feeling success completely gone by a moment of remembering. I heard her moving around and pulling her pants back on, and a part of me tried to prepare myself for her to leave.

But then her legs appeared in front of me on the ground as she sat cross-legged. She didn't touch me, but rested open palms on her knees, facing up. There if I needed her.

"Did you know all the girls in class practically drool when you turn to write on the board? I can't blame them. Your ass is especially nice."

Confused by her change in topic, I jerked my head up and found her with a neutral expression. Her eyes were kind and lacking all the empathy I expected to see there. She looked like she did when we talked over lunch. Minus a shirt.

"I didn't realize that." I knew girls whispered about how I looked but didn't realize they stared at my ass during class.

And then it hit me. I was done fighting back the memory because my mind had moved on to her question. She'd perfectly distracted me. Dropping my hand, I linked my fingers with her open palm.

"I'm sorry, Oaklyn." Even if we moved on, I still wanted to apologize for continually jerking back.

Her fingers squeezed mine and she said, "It's okay, Callum. You don't need to apologize to me. Whenever you're ready, just let me know what bothered you, so I know not to do it again."

"The nails down my back," I muttered.

Her expression didn't change, didn't shift like she felt sad as she imagined what I'd gone through. She remained neutral and gave me a nod.

"Do you want to stay in my guest room tonight?" I asked quickly, hearing how lame it sounded as soon as it came out. *My guest room?* "I know it's weird, I just want you here, and well . . ."

"I'd love to," she said with a wide smile. "I want to be here, too."

I breathed a sigh of relief and held my hand out for her. "First, lay with me a while. I'm not ready to leave this couch just yet."

Taking her hand, I pulled her up toward me and had her face me. Smiling at how beautiful she was, I brushed her hair back before leaning in to kiss her.

"I can't get enough of your lips."

"Good," she said, snagging another kiss.

"You want to watch a movie?"

She nodded, and I grabbed the remote and scrolled through the on-demand movies. We agreed on a rom-com, and then I pulled her back to my front, loving the feel of her skin pressed to mine. Throughout the movie, her fingers would trail up and down my hand or lace together with my own as she tugged it close to her chest.

I would breathe in her hair, loving the way it tickled my nose. If I could make her a part of me, I would.

By the time the movie was over, she was already passed out. I slipped out from behind her and then picked her up from the couch, her body curling into me as I carried her up the stairs to the guest room. Once I had her settled, on a whim, I decided to lay down with her. She, again, curled her body into mine as soon as I settled next to hers and I wrapped her in my arms. I hadn't meant to fall asleep, especially since I knew nights were rough when flashbacks happened during the day.

"Fuck, Cal. How can this be wrong when it feels so good? It feels good, doesn't it?"

"No!" I shouted, jerking up in bed. The air chilled my sweat-slicked skin. I jerked again when a hand landed on my arm.

"Hey," Oaklyn's soft voice reached me in the dark. "It's okay. It's just me."

"Fuck," I whispered past my panting. "I'm sorry." My body began to tremble as I came down from the rush of adrenaline. "I'm so sorry, Oak."

Her fingers slowly linked to mine, giving me a chance to pull away. The bed shifted as she scooted closer. On instinct, I leaned into her, allowing her to fall back and take me with her. I stretched my arm, letting the long strands of her hair drape over my fingers and rested my head on her chest. Her hair always seemed to be my anchor to reality. When we fooled around, my hand found its way into the strands, holding them tight as she wrapped her lips around my cock. As she kissed me and stroked her hand up and down my cock. I always held tight.

Listening to her heartbeat, I tried to match my breathing to it. Tried to match the slow rise and fall of her chest. Tried to get lost in the heat of her skin pressing to my cheek. My other hand leisurely stroked across her stomach, fighting the urge to wrap tight around her and squeeze her to me as if I could make us one. As if she were closer, I could use her strength and finally let it all go.

As I held her, she held me. Her fingers slipping softly between the strands of my hair, sending goose bumps down my neck and back. She never tried to push me to talk about it, never made a big deal out of the way my body trembled against hers. She just held me as I came down from my nightmare.

When the shaking finally stopped, she asked, "Do you want to head to your room?"

"Yeah," I agreed, embarrassed. "I don't want to, but it may be for the best."

Thank god she couldn't see the fire burning my cheeks in the dark.

"Okay." She placed a soft kiss to the crown of my head and we sat up. I hadn't expected her to hold my hand and lead the way, but she did like it was her own home. I showed her which door was mine and she didn't unlink our fingers until we reached my bed. With a gentle kiss to my chest she let go of my hand and walked toward the bathroom. She filled up one of the cups next to the sink and brought it back to me where I stood frozen, watching her movements in the dark.

"Drink. It'll help."

I dutifully took the cup and drank it all. She grabbed it from me and set it on the nightstand before ordering me to lay down. I almost laughed at the way she tucked me in, but it died before it started when she leaned over me and pushed my hair back from my face. Her golden eyes seemed to glow in the darkness and shine a light for me.

"You are one of the most beautiful men I've ever known, and I'm so grateful for any of the trust you place in me."

I lifted my hand to her cheek and brushed my thumb across the soft skin before pulling her down for a kiss.

"I'm a fucking lucky man," I whispered against her lips.

She gave one last kiss. "I'll be right down the hall. Have sweet dreams, Cal."

I did.

I dreamed of making love to her under the stars.

Chapter Twenty-Five

Oaklyn

You're on a stage. Just like an actress on Broadway.

They had to get naked and at least pretend to perform sexual acts too. This was exactly the same.

But no matter how many times I tried to remind myself of the all the things I'd said before, nothing rid me of the weight pressing down on my chest.

Staring at the ceiling, I tried to focus. I tried to make my body move in ways that made me appear turned on, like I was on the verge of an orgasm as I worked my hand between my legs.

What would Callum think?

I let out a soft moan, hoping the sound would hold me in the moment and not take me to Callum. I couldn't think about him when I was doing my job. And that's exactly what this was. A job. He had to understand that.

It wasn't like we were exclusive or anything, or had any claim on each other, but no matter how hard I tried to remind myself, my chest ached thinking about him. He already knew this about me.

He never outright said how much he hated it, but he'd stopped coming to the club. I could hear the irritation in his voice every time I mentioned work.

Instead of climaxing like I should've been doing, I was struggling to focus.

I forced my moans louder, writhing my hips harder, moving my hand faster, and then I tensed, faking the orgasm. I just needed it to end.

After the light finally turned red, I lay there on the bed, feeling the weight growing heavier and heavier as I tried to picture myself from Callum's eyes.

And for the first time since working there, I felt true shame.

It followed me out of the room. It hung over me as I removed my name from any more performances. There was no way I could be anything but sullen right then. After I managed to plaster on a fake smile and serve customers for the rest of my shift, I sat in the employee lounge, putting on my canvas tennis shoes when Jackson came strolling in.

"Please stay a little longer and agree to a sex scene with me," he asked, giving me his best puppy dog eyes. I almost laughed because he knew they didn't affect me.

With a heavy sigh, I shook my head and looked down to tie my shoe. "I can't, Jackson."

"Why not?"

Why not?

Callum. That was why. Not even the extra bill for my car repair hanging over my head was enough to outweigh Callum. I couldn't stop thinking about him and what he thought of me. I couldn't decide if I was wrong or right to turn down such good money for my teacher, someone who hadn't said anything about commitment and being serious. It felt serious. God, it felt huge, sinking into my bones, making them feel too big and my skin tight. But maybe it was just me. How did I know if he felt the same?

Here I was turning down good money based on what he may or may not have thought of me. Maybe I was just a student he was enjoying easy access to.

No. I knew that wasn't it. I knew Callum enough to know he at least felt something. Frankly, I felt enough on my own to not want to perform a sex scene with Jackson. Even if it would have only been pretending.

"I'm . . . ." How did I explain without encouraging more questions? "I'm seeing someone."

"What?" he asked loudly, moving to sit next to me. "How have I not known? Is it serious? Is it new? Does he know you work here?"

I chuckled at his rapid-fire questions. "Yes, he knows I work here." I answer the simplest question avoiding the others.

His eyebrows rose. "And?"

"And it just feels wrong now," I admitted.

"Oaklyn," he began. I looked up and found pitying eyes. "We need the money. It's not about the sexual acts. That's about the bottom line for things."

"I know."

"This is why I avoid relationships. I don't have the financials to give up working here because someone doesn't like it."

"You wouldn't take Jake up on a relationship if he came calling?" I asked with one eyebrow raised, daring him to say he wouldn't.

"That's . . . That's pointless to even think about." His fists clenched and unclenched before he changed the subject. "So, tell me about this guy."

"He's great. Really kind and smart. So freaking hot." I smiled just thinking about him.

"Where'd you meet?"

The smile dropped just as fast as it came, and I looked away, scrambling for an answer or deflection. "I, um. I can't say."

"Oh, come on. Tell me."

An idea came to mind to get him to stop pushing and I turned, keeping my face neutral to trap him. "Okay."

"Yes," he said, making a fist and pulling it into him.

"If you tell me about Jake."

His victory smile dropped from his face and I openly smirked. "I hate you."

I cocked an eyebrow and waited for him to begin or give up. I mostly hoped he'd give up.

His shoulders dropped on a heavy sigh. "He was a friend of a friend I got close to in college. We all got drunk and made stupid bets. I ended up having to kiss him and we all laughed, despite the way he kissed me back." Jackson breathed a laugh and licked his lips, as though he could still taste the kiss. "By the end of the night, he'd stumbled into my room and kissed me again. I blew him and he . . ." His Adam's apple bobbed. "He kind of freaked out and left. Came around a week later with a girlfriend, and we fell apart."

"I'm so sorry, Jackson."

"Now, we see each other and it's okay. If not filled with a lot of tension. But I'm pushing through it because he's given me no inclination of anything beyond polite, we-used-to-know-each-other vibes."

I gripped his hand in mine and squeezed, not needing to say I was sorry again. He knew I was sad for him and it didn't help anything. "What do you do outside of here? How do I not know?" I asked, changing the subject for him.

"I'm a spy."

"Fascinating." I exaggerated the word like I was truly shocked.

He just shook his head with a laugh before turning to me. "Okay. Now tell me where you met this guy."

I stared at him, weighing my chances of making it to the door and hoping he forgot about it before he saw me again. Probably slim. But this was Jackson. We'd formed a friendship with zero judgement. If there was anyone I could tell, it was him. "He's my teacher," I mumbled, but judging by his wide eyes and opened mouth, he heard me just fine.

"Shut. Up."

"He saw me here," I said before I thought better of it. Maybe I'd been dying to talk about it and now that Jackson knew, I was able to lift some of these confessions off my chest. "Before he found out I was his student. But even once he found out, he still came. I didn't know, and we became friends and I just . . . I just liked him too much to stay mad at him for not telling me."

"Shut. Up," he said again.

"You sound like a Valley girl." He flipped his imaginary hair and we laughed, but then he just stared. "Okay. Bring on the lecture about all I'm doing wrong and how wrong all of it is."

His shoulder lifted on a shrug, and he pretended to zip his lips shut. However, he broke the seal when he said, "Just be careful."

I wanted to say I was, but deep down, I knew I wasn't.

Being careful wouldn't be seeing your professor. Wouldn't be fooling around in his office. I opened my mouth to lie anyways when Charlotte walked in.

"Oaklyn!" She said my name with an exaggerated smile and I knew she wanted something.

"Yes, Charlotte?"

"Would you possibly, maybe, kind of want to hopefully cover my last three hours at the bar? My boyfriend is landing in town early and I was hoping to meet him at the airport."

"You have a boyfriend?" Jackson asked, shocked.

"Not all of us have a phobia of relationships."

"It's not a phobia."

I cut in before their banter could pick up any more than it already was. "Sure, Charlotte. I got to make up that money somehow."

"Thank you, thank you!" She came over and gave me a hug. "I'll be leaving here in fifteen. Is that okay?"

"Yeah, I'll just rest my feet back here for a bit and meet you out there."

She rounded the corner and Jackson excused himself too. He had a client waiting. Just as I was alone, my phone rang next to me.

"Hey, Cal."

"Come have dinner with me," he said first thing. "I went to the grocery store and I want to make something for you."

It sounded so nice and if he would have called ten minutes ago, my answer may have been different. "I can't. I'm sorry because I really want to."

"Why not?"

I paused weighing my options of possibly lying, but I didn't want to lie to him. "I'm working."

"Oh," he said before a long pause. "Are you almost done?"

"No, I still have a few more hours."

"Call off," he suggested, hope making his tone lighter.

"Cal, I can't. I need the money if I want to eat and still make the tuition payment."

Heat flooded my cheeks, embarrassed to admit how much I was struggling with money to someone so much more sophisticated than me.

"Okay," he said, his voice lacking all emotion.

"Please don't make me feel bad about this."

"Listen, Oaklyn. I try not to think about you working there, but it ends up being *all* I think about. I care about you. More than I should, and I'm just possessive. I don't know how to handle it because all I can think about is how I don't want you working there anymore. I don't want anyone else getting a part of you."

His words created a slew of emotions in me. Excitement that he felt that way about me. That he thought about me as much as he admitted. However, there was also this sinking in my stomach and irritation pumping my blood harder. Especially when his words—that should have been sweet and soft—came out mixed with his own irritation. Did that mean he didn't want to feel those things about me? That he was bothered by them?

"I get it, Cal," I said, trying to be understanding. "This isn't some chosen career I'm dying to do. I need the money, and this is my best option."

"Most college students tend to work at coffee shops for money," he muttered.

I ground my teeth, holding my biting retort back, not wanting to argue. I kept my tone low and tried for a calm I didn't feel. "That's not fair and you know it."

There was a long pause, and I began to wonder if he'd hung up.

"I know it's not, but it doesn't make it easier that you're there."

"Well, I'm sorry I need more than minimum wage and the minimal assistance from *both* my student aide jobs. I'm sorry my life isn't easy for you," I snapped, losing the battle for calm. "It's not easy for me either."

"I just wished you worked somewhere other than Voyeur where weird men couldn't stare at you getting fucked."

"That's pretty interesting coming from the person who has been a member for however long."

"That's different."

"No, it's not."

The phone call was getting out of control and our words seemed to toe the line of pushing too far. Thankfully, I was saved from another response when Charlotte rounded the corner.

"Listen, I have to go."

"Oaklyn."

"What, Dr. Pierce?"

He grunted as though calling him that had been a physical blow through the phone. "I'm sorry."

"Okay."

I hung up before he could respond. I didn't say anything to Charlotte as I passed by, unable to work anything past the lump in my throat.

Maybe the next three hours without talking would allow us both to calm down. I could hope. I had just got Callum, and I wasn't ready for a stupid argument to end it already.

Chapter Twenty-Six

Callum

I fucked up. Again.

I'd known it as soon as I'd opened my mouth, but I definitely knew it when she came into class and didn't look me in the eye. Not because she'd had her head down like she was hurt. No, she held her chin high and looked like she was ready to kick the world's ass. She sat in her chair, her lips pursed tight and refused to meet my eye. Even when I called on her to speak.

I knew what I'd said was wrong, but I'd lost my ability to rein in my emotions after I'd already been drinking earlier to cope with her working at Voyeur. It scared me as how easy I let the insults fly. I'd questioned how she supported herself from my high horse and it had been wrong. I'd been lucky to never have had to worry about money. Yet there I was, recommending Starbucks. I cringed every time I heard the words in my head.

I'd just never felt so possessive before, so afraid to lose someone. What would I do if she left me? Would I go back to never being intimate again? Would I even want to try without her?

The thought terrified me. Imagining myself back at Voyeur in a room alone watching strangers do things I never could. Imagining myself walking around my big empty house, alone. I couldn't do it after knowing all that she'd shown me.

Thinking on my feet, I quickly wrote a note on a Post-it and slipped it between the pages of a packet I was about to hand out. *I'm sorry. Please forgive me for being an ass.* The little yellow slip of paper only allowed for so many words, otherwise I could have written a novel on all the ways I was so sorry. I stood up and began handing out the packets, making sure Oaklyn got the one that held the note. Then, I finished class and hoped for the best. I was too scared to look over at her again to possibly see rejection all over her face.

It was scary enough waiting to see if she would stay or walk out the same way she walked in, completely ignoring my presence and pissed. I couldn't blame her if she did.

I tried to distract myself with packing up my things as the kids shuffled out the door, too scared to see if she'd already left. I had my answer when only a few people still lingered in the room and I heard, "I'll see you later. I need to ask Dr. Pierce some questions about the project."

"Okay, Oak. See you later."

I watched her friend walk out the door, followed by a few other straggling students and then I finally turned to look at her. She stood there, her whole body filled with tension. Her fists gripping the straps on her book bag, her jaw set in a firm line, her eyes cold.

But I knew—I saw—behind the chilled indifference, was hurt. A hurt I put there. I swallowed hard past the regret. Looking over, I made sure the door was firmly closed. I wished I could lock it and give us some privacy, but that could only lead to issues should someone try to enter.

"I'm so sorry, Oaklyn," I said, staring her down so she could see the sincerity. "I was wrong. I was an asshole and I was wrong. I had no right to ask you to leave your job to come have dinner with me. I had no right to pass any kind of judgment on what you do. I'm so sorry."

Her shoulders relaxed enough to ease the tightness in my chest. Her honey eyes warmed up a little more and she softened before my eyes, only showing the hurt, not bothering to hide. It was both better and worse.

"I get it, Cal. I really do. And it's not like I *want* to be there. I *need* to be there, to reach my goals."

"I know. And I respect you for your determination. I let my jealousy get the best of me. I'm just—" I choked over the words and had to clear my throat before continuing. "I'm worried you'll find someone better. Without all my issues."

I almost laughed at the situation I found myself in. An older professor confessing his fears to his student. In theory, I had all the authority, but there she stood, my student, a shining beacon who held my happiness in her hands, with all the power to crush or make me.

She snorted. "I'm more likely to meet a guy at school than at Voyeur."

"Don't even get me started on the boys at school and how hard it is to watch them watch you. Even if you do deserve someone your age."

I hadn't meant to say the last part, admitting how much me being older than her—at a more settled place in my life than her—scared me, but there it was. Just another fear slipping out to lay at her feet. After a moment, she closed the distance between us and only stood a foot away, looking at me with wonder and awe.

"I only want you." She took another step, now only a breath between us which felt like nothing when she gave me a shy smile. "I want Clark Kent. I want the man adorably in love with the stars." Another step until her breasts pressed to my chest and I pulled in a ragged breath, my cock twitching behind my slacks. "I want the man who looks at me like I'm more than any of those stars."

"You are," I immediately agreed. "You are so much more. I'm sorry for being a jealous asshole. I don't want to lose you."

"I don't want to lose you either, and I know I'm asking you to trust a lot, but I don't have another option. I don't really want to work there. It's not like it's my dying passion. I just need to . . . for now."

I stared at her, taking in her small features surrounded by sharp cheekbones. The dark eyebrows that made her eyes seem all the brighter. The almost non-existent dimple in her chin. The freckles you could only see if you stood right in front of her. All of it held my attention like it had from day one. "You are so beautiful," I whispered, brushing a lock of hair behind her ear.

"You're not too bad yourself." Her eyes dropped to my lips and then her tongue slicked out across her own.

I gave in to the desire and tasted them. I wrapped my lips around her bottom one and flicked my tongue across it. I went to do it again, but she opened her mouth with a moan and sucked me in. My tongue met hers and immediately my eyes fell closed becoming lost in her. It was so easy now. There were no pep-talks and stares before I could finally relax enough to close my eyes and become lost in the moment. It happened in an instant.

I didn't flinch when her hands slid up my arms, over my shoulders, until they dug in the back of my hair, holding me close. I didn't jump back when her hips thrust in to mine, brushing against my erection. I became so lost that I almost didn't realize when she began pulling back. She left a few more pecks against my lips before stepping away with a smile, her fingers to her lips as though holding my kisses in.

"We probably shouldn't get carried away. Wouldn't want anyone walking in on us."

Nodding, I tried to collect myself, taking deep breaths and willing my cock to soften. With one last deep breath, I turned to pack up my bag, ready to walk her out when the door burst open.

"Ready for lunch, asshole?" Reed asked, only seeing me when he barged in. It didn't take long though for him to notice her. She was kind of hard to miss. "Oh, hey. So sorry about that. We're old friends. I'm allowed to call him asshole," he tried to explain.

Oaklyn smiled at Reed and let out a soft laugh. "It's okay. No need to apologize."

Reed, the perceptive bastard that he was, walked closer, letting his eyes flick between us. Probably aware of every female student I had since I'd confessed my attraction to one of them. When he got closer, he reached a hand out to Oaklyn. "I'm Reed. It's nice to meet you."

"Oaklyn," she said, shaking his offered hand.

"Physics major?" Reed asked.

"No. Definitely not. Just here for an elective."

Reed's eyebrows rose at that, his mind clicking that this was the student who tied me in knots. He stared for a moment longer taking in all her features, and I wanted to wedge between them so he couldn't look at her anymore. It may have been non-existent, but in my mind the silence lasted forever, and I needed to get Oaklyn away from Reed before he said something damaging.

"I hope you have a good rest of your day, Miss Derringer."

"Thank you, Dr. Pierce."

I almost groaned when she bit her lip holding my gaze before leaving. My eyes were glued to her until the door clicked shut. Even then, I still stared.

"She's hotter than you said."

I didn't even bother denying it. It would've been a waste of energy. Instead, I grabbed my bag and walked past him.

"Fuck off, Reed."

Lying in bed, I struggled to stay focused on the book in front of me. My mind constantly wandering to Oaklyn. It always wandered to her. Even when I hadn't known what she tasted like, felt like, it had still been focused on her. Even now, I couldn't fully explain what it was that drew me to her, what kept pulling me back. Maybe fate, an energy that my body recognized, knowing she would be the one to change me? I didn't know, and I really didn't care.

Tossing the book aside, I grabbed my phone and scrolled until I found her number. A text message wasn't too much.

Me: How's studying?

Almost immediately she responded, and my smile grew.

O: Good. How was your lunch?
Me: Good.

Especially since Reed had offered me a break and hadn't brought her up again.

O: Does he know about me?

I considered lying, but I didn't want to lie to her. My thumbs hovered over the screen as I considered my words. Trying to see the outcome that may have occurred for every response I thought of.

Me: He knows I'm attracted to you.
O: Does that worry you?
Me: No. Why?
O: You have a lot to lose, Callum.
Me: Reed wouldn't say anything. He's my best friend.
O: We should be more careful. I won't be the cause of you losing your job.

I almost responded that she was worth it, but I didn't want to overwhelm her with the desperate feelings that consumed me.

Me: Don't worry about me.
O: But I do. Maybe we should keep the classroom kissing to a minimum.
Me: I guess
Me: Party pooper.
Me: So, where do you suggest we get our kisses in?

She didn't respond. I almost set my phone aside she took so long to respond. My mind became lost in the possibilities of what I'd said that had made her stop talking. Maybe she had a phone call. Maybe I was over thinking it all.

I jumped when my phone vibrated in my hand. Seeing "O" on the screen, I immediately swiped to answer.

"Hey."

"What are we doing here, Callum?"

I paused, processing her sudden question. "What do you mean?"

Her heavy sigh reached through the phone and upped my anxiety about what she could mean.

"I don't want to be one of those people who asks where we'll be later, but this situation is different. There's a lot at risk. I like you. A lot. I know this isn't a normal relationship with dates and a chance at a natural progression like any other couple. But what are we doing?"

"Oaklyn." I swallowed and thought through my words, needing her to know how serious this was for me. "You know I would take you on dates if I could. I would sweep you off your feet. And I will. Later."

"But what does that mean? Later?"

"You won't always be my student, Oaklyn."

Silence greeted that statement, and I bit my tongue to keep from speaking as she processed that I'd thought that far into the future. I could at least admit that I had, I just wouldn't admit to her how far I'd actually thought.

"Okay. I like the sound of that," she finally said, making my face split into a grin. "But . . . "

My smile slipped a little at that simple word. Rarely anything good came after *but*.

"What if people see us on a date later?"

"They can assume but won't know. The possibility of assumptions won't keep me from something I want and care about so much." My answer came out more passionate than I intended, but I wouldn't take it back. Especially when I heard her soft response.

"I care about you too, Cal."

A heavy silence filled the line and I thought about what I really wanted to say to her. What my words really meant. So much more than 'want' and 'care'. Did she feel it? Did she want to say more, too?

She cleared her throat breaking the moment.

"Well, I should probably get going. This professor is making us slave away over a star project."

"He sounds amazing," I said, letting her escape the serious moment. Even though we were back to a lighter topic, again, her words reached me with more meaning than I think she intended for me to hear.

"He's the best."

Chapter Twenty-Seven

Callum

"Come over this weekend," I said against Oaklyn's neck. I watched her walk into the conference room where the printer was. She had her back to me, and I snuck up behind her, loving the way she sucked in a breath when my fingers brushed her hair away from her neck. "Dress up. It will be a pseudo date. Please," I whispered, quickly pressing my lips against her smooth skin before stepping back.

"Yes," she'd agreed.

I'd rushed back to press one last string of kisses up her neck, loving the moan that vibrated against my lips. I wanted to stay, pinning her to the desk, but the door wasn't locked, and we wouldn't be able to explain that away.

So, I stepped back and said, "Tomorrow," before walking back out the door.

I couldn't stop thinking about our conversation the other night about dates. Imagining her all dressed up, a shy smile in place as I walked into a restaurant with the most beautiful woman on my arm. I needed to give as much of that to her as possible.

Saturday night, I'd pulled out all the stops. I had candles on the dining room table, in the kitchen, in the entryway, and lit the fireplace in the living room trying to set the mood. Trying to hide the fact that we were still at my house rather than the decadent restaurant I really wanted to take her to.

But none of it mattered when I opened the door to the most beautiful woman I'd ever seen. Her golden eyes seemed to glow under my porch light, wide and filled with nerves. It was an intoxicating mix with the black dress she wore. Sleeves stretched down her forearms, but her shoulders were left completely exposed. It was fitted up top, just hinting at cleavage before flaring out above her waist. I stepped back with my jaw hanging open to let her in and looked down at a small expanse of thigh exposed before being met with over the knee suede boots.

Her fingers touched my chin, lifting it back up to close my mouth. I breathed a laugh, still unable to form words.

"Like it?"

"I fucking love it. You look beautiful." Her makeup was still subtle, and her hair pulled back in a pony tail that looked both sophisticated and still hinted at her nineteen years. "Come on in. Dinner's ready."

Her eyes looked all around, wide with excitement as she took in all the candles.

Her smile from across the table as we ate, talked, and laughed filled me with pride that I'd put it there. She joked, asking me where I hid the tin containers the food came in. It had to have been one of the easiest dates I'd ever had.

She set her silverware aside and took a drink of water, watching me the whole time. It was intoxicating watching the candle light flicker across her features.

"Thank you for the flowers," she said. I'd given her a dozen roses once we entered the kitchen and she beamed, saying no one had ever gotten her flowers before. I loved being a first for her.

"I'm glad you like them."

"My dad always got my mom flowers. Sometimes they were the ones they were about to throw out at the store and sometimes they were even just wildflowers around his building at work. Mom said it didn't matter. It was the fact that he'd thought about her."

"How are your mom and dad?"

"Good. Busy as always. Life hasn't seemed to change too much for them over the years, minus having to support me. But they still work a lot to stay afloat."

I hated that she'd had to struggle, but her smile when talking about them, didn't make it seem like it had affected the love too much.

"How are your parents?" Oaklyn asked.

"They're good. Just got back from a trip in Italy. Dad had some brief business to do, and my mom talked him into staying the whole week. She called me last night to tell me all about it for over an hour."

She laughed at my eye roll. "You seem close to them."

"I am. They're good parents and always strove to give the best to me. They just want to see me happy."

Her eyes dropped to where her thumb was rubbing at the side of her glass before she spoke. "What do you think they would think of me?"

Probably not happy that she was my student, but I didn't say that. "I think they'd like you because you make me happy."

She peeked up at me from under her lashes. "Good."

"It's very good."

"Are they visiting you any time soon? Not because I'm trying to hint at a meet and greet," she rushed to explain. "I just know you haven't seen them in a while."

"They may at the end of the semester. They were just here for Christmas." I took a drink of water and tried to decide if I wanted to confide in her, but it was a no-brainer. I always wanted to confide in Oaklyn. She was my safety. "They actually mentioned me coming home."

"I thought you didn't go home," she said, sitting upright, concern covering her face.

"My cousin, Sarah, is getting married." I took another drink of water trying to ease the tightening in my throat. She didn't say anything, but I could see the question in her eyes. "Sarah was his sister."

"Are you okay?"

I paused before answering, taking stock of my body. Other than the nerves of speaking about it, I was calm. No sweating. No racing heart. No shaking. I *was* okay. "Surprisingly, yes."

"Good," she said smiling. "What are you going to do?"

"My original thought was no, but I feel like I'm in a better place, like maybe I could. I always assumed I'd never go back to California, but maybe . . ." I hadn't been sure I was going to say anything, but just seeing her across from me, feeling her happiness for me, I had to. I had to ask. It was an urge I couldn't swallow down. "But I thought, maybe, with you by my side, I could face it."

Her eyebrows rose toward her hairline. "You want me to go home with you?"

"If you want to," I rushed out. Her eyes were wide and not really giving any of her emotions away and nerves began to set in. "It wouldn't be until October."

She didn't say anything, and I couldn't look away. Concern shot through me when wetness glazed over her eyes and my mind scrambled to figure out why. She scooted her chair back and stood, and for a moment, I feared she would leave. I'd pushed her too far, said too much. But with her lip firmly planted under her teeth, she walked over to me and pushed me to lean back in my chair. Then she threw a leg over my lap and planted herself there, a smile hinting on her lips. There was no hesitation on my part as my hands fell to her hips, securing her against me, loving the pressure of her on top of me. I scooted back a bit to give her room before she reached out to hold my cheeks and lean down to kiss me.

She kissed me gently and I let her lead the way, getting lost in the soft grazes she gave me. Too soon she pulled back, but just enough to look me in the eyes, hers flicking back and forth before she whispered, "I'd go anywhere with you."

I didn't wait for her to take the lead then. I dove in and began devouring her lips, eating her promise straight from them. I wanted to take her everywhere with me.

I loved her.

The truth of it had lingered inside me for a while, but right then, it consumed me.

To keep from letting it slip past my lips, I kissed her harder. Her hands dragged down my chest and she scooted back, working my buckle before opening my pants. I jumped a little when her soft hand wrapped around my cock, but not because I was scared, but because her touch shot electricity through every part of my body, making my skin come alive. She stroked me up and down, not hard enough to make me come, but enough to make me desperate for more.

I gripped her bottom and held her as I stood. After I'd shoved the plates to the side, I sat her atop the table and worked my lips down her neck, sucking at the pulse beating frantically. I dipped down into her cleavage as far as the dress would go and then I tugged the material down, making her pert breasts pop free.

No fucking bra. Thank god.

Wasting no time, I latched onto her pink nipple, tasting her skin. She thrust her hips up and wet heat came into contact with my cock. My body jerked and pulled back to look up at her. I could only imagine what my eyes looked like. Wide, frantic, nervous, excited, terrified.

"No panties?"

She shrugged, and one side of her mouth ticked up in a half smile. Swallowing hard, I stared down at her, her hand making its way into my hair and tugging me to her lips. She bit, licked, and sucked pulling me back into the moment. I cupped her warm breast in my hand and swallowed her moan when I pinched her nipple. I did it again and her hips jerked up, bringing the wet heat straight in line with the head of my cock.

The world froze for what seemed like days while I tried to unscramble the emotions tearing through me. But then her tongue flicked across my chin, followed by a bite and I groaned, my hips thrusting forward again of their own free will, slipping another inch inside of Oaklyn.

My chest heaved, a mixture of panic and desire. She gripped my face and tilted my head back until I was staring at her. She seemed just as nervous as I was. Her eyes flicking across my face, her tongue slicking out to wet her dry lips, her breaths coming just as fast as mine.

"Look at me," she breathed the command and then lifted her hips, letting me slide in a little more. "It's okay, Callum. It's just me. Don't look away from me."

Using her eyes as my focus, the flickering candles around the room illuminating her beautiful face, I pushed all the way inside her. Then I pulled back until only the head of my dick remained nestled in the warm, wet folds of her pussy, and pushed in again. And again. And again.

She never once looked away. Even when she leaned down to kiss me, her eyes stayed on mine. Her wet heat enveloped me, welcomed me, gave me the sweetest gift. Emotions squeezed my chest, making it hard to breathe. Desire ignited throughout my body making me feel more alive, more everything than ever before.

"It's okay. It's just me. It's okay." Over and over her voice guided me. Her desperate whispers shifting into moans as my hips picked up the pace.

"Oaklyn," I said her name like a prayer, like she was my mecca, and I'd finally found my way there. I pulled her to me, her chest flush with mine. Her thighs tight around my hips, her hands still clutching at my cheeks. "You're so fucking tight. So wet." I closed my eyes on a thrust, feeling every inch of her clutched tight around me. "God, you feel so good."

"Don't stop," she pleaded.

"Not a fucking chance."

I hadn't even considered it. My mind too focused on the wet glide of her core around my dick. The way it squeezed and milked me. The fire it lit in the base of my spine and a pleasure I felt through my whole body. The pleasure of choice. I chose to be inside her. I chose to feel this pleasure. I had control over it.

I had control, and no one was taking that from me.

"Oaklyn," I said again. My throat almost closed up and fire burned the backs of my eyes at the same time that it shot down my spine. I became lost in her, lost in the moment, the magic of it all.

"Please, please," she cried against my lips, each one more desperate than the last until her whole body stiffened and her eyes slid shut as her jaw dropped open. She clung to me and moaned through her orgasm.

"You're so beautiful when you come."

I pinched her nipple, completely in awe of her in that moment. Never having felt like more of a man than when I watched her flush from the intensity of her orgasm.

It sparked my own, and I buried my head in her chest, squeezing my eyes shut and fucking her faster. Completely lost in the pleasure that zipped through me.

"Yes, Callum. Fuck me," she encouraged, taking every thrust.

My body broke out in goose bumps as my hips jerked, my balls pulling up tight. I groaned against her neck, holding her to me as I emptied myself inside her.

As my breathing returned to normal, I finally began to feel her hands running though my hair, her soft kisses to the side of my head, and the soft cries shaking my body.

"Shh. Shh. Callum. It's okay."

I should have been embarrassed. Still buried inside her, coming down from my orgasm, and crying into her neck. But it was Oaklyn, and she'd given me something I never thought I'd ever have. Comfort, acceptance, patience, pleasure.

Pleasure that I had control to stop if I wanted to. Pleasure I chose to have and not because someone made me.

"Thank you. Thank you." I said it over and over, letting the bliss slowly ebb. My dick softened and slipped from her heat. I finally let go of the tight grip I had along her back and wiped at my cheeks. When I looked up, her own cheeks held tracks of tears and I loved this woman all over again. "Thank you, Oaklyn," I said again.

"Thank you." She grabbed my cheeks again and placed a gentle kiss to them before slipping off the table. She held my hand and pulled me along as she blew out each candle. I followed behind obediently, willing to go wherever she took me.

Once they were all blown out, she led me upstairs to my bedroom. Before we laid down she turned to me. "Is this okay?"

"God, yes. I wouldn't want to be anywhere else but here with you."

She bit her lip, smiling as she looked down. I took off my shirt and pants, pulling my boxers off along with them. Nothing seemed impossible, including laying naked next to her all night. I may have ended up waking up to a nightmare, embarrassing myself, but I wanted to try. I wanted to do it for her.

When I laid down she backed toward the bathroom door saying, "I just have to, um, clean up."

My eyes dropped to her legs and I imagined my cum slipping out and coating her thighs. Groaning, I flopped back to the pillow and listened to her laugh.

"Also, I'm clean and on the pill."

My eyes shot open. "Shit. I didn't even think about that. I'm sorry I put you in that risk."

"It's okay," she said. "I knew what I was doing. I didn't want anything to distract us from the moment and I knew I was safe."

"Thank you."

When she came back, she slipped out of her dress and climbed into bed beside me. I curled into her and lay my head on her chest, listening to her heartbeat.

It beat against my cheek as her fingers sifted through my hair. She didn't say anything but held me as I clung to her. Before I was lulled to sleep, I turned to place a kiss to her skin, whispering one last thank you.

Chapter Twenty-Eight

Oaklyn

Wet kisses down my neck woke me the next morning. It was a hell of a way to wake up. Callum's hand covered my breast and flicked my nipple. I moaned and arched back into him, feeling his erection poking at my bottom. Without thought, barely awake, I snaked my hand behind me and gripped his shaft. His whole body jerked and then froze. Immediately, I let go and rotated to face him, wanting him to see me.

When he refused to meet my eye, I pretended like I hadn't noticed, not wanting to force him to acknowledge his reaction. Instead, I kissed the slight dimple in his chin and whispered a good morning against his skin.

"Good morning," he said, his body relaxing again as he pulled me into his chest. He finally looked at me and his blue eyes seemed brighter in the morning light pouring in the windows. Somehow happier, less weighed down. I held his stare and kissed him, not wanting to look away because I couldn't if I tried.

"How did you sleep?"

"Like the dead." He smirked and nipped at my nose playfully. "You wore me out."

I laughed and matched his position of my arm around his back, scooting up just enough to get better access to his mouth. I nipped at his lips, flicked my tongue along the seam, urging him to open up. And he did. His head tipped to the side to get better access to my mouth. His large palm spread wide on my back, holding me as tight as he could to his chest, mashing my breasts against him.

We made out like we were starving and the other was our only sustenance. We both moaned when his cock slipped between my thighs and rubbed at the folds of my pussy.

"Can we . . . ." He began breathlessly. "Can we try again?"

I gave him a teasing smile. "I thought you were worn out."

"Not *that* much," he said, rolling on top of me.

This time was more intentional than last night. Last night was a heat of the moment, taking advantage of becoming lost in each other. This morning, lying naked in his arms, I spread my legs to allow his hips room to rest against me. He supported himself on one arm and scooted back enough to reach down and grip his cock, placing it at my entrance. I didn't blink when he swiped the soft head up and down my folds, making my hips jerk up to meet him.

His lips parted, breaths panting out of them as he notched himself inside me just enough to let go and pushed in one slow inch at a time.

"I could get used to it here. Make your pussy my home."

"It's yours."

He framed my head between his forearms, his flexing biceps on each side of my face, but I barely noticed because he moved inside me. He stared at me with awe, like I was the answer to everything he'd ever been searching for. Had anyone ever felt so cherished?

My thighs strained from the tension the pleasure created. He rocked his hips, grinding against me causing me to gasp.

"Does that feel good?" He smiled and did it again. And again.

"Callum. Please."

Sweat beaded on his brow and his pace picked up, the rhythm becoming less smooth than a moment before. He pushed hard, and I cried out. I lifted my leg over his hip, needing to feel him deeper. He leaned down and finally kissed me, moving his other hand to my thigh to hold me in place as he really began to fuck me.

"Oaklyn. Oaklyn." He said my name like a prayer and each time he moaned it into my flesh, it sent another wave of pleasure to my core, pushing me closer and closer to the edge. I held onto him tightly, loving the feel of this strong man flexing above me, his chest hair abrading my nipples, bringing them to life.

As he began to lose control, he bit down on my neck with a long moan. The frantic pace was hard and deep and hit my clit each time. I rose and rose until finally my whole body pulled tight and exploded. I moaned out my release, loving the sound of his mixing with my own, like music unique to us. To our pleasure, to our love.

When I opened my eyes, he was staring down at me again, so intense, and so light, and just happy. Reaching up, I wiped a bead of sweat from his temple and buried my fingers in his hair. I couldn't help but smile at him, loving how beautiful he was, how beautiful he made me feel.

I loved him.

The reality of it hit me, and I think I always felt it there, building beneath the surface, but watching him return my smile, still buried inside me, there was no denying it. I loved him.

My smile switched to a laugh and he laughed with me until both of us had tears forming in our eyes from all the emotions creating a bubble around us. When he slipped out of me, we moaned in unison, and he leaned down to kiss me before falling to his side.

"Can we do that all day?"

"I wish, but I can't. I have a meeting with my advisor today."

"On a Sunday?"

"Yeah. He wanted to show me around the athletic center and meet the physical therapist there. Said Sundays are a good day because it tends to be slower, and he had more time to walk me around."

"That sounds like a good opportunity just to get your name on his radar."

"It is."

I almost opened my mouth again to explain to him I was interviewing for the internship today, but I didn't. A part of me wanted to share my nerves, share my excitement, but then I'd have to face the disappointment with him too, and I didn't want to admit failure to any more people than I had to.

Besides, we could celebrate together when I surprised him with hopefully good news.

"What about after? Another dinner?"

Rolling my lips between my teeth, I tried to think of anything other than the truth, but while I didn't mind not telling him things, I wasn't going to outright lie.

"I can't. I have to work tonight."

It was as if I could feel his body shut down. His hold on me loosened and he rolled to his back to look at the ceiling. I hated it and a part of me wanted to apologize and say I'd call off, but I couldn't do that forever. It was a fact of who I was and something we just had to deal with. No amount of apologizing would make it any easier or better. So, instead, we both did one better and just ignored it. He denied and hid his frustration and I denied and hid the way I noticed it.

"Okay," he said, his voice flat and missing the excitement from before. "Tomorrow. After school."

"Yeah," I agreed. I tried to build up the excitement, but there was no getting it back. I looked over his profile, taking in the muscle clenching at his jaw, and I wanted to do anything to make him feel better.

I love you almost spilled from my lips, I had to actually bite my tongue to make it stop. But I had to, because that was not the reason I wanted to tell him how much he meant to me. I didn't want to tell him to make him feel better in the moment, or to let him know I would never want anyone other than him. I wanted to tell him when the feeling consumed us both. When the love became too much, not the frustration.

Instead, I rolled over him and put all of my unsaid words in a kiss. He kissed me back just as hard as though he had his own truths to share.

We made out until I had to leave, and even then, he kissed me every chance he got until the door shut behind me, and I headed home to get ready for my interview.

The interview had gone amazing. I'd walked around the few athletes working out and listened to Dr. Jones explain what my job would entail. He showed me the room where I would mostly be assisting the other team PTs, but said I'd also eventually be out helping athletes with their exercises in the weight room. All of it felt so exciting. Like it was a huge step toward the future.

He asked me about my experience, which was minimal, and about the classes I'd taken in high school. When he'd given me a pop quiz over some basic anatomy and typical injuries that occurred with each part, I'd answered almost all with flying colors. He'd turned to Dr. Denly and mumbled a "not bad." I'd had to look down to hide my smile. With a few book recommendations he'd asked I read over the last two and half months of the semester, I left the gym seeing the light at the end of the tunnel shining brighter than ever before.

I'd driven straight to Voyeur in hopes of maybe starting early and seeing if I could get Charlotte to let me work the bar extra hours again. It ended up being my lucky day because apparently, Charlotte had called in sick and Daniel was behind the bar looking frazzled by the crowd.

I'd taken over and made sure to be extra friendly with each customer I served, milking as much of a tip out of them as possible. It had been hard enough to perform when I'd begun any type of physical relationship with Cal, but now that we'd slept together, now that my emotions were barely being contained inside of me, it was impossible to even consider it.

I just had to hope the extra tips would be enough to cover the next payment I had to make for tuition next week.

Chapter Twenty-Nine

Callum

I hadn't called her the next day, and I'd been evasive in my text messages.

I hadn't seen her either. In fact, I called in sick.

I wasn't sick.

I was hungover.

After she'd left, I'd begun drinking at lunch, just sitting around imagining her at Voyeur. What she was doing. Who she was with. Who was watching her. I'd stayed in my empty home and drank one glass after another, feeling my control quickly evaporating. It'd been years since I'd let myself slip into a loss of control, since I'd let my anger determine my actions. I'd fought hard to gain it and there I was letting it eat me alive.

How far would I slip before I did something I'd regret, said something I'd regret? Would I be able to hang on until she finished working at Voyeur? How long would that be? What would I look like as a person by that point? What would *we* look like?

When I finally saw her in class on Tuesday, she smiled at me like I wasn't a broken man barely holding it together. She looked at me like I was normal, like I was whole, and it took everything I had not to go to her and kiss her. How was I supposed to make it through the rest of the semester without looking at her with my whole heart in my eyes? It was so much more than attraction. Each time I saw her, my chest felt like it was going to explode with emotion for her. She was my Halley's Comet. Only coming once in a lifetime.

"Miss Derringer," I called to her as everyone packed up to leave. "Could you please come to the physics office with me? Donna needs you to sign some papers."

She walked by my side in silence. The tension between us palpable. As though if we spoke, the tension would snap wide open, scream to everyone around us that we were intimate. That we were fucking.

As soon as I found a hallway with no one in it, I turned.

"Where are we going?" she asked.

I didn't answer, reading every sign on the door looking for the right one. Maintenance Room.

I looked side to side one more time and opened the door, pulling her in behind me. At the click of the latch, I turned her and pinned her, my mouth immediately on hers, needing to taste her. I'd missed her and hated that I'd stayed away, that I hadn't called, that I hadn't reached out to her. She gasped for air when I finally released her lips, moving down her throat.

"Are you okay?" she breathed the question. "Donna said you were sick. Why didn't you tell me?"

"I'm sorry," I mumbled into her shoulder, unwilling to remove my lips from her skin. "I didn't want you to worry."

"Callum, I—"

But her words were cut off because I'd tugged down her over-sized sweater and bit her nipple through the lace of her bra. I felt like a teenage boy, desperate to be inside her now that I'd had her.

She moaned when I pulled the lace aside and laved at the tender bud and sucked it between my lips. Her hands fumbled with the buckle of my pants and I dug my hand into her hair like it was my anchor in this moment. Like it kept me from falling back into my past.

"Callum," she breathed. "Who's about to suck on your cock?"

My hips thrust forward against her searching hand. "You," I moaned.

"Say my name."

"Oaklyn. The most beautiful woman in the world is going to fall to her knees and wrap her sexy as sin lips around my dick and suck me."

She moaned as she slipped out of my hold, falling to her knees to suck me inside her mouth. She flicked her tongue along the underside, tonguing the slit on the head.

Even in the dimly-lit room, I could look down and see her staring back up at me, holding my eyes, reminding me that it was her. Fuck, I loved her so much. Loved her for knowing what to do. Loved her for everything she was.

"Oaklyn. I need to be inside you."

She let go of my shaft with a pop and stood, turning around to face the door as her hands went to her leggings to pull them down.

I halted her movement. "No."

A shiver wracked my body and I swallowed hard, fighting off the memory, the shame attached to it.

She immediately turned and put her hands on my cheeks, making me look at her. "It's just me."

Her soft voice, calmed the churning of my stomach and tethered me to the present. I stared into her golden eyes and held them as I leaned in to press a kiss to her lush lips. Then I pushed her back against the door again and worked her leggings down her legs, only getting one foot out before I grabbed her bottom and hoisted her up high enough to fit my cock to her opening. I worked her slowly onto me, spreading her wetness with each push until finally I was fully inside of her.

With our foreheads pressed together, eyes locked on each other, our breath mixing between us, I slid out and back in. She held my gaze the whole time. Her wetness grew until it coated my balls, and I began pounding into her faster. Trying to hold her hips away from the door to keep from making any noise. It didn't take long before we were both on the edge of the precipice, her brows furrowed with the effort to not let her lids slide closed.

Electricity zipped down my spine and pulled my balls up tight. Leaning in, I locked my lips to hers and moaned out my pleasure. I gripped her hips, holding myself as deeply inside of her as possible as her cunt spasmed around my cock, her sweet moans of pleasure only serving to intensify my own.

My body shook in aftershocks and our gasping breaths echoed around us, seeming so loud that the entire campus could hear, but I knew it was just us in our bubble.

Satisfaction settled in my bones, reminding me that she was mine. That this was where I wanted to be. That she was my salvation.

I slipped out of her and set her down before grabbing a paper towel from a shelf and cleaned her up. She smiled and gently kissed me through it.

"I missed you yesterday. I'm assuming you're feeling better now?"

"Much."

Once we were both situated again, I asked, "Do you want to come over tonight?"

She looked away and I knew before she even said it.

"I can't. I have to work."

I fought to keep my expression neutral but failed. It was hard enough to deal with it before, but now that we'd had sex—made love— it damn near crushed me.

"I'm sorry, Cal."

"It's okay," I lied. "I understand."

She gave me one last kiss and then I told her I'd go ahead of her and message her that the coast was clear. She had to go to her next class and told me she'd see me tomorrow.

I somehow finished out the day with less than stellar concentration. My mind constantly on Oaklyn, ruled by the jealousy that created a rage that scared me. My control seeming to live on the edge of here and gone.

How long would I be able to walk the line before I snapped? What would Oaklyn do when it did? What if I walked that line and ended up falling into a hole I couldn't get out of, just for her to leave me? The whole day these thoughts swirled around me. When I got home, I immediately went to the kitchen for a drink, but then paused looking at the time. Almost eight. She'd be working.

Hopping in my car, I headed to Voyeur. If she was performing for me, then she wouldn't be for anyone else. I'd buy her whole damn night to keep her from others.

She saw me enter and a smile lit up her face that reached me from all the way across the bar. I fought to pull her across the counter and kiss me once I reached her and instead ordered a water. I downed it and wasted no time.

"I'm going to put in a request. Make sure you take it."

"I don't have my name available tonight."

My chest swelled with that information, joy filling the holes that had popped up the past few weeks. Looked like I didn't need to buy her whole night because she wasn't performing for others, but I still wanted to have time with her. Just because an employee didn't have their name available, didn't mean you couldn't still request them.

"Make sure you accept the request," I said with a nod as I stood from the stool.

She smiled, hopefully just as excited as me for the next hour.

I went to the iPad and entered the information, feeling like the scenario was perfect for us.

When I finished and walked into the main area again, I searched for Oaklyn since she was missing from the bar. I found her out on the floor among the patrons and rage slammed into me like a freight train, almost knocking me down, stealing the air from my lungs.

She stood at a table, delivering drinks, smiling, leaning down, exposing her creamy cleavage so a man could whisper in her ear, his eyes glued to her breasts. She laughed at whatever he said and then spoke close to his ear. I wanted to rip the man limb from limb.

I forced my body to turn and head to the bar where I threw back a double shot of whiskey, needing anything to calm my nerves. By the time my wrist band vibrated to let me know the room was ready, I was able to breathe again, but my muscles still twitched with tension. It didn't matter because the next hour, Oaklyn was mine.

I walked back to the room and situated myself in the darkened corner, staring out over the row of desks and the teacher's desk up front. After only a few minutes Oaklyn came in, her long, bare legs drawing my attention first. She looked so young strolling into the pseudo classroom in cut off jean shorts and chucks, but the loose lacy top that barely contained her breasts promised me she was all woman.

She looked around the room as she approached the front, taking in the setting before turning over her shoulder to look at me with a smirk.

"Fantasy of yours?"

"Pretty much all I think about in class every time you're sitting there in the front row." I stood and began making my way to her. "Don't act like you don't think the same thing when you come in with your lips painted red, making me pay attention to you. Making me remember the way they look stretched around my dick."

"Maybe," she said, shrugging.

"Tease."

"What are you going to do about it?"

I stood right in front of her, her head tilted all the way back to stare up at me. "Have you ever been spanked, Miss Derringer?" If I shifted my gaze below her chin and blew hard enough, I'd be able to shift her shirt and see her pert nipples. Is that what other men in the room could see too? I could feel my face flinch but pushed for a neutral look awaiting her answer.

Her tongue slicked across her lips and she shook her head. "Another fantasy?"

"I have no idea, but I'd love to try with you." Honestly, I had a hard time thinking past anything other than being inside of her as much as possible. Being with her as much as possible. Keeping her as my own as much as possible.

She wrapped her arms around my neck and stood on her tiptoes to kiss my chin. With her fingers in my hair, she directed me down to her lips. "Maybe we'll have to figure it out sometime, *Dr. Pierce.*"

With a growl, I began feasting at her lips, tasting her, claiming her. I gripped her slim waist and hoisted her up on the desk and wedged myself between her thighs. She rocked her hips against my erection behind my slacks and stars burst before my eyes.

"Callum," she whispered. "Yes."

I placed a few more desperate kisses to her lips, but then stopped to pull back and just take her in. She was so beautiful and so full of life. The way she looked up at me, her eyes glazed in passion and desire, a spark of something else hidden in them and I wanted to know. I opened my mouth to ask but froze wondering how many others she'd given that look to. Jackson? Anyone behind the glass that had requested that they wanted the performer to look at the wall so they could feel more a part of the scenario?

I leaned down to kiss her again, trying to erase the thoughts from my mind, but they were like drums in my head, and I couldn't let them go no matter how hard I tried. And like a glutton for punishment, as though knowing she worked there wasn't enough, I asked anyways.

With my lips pressed to hers, I pulled back just enough to ask, "Have you done anything with anyone?" The thought of Jackson even pretending to have his hands on her sent a rage boiling through my blood.

She stopped kissing me all together and pulled back completely. She wouldn't even look me in the eye and I prepared myself for the worst. I prepared myself for the yes.

"No, Cal. I've turned down all requests." I wanted to smile at her answer. The euphoric feeling spread through me and my lips twitched to show my pleasure. However, her pained expression halted the smile. She wasn't hiding because she was scared to admit she'd done something. She was hiding because she was embarrassed that she had to even explain. I'd made her feel that. I'd made her look down and hunch her shoulders because of my own insecurity. I did that to her and it was almost more painful than the thought of her being with another man. "I've been working the bar. Extra to closing almost every night I can just to make up the cash because I have a payment to the school soon."

"Let me pay for it." It slipped off my tongue and fell between us. I hadn't planned to say it, I hadn't even really thought of it before, but I wanted to make her life easier. "Let me pay for the rest of the year." I wanted to help, and it seemed like such a perfect win-win situation. She didn't have to work here anymore, and I paid her bills.

To Oaklyn, it was the wrong suggestion. Her head jerked up toward me and her lip curled up in disgust. "What? No!"

"Please, Oaklyn." Why wouldn't she let me do this for her? Why was she being so damn stubborn?

"Absolutely not." She hopped down off the desk and paced away from me. I watched her back get further and further away. I looked around the room, through the glass wall and imagined some other person behind it watching her. I imagined them jacking off or having sex while they watched Oaklyn fuck herself. Each thought built up and up, bubbling to the surface, begging me to release the pressure, let my control slip completely.

"Oaklyn."

"No." She faced me with hard eyes. "You're not paying for anything."

"But you'll let some stranger pay for your schooling by watching you have sex, but not me?"

Oaklyn's head jerked back like I'd physically hit her, her jaw dropped in shock. "Am I a prostitute to you? Do you want to pay me for sex?"

"No," I growled, angry that she'd taken it that way. "I just can't stand other people doing it."

"I don't fuck for money!" she shouted. "And I sure as shit don't want your money because we *do* fuck."

"Real big difference there," I said, my tone dripping with sarcasm. And even my own insides curled in disgust at my words. What the fuck was I doing—saying? Closing my eyes, I shook my head and realized I was toeing the far side of the line, one leg already hanging off the cliff. My fear of losing it and hurting her was taking place and I hadn't done anything to stop it.

It was like seeing how close to the edge I was knocked me back a few steps, like it firmly planted both feet down on the safe side of losing control and I tried to recover. I tried to fix it, but when I opened my eyes to look at her, her face was painted with pain and hurt that I'd put there.

"Please, Oaklyn," I begged even though I felt like I'd already lost the battle. "I know you're strong and prideful. I know you can do this on your own, but you don't have to. Let me help."

With her chin quivering, she shook her head. "I can't."

The anger bubbled, but low enough that I was aware of it and how easy it was to flow over. But still enough that it reminded me of the damage I could do, and it hit me. Like a sledgehammer to the chest, it hit me.

"I can't either."

Her chin dropped in shock, her eyes wide and blinking quickly, trying to change the picture before her. I had to clench my jaw when tears glazed over her eyes and pooled on her bottom lids before falling, leaving silvery tracks down her cheeks I yearned to wipe away.

"Callum—" Her words cut off on a choked whisper.

She was beautiful, and I kept flashing back to the way my question had made her feel ashamed and embarrassed. I kept flashing back to the hurt on her face when I insulted her, reducing her to a prostitute. Remembering how easy the anger won and changed the way she looked at me. I couldn't do it to her.

"Oakl—" Her name got caught in my throat and I had to clear it and try again. "Oaklyn, you mean the world to me. You've given me the vision of a future I never thought I'd ever have, that I didn't think I was worthy of. You're so young, so full of life, and I was lucky enough to have you share that with me. When I look at you, my world feels more right, I feel more at peace than I have in years. When I look at you and see the way you watch me, I feel like someone else. Someone normal who will have a normal future. I feel good when you look at me." Slicking my tongue across my dry lips, I struggled to get the truth out. "And if we continue on this path, that will disappear."

She shook her head, not understanding. How did I admit how far I'd fallen? Swallowing hard, I ran my hand through my hair, staring at the floor.

"My insecurity with you working here—my jealousy is taking its toll on me. I've been . . . Drinking more. A lot actually. I know you've seen some, but it's so much more than that. I can feel my patience slipping faster, the control I've worked so hard to gain is just slipping between my fingers like sand, and I'm barely hanging on." I threw my arms wide, presenting the night to her. "I mean, fuck. Look at what just happened. Look at what I said to you. I can't keep doing this just to destroy you. I know it's not forever, but I can't wait and destroy us in the process. What would we both look like by the end? Pieces of who we started as?"

"Callum, we can do this. We can make it work. I promise, we will find a way," she pleaded with me, stepping up to wrap her hands around mine. The soft heat of her skin shocked mine, traveling up my arms, trying to make my heart beat, but it felt hollow, like it was lying there useless, dying. Her eyes shone brighter from the tears, sparking my own. The lump that had been lodged in my throat broke free and wetness slid from my eyes. My nose itched, and I hated that I couldn't be stronger. That I couldn't just control my emotions.

"I can't let my jealousy and fear—my inability to rationalize and rein in those emotions—tear you down. And I can't deal with knowing you are sharing something so desperately precious to me with others. Even if it's pretend. Even if it's just a job."

Her face crumpled, and I squeezed her hands in mine, fighting from pulling her in my arms and lying to us both just to make her stop crying. But that would be just for now, I'd only be postponing the inevitable.

"Please don't do this," she begged through her tears, tearing me apart.

I took a moment, trying to work past the pressure on my chest, trying to control the tears sliding down my cheeks. "You deserve someone strong enough to deal with it. You deserve someone who doesn't rely on you so much. You're just a teenager, just starting your future with so much fire. You deserve more than someone who hefts their baggage on your shoulders. You deserve more than me."

"I don't. I do—."

"You do."

"I only want you, Cal. Please."

I lifted a hand to her cheek to wipe away her tears, but they were just replaced with more. "Oaklyn, I can't swallow the thoughts of you working here. I'm selfish and scarred and I don't want to hurt you with my issues, and that's what this is. *My issues*. Not you. Logically, I know you wouldn't do anything, but the fear of it is tearing me apart. It is *eating* at me, and it's going to spread like a venom I'll take out on you." Taking a deep breath, I said it one more time. "I can't do this. I can't handle my emotions with you working here."

Her face crumpled all over again, and a part of me hoped maybe she would give in and let me pay. She took a deep, shuddering breath, and lifted her chin, tears still falling.

"And I can't let you pay for my schooling. It would tarnish everything good you said about us. Everything good we've done would be ruined because I'd feel like a whore."

"You are not a wh—."

"I would feel like one."

"Oaklyn. I'm so sorry."

"Me too."

With that, she stepped into me, wrapping her arms around my waist, burying her head in my chest, and I held her as close to me as possible. Trying to keep a part of her with me even when I walked away. I leaned down and pressed my nose into her hair, trying to imprint the smell of her in my mind so I wouldn't ever forget. Her shaking shoulders and quiet cries cracked my chest open and crushed everything soft inside.

My own tears slipped in her hair as her hands ran up and down my back. I made sure to feel every stroke. Cherish every touch. It might be the last time I let anyone get so close.

She tipped her head back and rose on her toes to press her wet, trembling lips to mine. Immediately my eyes closed. I tasted her, memorized her, let my tears mix with hers.

All too soon, she pulled back, and dropped her head, hiding behind her hair. Her arms no longer wrapped around me, but around her own waist as though she was protecting herself from any more pain.

Hopefully, when I walked out the door, she wouldn't have to protect herself anymore.

When I walked past her, I stopped and pressed a lingering kiss to the crown of her head, her soft cries at my back as I exited the room.

I left Voyeur for probably the last time and headed home to lose all my control in private, trying to find comfort in the fact that she wouldn't be there to feel it.

Chapter Thirty

Oaklyn

Each day I felt like I couldn't sink any lower. Each day I was sure the ache would ease a little, making breathing a little easier, make moving less painful like every muscle in my body had given up.

It never did.

Instead, it intensified each day I had to be around him but couldn't be with him. Because even though Callum and I had decided neither of us could settle, we still saw each other every single day. And it made the pain that much more difficult to beat. That much more difficult to forget.

I missed him. Missed him as my friend. Missed his kisses, his touches. I missed all the future had had for us. All of it gone. California, gone. The explorations we would have had together—gone.

A week after he'd walked out of Voyeur, I'd tried to force myself back into performing. I'd entered my information to perform a solo performance. I'd simply had to masturbate under the covers. Simple. Nothing hard or very exposing.

With my hand moving under the sheets, not even bothering to actually touch myself, I'd never felt as bad as I had in that moment. Long after the light had flicked to red after the performance, I'd laid in bed and thought about Callum, the weight of his memories holding me down, crushing me. I'd immediately taken my name off the list of performances and returned to my spot at the bar.

The next day, Jackson had convinced me to do a performance with him. We'd only needed to watch a movie and have dry sex. No kissing. No nudity.

Halfway through, I'd started crying on his shoulder. He'd held me and moaned louder to hide any sounds I'd made. He'd held me long after the performance was over, telling me he was sorry. He didn't even need to ask if it was Callum. He'd rubbed my back and told me it would eventually get better. That he'd known from experience it was possible to survive without the one you truly wanted.

I wanted to believe him, but it felt impossible when I watched Callum in classes.

I'd barely taken any notes the past week in class as I watched him, desperately wanting him to look at me, but terrified of what I'd see in his eyes when he did. In the office, he never asked for my help. He always pawned me off on the lab manager or had Donna send me home early.

I hated it. Hated everything about the whole situation. Hated seeing him look so haggard and know I'd been the cause of it. Hated knowing I'd set him back and that he'd begun losing his control.

Somehow, one night lying in bed, my frustration with my parents grew again. I'd never have had to work at Voyeur if they hadn't spent my money. Then I wondered if Callum and I would have ever happened. The idea of never having felt Callum's lips on mine, his body on top of me, inside me. The idea of never having felt his smile and happiness directed at me, felt unimaginable. My love for him felt destined no matter the circumstances. Did that mean my pain was destined too? Were we always meant to fail?

I shook off the memory as I prepared to walk in to the office. With a deep breath, I pushed the door open, forced a weak smile at Donna and slowly approached Callum's door. I always asked if he needed me even though every day he answered with a no, not even looking up from his papers.

Today when I looked in, I almost threw up the pop I had before arriving.

Shannon had her butt perched on his desk, her back to me as she smiled down at him. What was worse was his smile back at her. Sure, it looked forced, not reaching his eyes, but even a forced smile was out of my reach. His eyes flicked to me standing in the doorway, looking at me for the first time in weeks.

The blue was dull, hollow of any shine that used to be there. Dark circles under his eyes made the darkness seem all the more apparent. For the first time in weeks, even with his lips stretched into a smile, I saw my own pain reflected back at me. Just as quickly, he dismissed me, looking back up at Shannon, and I walked away as fast as I could.

I couldn't watch. The pain was bad enough without the image of him with another woman.

Trying to erase the picture from my mind, I worked harder, turning each beaker and flask to face perfectly straight. Any excuse to hide in the storage room a little longer.

The door opened behind me and I knew, just fucking knew it was him. Maybe it was the pause of his steps when he noticed me in there. Maybe it was the way my body sensed his and came to life just from his energy being close to mine. I didn't know, but my muscles jerked when the door clicked shut and we were the only ones in the room.

My chest heaved over my rapid breaths, trying to keep up with my frantic heartbeat. The last time we were alone, we'd shattered, and I still hadn't recovered yet. My hands trembled from the nervous energy coursing through my limbs, so aware of him standing behind me. Off to my left, a glass slid off a shelf and I imagined his strong hands gripping the equipment and remembering how he'd gripped me.

"It hurts, doesn't it?" His voice was soft, deep, quiet, but it rattled through my body like a scream. "To watch someone that means so much to you be with someone else."

I whipped around so fast, the end of my ponytail flicked my face. Angry heat flooded my face and a fire that he would hurt me so intentionally burned me from the inside out. "You did it on purpose? To teach me a lesson? Like I don't know?"

"God no. No, Oaklyn." He looked me over, alarm contorting his face into a frown. "I don't want to hurt you," he said, stepping closer to me.

His soft confession hit me in my chest. I knew he didn't want to hurt me. That was how we got there in the first place. I closed my eyes, unable to stare at his beauty without remembering all the reasons I loved him.

Because I still loved him. No amount of pain was taking that away.

Wetness escaped my closed lids despite how hard I tried to hold it back. They turned to full sobs when his thumb came out to swipe at my cheeks. My chest shook, and I leaned into his palm, finding a false comfort in his hands on me again. Even if it meant nothing, I'd missed his touch. I missed him so fucking much.

My eyes were still closed when I felt his heat inches from me, when I felt his breath on my wet cheeks.

"I'm so sorry, Oaklyn. So fucking sorry."

Turning my head, I held his hand to me and kissed his palm. Taking the final step to connect us, I finally opened my eyes and looked up into his. We stood like that, his hand on my cheek, my hand on his, staring at each other, cherishing the small moment of connection even if it was all a lie.

I could have stayed in the room forever if it meant he was by my side.

He leaned down, and I met him halfway, pressing my lips to his. We didn't go any further, just pressing as close as we could, trying to make it last.

But all too soon, he pulled back and whispered, "I'm so sorry."

Then he walked out, leaving me again crying alone in a room.

I almost missed my phone vibrating in my pocket but pulled it out to see my advisor had sent an email.

Miss Derringer,

Congratulations! You received the internship with the sports therapy team. Let's set up a meeting later next week to discuss the details.

Dr. Denly

My first inclination was to run to Callum, to throw myself in his arms and celebrate, but with my hand on the doorknob, I stopped, the truth of our situation hitting me all over again.

I couldn't help but remember the morning after we'd slept together, when I'd had my interview. I remembered how I'd thought we'd celebrate together. How wrong I'd been. How different it was than anything I'd ever pictured.

Maybe I should have told him my plans, told him I had a light at the end of the tunnel.

However right then, it all felt too late. Like nothing was ever going to make a difference and bring us back together.

Instead, I pulled up Oliva's name on my phone and messaged her. I needed to do something to keep me from falling at Callum's feet and asking him to hang on a little longer.

> **Me:** I got the internship. Can I come over?
> **Olivia:** OMG! That is amazing! Yes, come over and we can celebrate. I have some dranks stashed in my room.

I finished up what I was doing and told Donna I wasn't feeling well. I couldn't run the chance of running into Callum again. The shining sun almost mocked my dark mood as I made my way across campus. Spring break was only a couple weeks away, but the nice weather was already starting. Had Callum and I already run our course in three short months?

Olivia opened her door and threw her arms around me.

"Oh, my god. Oh, my god. You did it! I knew you would," she squealed rocking us back and forth. Her excited shouts died as fast as they came when she pulled back to see my eyes filling with tears. "Oh, my god. Oaklyn." She gripped my hands in hers and tugged me into her room. The slam of the door behind us broke the wall holding back my emotions and I crumbled. All the tears I'd been holding back poured out. "What's wrong? What happened?"

"I've messed up, Oliva," I said, sitting on the bed next to her.

"Is it Voyeur?" Her back went ramrod straight, ready to go to battle for me. "Did something happen? Do we need to call Uncle Daniel?"

"No. No. Nothing like that." I wiped at my eyes and took deep breaths, hoping she would forgive me keeping secrets from her. "I—I have to tell you something."

"Okay."

"I've um . . . I slicked my tongue across my lips and stared down at my fidgeting fingers. "I've been in a sort of relationship with Callum. Dr. Pierce."

Olivia didn't speak, and I was too damn scared to look up and see the judgement in her eyes. Hearing it out loud made it seem all the more real, which led to it being all the more painful since it was over. I took a deep breath to help control the panic that grew, taking up too much space, the longer her silence lasted.

"You lucky bitch," she finally said.

I jerked my head up, my eyes wide. Not at all prepared for that response. "What?"

Her lips tipped up in a smirk. "If you're looking for a reprimand, it's not going to come from me. That man is sexy as sin, and if he even showed a little interest, I'd probably have a sexual harassment suit against me."

A laugh sputtered from between my pinched lips. Of all the things I expected to happen when I showed up, I hadn't expected to laugh.

"And you've been holding out the deets. How dare you. Now, that, I will give you shit over. When you're boning one of the hottest teachers on campus, you tell your best friend."

A barely there laugh escaped. "It's not exactly a relationship status you can post on Facebook."

"True," she said, nodding. "But wait, what happened? Why are you here crying?"

"We broke up."

"Sweetie," she said, pulling me into her arms. "I'm so sorry."

Burying my head in her shoulder, I got the rest of it off my chest. "He knew I worked at Voyeur."

Her rubbing hands stopped on my back. "How?"

"He, uh . . . he went there." Olivia gasped and tried to pull back, but I held her close, not ready to face her yet. "You can't tell anyone. I'm breaking the NDA even talking about it."

"I would never." Her stroking hands continued again, and I pushed on.

"He couldn't handle it. He was jealous and tried to hide it, but it became too much. Eventually, he offered to pay for the rest of my school, so I could quit Voyeur, and I just couldn't." I pulled back from her shoulder and waved my hands animatedly. Mad all over again over the situation. "He said, that I was being stubborn for not letting him pay. That he already paid for my time, so why not just let him pay for my school and eliminate the issue of Voyeur all together."

"Well, why not?"

My eyes shot to hers, completely unprepared for her response. She, more than anyone, should know why I wouldn't take money from someone. "What?"

"I mean, it's not a loan, so it's not like you'd have to pay it back. It's like he's paying for your time up-front."

"So, I can be his whore. He'd be paying me to perform just for him."

"You wouldn't be his whore, Oaklyn," she said exasperated. "And I mean, it's not like you don't perform for him anyway. With him paying for school you could continue to perform just for him," she suggested, her eyebrows bobbing, "and not have the weight of Voyeur hanging over your heads. I honestly don't see how it could go wrong. You're tired all the time from working your ass off, I'd get to see you more, you'd be less stressed trying to find time to study. All of these sound like pros."

I didn't even know what to say. My jaw hung open, and I blinked over and over, trying to replace the situation. How could Olivia take his side? "You know why I can't take money from people. Money ruins relationships."

"Listen, Oaklyn. You know I love you and that's why I'm going to be honest with you. You say having him pay for your school would ruin your relationship," she hesitated, looking concerned for how I was taking her honesty. "But it seems like it's ruined anyways."

My mouth opened and closed like a fish, unable to form words.

"Olivia, I—" I didn't know what to say. It felt wrong. "I can't let my professor pay for my schooling."

"But it wouldn't be your professor paying for school. It would be your boyfriend taking care of his girlfriend."

"It's not the same," I fought.

"It is."

"It doesn't feel the same."

She looked at me with sad eyes. Pitying me.

And I hated admitting it, but putting myself in her shoes, I'd look the same damn way at me. I was being stubborn. I had one thought and I couldn't see past it. I was so determined to make it on my own, that I'd shot myself in the foot to get there.

"Olivia, I fucked up," I said, repeating the same words when she opened the door, and began crying all over again.

She held me in her arms, rocking me back and forth, telling me it would be okay. Telling me I'd find a way to fix it.

"How? How do I go back to him after hurting him so much? How do I fix this? What if his offer doesn't stand? What if he doesn't want me anymore?"

"Oaklyn," she breathed a laugh. "I highly doubt he put his career on the line to be with you to change his mind so quickly."

"But I hurt him." And he'd been hurt so much before. It made me sick to think I added to it.

"If you make it work, I'm sure you will again. And again. I'm sure he'll hurt you at some point. People tend to call that a working, loving relationship," she said, nodding her head sagely.

Somehow, she made me laugh again. Not much, but it was better than the ache I'd walked in with.

"But, dude," she said excitedly, shaking my shoulders. "You got the fucking internship."

"Yeah. I guess I did," I agreed with a small smile.

"Let's celebrate." She crawled off the bed and dug underneath, unearthing a bottle of vodka and cranberry juice. She poured us each a drink and we sat back on her bed getting comfortable to watch a rom-com.

Between laughing and getting drunk, I came up with a plan. I wasn't sure if I could go to Callum and take him up on his offer, but I had other options that I could come to him with to at least try and repair the damage I created because of my pride.

Callum

"Is this the right knob, Dr. Pierce?" Andrea asked. We'd been out under the stars for thirty minutes, but with her flirty voice and constant batting eyelashes, it felt like it was thirty hours.

"I can help you if you need me to," Kenneth offered as he stared at her ass.

My head pounded as I readjusted the telescope again back to where it needed to be. "Just don't touch it this time, okay?" I was barely holding back my exasperation with the situation.

"But what if I want to touch it?" she asked, trying to portray innocence.

"I'd let you touch it," Kenneth chimed in.

Breathe in for five seconds. Breathe out for five. In for five. Out for five.

"Let's just find your star and write the description," I said with a forced smile.

I hadn't had a drink in two days. I thought maybe if I could limit my drinking and still keep a tight rein on my emotions, I could go back to Oaklyn a better man. Instead, over the past two days, I'd been on edge. Snapping at everyone. Poor Donna just gave me looks that said I could be pissy all I wanted, but I better stop taking it out on her.

It wasn't fair to anyone around.

Maybe I was being just as stubborn as Oaklyn in thinking that I could somehow numb myself to these emotions, even without alcohol, and that would make everything better.

Earlier in the stock room had proved how futile that thought was. I knew she was in there alone, and I went anyway. A glutton for punishment, knowing nothing good would come of it. I'd still been a selfish bastard and kissed her. I just hated seeing her so hurt. Needed to kiss her pain away, tell her how sorry I was again.

Each day in class she walked in like a zombie, looking as bad as I felt. I hated it. Hated every single thing about all of this. Mostly, I hated how weak I felt. Like I was putting us through this because I was a weak, damaged man. You'd think it would push me to do something about it, but it all felt like a waste. I thought I had done something about it before, and yet there I stood in the middle of a park with two of my students, trying to not just pack up and tell them to stop wasting my time, so I could go home and return to drinking myself to death.

It wasn't me. I loved teaching. I loved this project and seeing the students' awe at seeing the stars in a way they never had.

I'd lost that version of myself somewhere in the past few months. Instead, I tapped my thumb on my thigh, impatient for Andrea to finish scribbling some note in her book so we could get the fuck out of here, and I could go home to drink.

"Done!" she proclaimed victoriously.

"Fantastic," I said, already breaking down the telescope. "You guys can go ahead and leave, and I'll get this all packed up."

"Do you need any help, Dr. Pierce?" Andrea said, kneeling down too close beside me to grab a part.

"No," I snapped, causing her to snatch her hand back like I'd slapped it. "No," I repeated, gentler this time. "Thank you, but I have everything. It's late. Go ahead and head home."

As soon as I got everything in my car, I raced home. I left the case in the car and opened my door, tossing the keys to the table and shrugging off my coat, letting it lie on the floor.

Grabbing a glass, I went to the kitchen to snag the extra bottle of liquor in the top cabinet, having drank everything from my wet bar already. I filled half the glass and drank it in two swallows. I filled it again and thought about Oaklyn. I thought about how soft her lips had felt on mine. How golden her eyes looked when they were glossed over with tears.

I drank the contents of the glass and refilled it.

I thought about how her cheek pressed into my palm, searching for comfort I didn't know how to give anymore.

I drank again. And refilled again.

I thought about how her cries had echoed off the glass in the stock room, all of it bouncing back to pierce my heart all over again.

I drank again but halted when I went to tip the bottle and fill my glass.

Blood pounded in my ears. My fist gripped the neck of the bottle too tightly. A fire that burned in my stomach rose to my chest, making my lungs singe like they were on fire. Twelve years after therapy. Twelve years after breathing exercises, making myself feel like I was in control of my emotions. Twelve years of feeling like I was finally in control of my actions, burned to the ground, taking me with it.

And not just me. Oaklyn too.

A growl started in the depths of my soul and worked its way up my chest. It came out a rage-filled scream, and I unleashed. I tossed the

bottle into the kitchen sink, and to release some of the tension pulling my muscles too tight, I threw the tumbler at the wall, the piercing
sound of shattering glass raining down on my hardwood floor finally
broke me out of my stupor.

"Fuck," I shouted, digging my hands into my hair and tugging.
"Fuck."

Over and over it was all I could think. I was so fucked. This whole
situation was fucked. I looked over at the glass on the floor and everything drained from me. I should have cleaned it up. I should have
cared. But I didn't.

I turned away from it and headed upstairs to hopefully pass out
and not dream of Oaklyn and what a mess my life was falling back into.

Chapter Thirty-One

Callum

Two weeks after ending it with Oaklyn, I was still drinking too much, trying to figure out if it was better or worse without her. Better for her, at least, because I couldn't take my temperamental moods out on her.

Two weeks and I was getting more and more exhausted, the hangovers weighing me down, effecting my classes. Each time I had to watch her sit there in class, looking beautiful, but just as tired as me, I wanted to run to her and make it all better. But I wasn't in a place I could. If I thought I was a mess when we'd ended, I was a god damn catastrophe now.

Breathe in for five, out for five. Repeat.

Five more times and I felt somewhat ready to exit my car and head to class.

All that control came to a screeching halt when I looked up through my windshield and saw Oaklyn with Jackson. He'd pulled to the curb and she got out, looking tired, but still conjuring a real smile for him. He went around to the sidewalk and pulled her into his arms. She went willingly, holding him to her, too. I squeezed the leather around my steering wheel, listening to leather creak under the pressure as I watched him lean down and press his lips to the top her head.

He stepped back still holding her hand until he walked too far away their fingers slipped from one another's. Were they a couple? Had she moved on and let him comfort her?

Bile swirled in my stomach, threatening to burn its way up my throat.

How could she be with him? So soon? After she'd told me she didn't want anyone else? Were they together?

I imagined seeing her in class. Wondering how I'd focus. How would I be able to look at her and not lose my shit in front of everyone? Demand that she give me an explanation.

I couldn't. I couldn't do it.

Starting my car, I punched in the number for the office letting them know I wasn't going to make it in today. I didn't have to pretend to sound sick, I was broken and nothing about me was hiding that.

Back at home, I slammed the door to my house, tossing my bag to the floor as soon as I entered, and marched over to the mini-bar. Not bothering with a glass, I unscrewed the top of my bourbon and started drinking.

The morning sun shone into my dark home, turning the framed picture across from me into a mirror. My foggy reflection stared back at me. I pulled my lips from the bottle and really looked at myself.

A twenty-nine-year-old man drinking straight from the bottle before nine in the morning.

A twenty-nine-year-old man who gave up the woman he loved because he had no discipline over his emotions.

A twenty-nine-year-old man letting the past rule him rather than taking control. And not the false control I had before. *Real* control. Control that stayed even when things went wrong.

How long was I going to let this ruin me, make my decisions for me?

Yes, I trusted Oaklyn enough to get close to her, to make love to her, but I could push myself to be with others—learn to trust them. I could choose what I could and couldn't do.

I hadn't done enough to get there on my own, and I'd laid all my intimacy at her feet like I'd be alone forever without her. While I didn't want anyone other than her, it didn't mean she was the end all, be all to my future.

I couldn't keep doing this.

I couldn't keep letting other's actions rule me.

Swallowing the last swig of bourbon, I walked to the kitchen and began dumping the rest of it down the sink. Watching the brown liquor swirl down the drain was cathartic. It felt like the first step in the right direction.

Step two had me running up the stairs two at a time to reach my bedroom. I burst into my room and quickly stuffed some clothes and toiletries in a carry-on. Done with that, I pulled up my phone and made the arrangements. Then I called an Uber because I was drunk at ten in the morning and the admission was another punch in the gut, letting me know I was making the right decision.

By the afternoon, I looked out another window, watching a different scenery roll by. One I hadn't expected to see ever again.

The car parked outside the large home and I grabbed my bag and strolled up the sidewalk. Lifting my hand to knock, I paused. Once that door was opened, I couldn't go back. She'd force me to stay as long as she could. There would be no running or escaping.

I took a deep breath and knocked.

The door flung open and she stood there with wide eyes.

"Hey, Mom."

"Oh, my god. Cal." Her hand flew up to her mouth and her face crumpled as she began to cry. I stepped in and pulled her into my arms.

"Mom," I laughed. "This isn't the welcome a boy wants from his mom."

"I just—I can't believe you're here. You're home."

She pulled back and had to stand on her toes, but she kissed my cheeks over and over again until I pushed her away. "Stop. I just saw you a couple of months ago."

She wiped at her eyes. "Well, come on in. Your father will be happy to see you."

She kept looking back over her shoulder like I'd disappear. It wasn't like seeing me was a huge deal, it was the fact that I was home. California had always been their home—our home—but I had left as soon as I could, and I knew it hurt them that I hadn't come back. My parents loved me and had wanted to spend the holidays with family but had accommodated me and my fears.

They knew I related California to my past. So, for me to stand there, despite what had happened, meant a lot.

"Look who the cat dragged in," my mom announced.

My dad looked up from his chair in the living room where he was reading the paper and did a double take.

"Cal," he said in wonder. Then he tossed the paper aside and came to wrap me in his arms. "Welcome home, Son."

"Thanks, Dad."

My mom sniffed from the side but shook it off. "Well, let's not just stand here blubbering. What can I get you to drink?"

"Just a water, Mom."

I was determined to not let my anxiety control me. So, water from there on out until I got my shit together and finally faced some demons.

Mom came back and sat on the couch, just smiling at me.

Thankfully, they had moved after everything had happened. The nightmares had been too intense to stay. While being in California was hard enough, I never wanted to test my strength of being in my old room.

"You know I'm so happy to have you here, but why now? I can't help but feel like something's brought you here," my mom said.

I took a long drink of my water trying to ease my dry throat. "I, uh—I met someone."

Her face lit up like she could already see the grandbabies in her mind.

"Calm down, Mom." My hand rubbed at a knot of tension at the back of my neck. "It's complicated, to put it lightly."

"Complicated, shmomplicated," she said, waving her hand. "If you love her, you make it work."

"Which is why I'm here. We uh—" I took a deep breath, trying to figure out where to start. What did I confess first? "She's young. It made me very aware of the issues I was laying at her feet. I hated that I was putting that on her when she had her own things to deal with."

"Oh, baby. You are not your past." She'd said it to me as many times as she could squeeze in.

"I'm trying to realize that. That's why I'm here. We broke up and I kind of spun off the handles."

"I thought you looked a little worse for wear."

"Charles!" My mom gasped, slapping my dad's leg.

He just shrugged at her. "The boy looks like he hasn't slept in months."

"Thanks, Dad. It's actually only been a couple weeks."

"So, explain the complicated," my dad said, knowing it was a bigger issue than I was telling them.

"She's young."

"Legal?" he asked, eyebrow raised. My parents were understanding, but not that understanding.

"God, Dad. Yes." I breathed out a laugh. "But just starting her life." My parents sat there, giving me time to think, knowing there was more. I thought about what I wanted to say without giving anything away. "I'm possessive of her—jealous in a way I've never felt before, and when my jealousy sparks, I lose my mind. There's no rational thought. There's no reasoning. I lose myself in my mind and my issues and I lose my temper. I'd lose it on her. Say things. Mean things and I hated it." It hurt even more to say out loud. "She's too young to take on my issues."

"Callum," my mom said, admonishing me. "A woman can make her own decisions. A woman can walk away when she needs to."

"But what would I have to do for her to make that decision? How far would I fall?" My mom frowned and reached across the space to grip my hand. Just her holding my hand comforted me. "That's why I'm here. I can't keep letting my past rule me. I can't keep hiding and hoping that ignoring it will make it better. I'm tired of it, Mom."

She swiped at a tear that managed to escape. I knew she still held so much guilt over what had happened, and I didn't want my inability to let go keep holding everyone else back. I needed to face it. Deal with it.

"I was hoping Dr. Edgemore would be able to see me this week," I said, referencing the therapist I saw before I left California.

"I'll make sure he does," my dad confirmed.

"How long are you staying?"

"Two weeks. I have a week of vacation saved up and then next week is Spring Break."

"Two whole weeks." My mom clapped her hands in excitement. "I can't wait. Plenty of time for you to tell me about this girl."

I smiled, just thinking about Oaklyn. "She's great. Beautiful, smart, determined, funny. She's so much of everything, I can't even narrow down the adjectives."

"She sounds lovely. I can't wait to meet her. Maybe we can visit and all go out to dinner."

At that, I looked away wincing. I'd run out of time on keeping the biggest complication a secret.

"What? Are you embarrassed by us?" my mom asked, joking.

"No. We uh—we can't exactly date."

She cocked an eyebrow and stared, trying to consider all the reasons. "Is she married?"

"No. Jesus, Mom."

"Well, what is it?"

My heart raced in my chest making me light headed. "Um, she's uh—my student."

Her eyes shot wide, and she gasped, "Callum Pierce."

"I know. I know, Mom. I didn't mean for it to happen. I didn't know, and I fought it. God did I fight it, but she's just so much. And with her, for the first time ever, I saw a future. I saw her with me in a future and I couldn't fight it anymore."

Her shocked look softened to sympathy, and I knew it would be okay. She understood, and at the root of it all, if it was legal and consensual, my parents wanted me safe and happy.

"It's not like you weren't my intern when we first met," my dad muttered to my mom. "We had to keep our . . . Activities secret too."

She blushed, and I cringed. "Ew, Dad."

He leaned over and kissed my mom on the cheek.

That was the love I wanted—the future I wanted.

There was no way I was getting to it in the state I was in right now. If I ever wanted my dream of Oaklyn and I working out later, I needed to be a better man.

Remembering her in Jackson's arms, my shoulders slumped, and I wondered if I was too late.

But it didn't matter. I'd fight for her if I had to.

First, it was time to face everything and be a better man.

I was ready.

Chapter Thirty-Two

Oaklyn

Two weeks.

I hadn't seen him in two weeks.

I thought I missed him before, but nothing compared to when he'd disappeared. We'd had a sub for some classes and mostly emails and notes for the others he missed. I tried to subtly asked Donna where he was, but she's simply said vacation. I wanted to demand where and why. Instead I gave a simple nod and walked away.

I could have messaged him, and I must have typed up at least a thousand texts, but never sent them. I was sure he was okay. He had too many people caring about him to not be okay.

But tonight, all my concerns would be answered. I'd be able to see for myself if he was okay. It was the night he was going to help me with the telescope for the class project. I'd begun looking up other plans because I didn't know if Callum would be back or if he'd even want to assist me anymore. Maybe he'd pawn me off to another teacher.

Then the email arrived yesterday morning as a reminder to be at the park by eight at night to do the final portion of the class project. I checked the schedule at the same time and my heart sank at seeing another student had signed up for the night. The possibilities had fluttered across my skin when I'd thought it would just be him and I. But, nope, Joey would be there too. Stupid Joey.

Getting off the bus, I walked the last few feet to the park. I pushed the code into the gate and closed it behind me. The park closed at dusk, so we'd be the only ones around. Oh, and Joey.

Standing inside the entrance, I took a deep breath, preparing myself to see him. Preparing myself to act natural and not fall at his feet, explaining the last two weeks and beg him to take me back. I had so much to say. So much I wanted to tell him—had planned on telling him before he disappeared on me.

Deep breaths.

I walked around the bathrooms and saw a figure atop the hill and began heading toward it. Maybe I was the first one there.

He was bent over a box, his broad back stretching his jacket tight and I yearned to reach out and run my hands across it. Fuck, I missed him.

"Hey," I said softly.

He stood and turned, facing me, taking me in. "Hey."

One cheek ticked up, almost hidden behind thick scruff bordering on a beard. It looked good on him. While he scanned me, I did the same in return, and I could tell he was nervous, but at the same time not. His shoulders seemed to be less tense, his eyes holding less back.

He seemed better than I'd ever seen him before.

It hurt to see him doing so well, but I swallowed it back and forced a smile. "Should we get started or wait for Joey?"

"Joey couldn't make it. Canceled last minute."

"Oh." We were alone, with no interruptions, for the first time in a month. My stomach fluttered with excitement, but also churned with nerves. Was I the only one nervous? He seemed so calm, so relaxed, if not a little fidgety. "Okay."

"Come here, let's find us a star," he said, his eyes light and smiling. My body trembled with each step closer to him.

"You're going to look through here and adjust the focus here." He continued to point at the different parts of the telescope, explaining what each did. I tried to listen, but I was so aware of the way his long fingers worked the knobs. I was too aware of the way he looked at me, the way it seemed to burn across my skin. Was I making it up? Was I really feeling it?

His hand reached around me to a knob, almost making me choke on my tongue when his heat seeped through my shirt, burning my skin. He stayed close for longer than was necessary, letting his fingers linger on the telescope, and I had to fight from leaning back into him. My body trembled when I imagined how it would feel to have his hard muscles pressed against me again. But then he backed away, and I expelled the breath I hadn't known I was holding before leaning down to look at my star.

It looked simple; just a tinge of blue.

"You seem unimpressed," he laughed, the sound rippling down my spine.

"I thought it would be more like all those shows or the pictures in our books. More colorful."

"The pictures you see in books usually have a different lens applied to the photo, detecting different electromagnetic radiation. Most common is infrared." He said some other big words, his hands moving around animatedly, but I didn't understand many of them.

I tried to keep a serious face, like I actually followed what he was saying, but in the end, I laughed. Watching him talk about astronomy was beautiful. He had so much love for the topic, and I loved seeing him so excited.

"What's so funny?" he asked.

"You're letting your nerd-side show."

"It's sexy isn't it?" he said, half-joking. Crickets chirped in the silence that followed. A cord pulled tight between us, feeling ready to snap, on the verge of something breaking. I couldn't tell if it was for the good or bad.

"Where were you?" It fell from my tongue. I didn't mean to ask, but I couldn't say I regretted it.

His Adam's apple bobbed before he turned fully toward me, his face serious.

"I went home. To California."

"What?" The breath whooshed out of my lungs. I thought he would never go back there. "Are your parents okay?"

"Yeah, yeah. They're fine. Just time to visit."

"Wow. California. That's amazing, Callu—. Dr. Pierce." I didn't have a right to call him by his first name anymore. He was just my professor now.

"Callum." He corrected, stepping closer. My breath got trapped in my lungs as I watched him approach, only a few inches between us. I waited on edge for him to lift his hand and touch me, but it never came. "You can always call me Callum."

"Okay," I said on my exhale. My head swam at his nearness.

"It was time. To go home."

I nodded dumbly, not sure what to say, but wanting to know everything.

"I was a mess, and what I was before was just a mess hidden by a fine veneer. I thought I had gained control over myself—over my past, and it was a lie. Every little thing that brought it up sent me into a tailspin. Which I could ignore because it had been just me." He breathed out a laugh and smiled at me. "Then there was you, and my loss of control became an issue. I could no longer ignore it and bury my head in the sand. I was faced with how my actions would affect my future. And Oaklyn, I want a future. A future I can choose. A future not haunted by my past."

I didn't realize I was crying until his thumb came up to wipe at my tears. I leaned into his palm, letting the warmth of his touch comfort me in a way I hadn't had in almost a month. "I'm sorry. I didn't mean to cry. I'm just happy for you. You seem happier."

"I am and I'm not. I saw a therapist at home and he recommended one here, so I'm hoping to get to a better place and stay there. But there are other things that hold me back." His hand still lingered on my cheek, and I fought to not turn my head and press my kiss to his palm. To step into him and press myself against his warmth.

"I quit Voyeur." I couldn't hold it in anymore. I'd wanted to tell him as soon as I'd done it. I had walked into class floating on hope that we were going to recover. And he hadn't been there. So, I blurted it out now.

"What?" he asked, just as shocked as me that I'd tossed it out there. "When?"

"About two weeks ago."

"But—but what about school? What about Jackson?"

I shook my head trying to understand, and his hand dropped. "What about Jackson?"

"Aren't you two together? I mean, I saw you getting out of his car before I left. He had his arms around you and kissed you."

His words sounded like barely restrained anger, and I racked my brain before flashing back to the day he probably saw us. I remembered Jackson's hug as he said goodbye. I could only imagine what he thought.

"No, we're not together. He was giving me a ride to school after I quit. I'd sold my car the day before and he offered to drive me."

"You sold your car? Why?"

"It was enough money to get me through the end of the year, and I could quit Voyeur. It became . . . painful to be there." When I paused to look at him, he grimaced. "Don't wince like you have any responsibility for my feelings working there. It's not like I loved it. Voyeur was a means to an end, and I didn't want it anymore, so I found a better solution."

I slicked my tongue across my dry lips. "I'm sorry Callum. I'm sorry I was so stubborn and refused to see other options. I should have let you pay. I shouldn't have let you walk away because of my pride and misguided assumptions with money. I've seen money ruin too many relationships, and I couldn't have it happen to us." I laughed softly at that. "But I guess it did anyway. And honest to god, if my car wouldn't have been enough money to quit, I would have come to you. I was done being away from you. I miss you."

"Oaklyn," he whispered my name in relief. Relief that it was over.

We'd both made strides to get back to each other.

"Also, I got an internship with the college's physical therapy team. It starts in the summer."

"That's amazing."

My chest swelled at his pride in me.

"Between that and scholarships, grants, and loans, I should be okay. I may have to use candles and eat Ramen until everything comes through, but I'll be okay."

He laughed with me and stepped in close, pulling the breath from my lungs. Fuck he was so close. My breasts heaved, brushing against his chest. My skin lighting on fire, yearning to touch him.

"Callum," I whispered his name on a broken breath. I wanted to pull him close and never let go.

"I'll feed you," he said before leaning down to peck my nose. "Not because you need me to, but because I miss eating lunch with you and I love watching you enjoy food the way you do. Also, because you make me amazing brownies."

"What?" I asked, unsure I was hearing him right. Wanting it to mean what I thought.

"I love you, Oaklyn. So much and the past month has killed me, but I don't regret it. I don't because I'm a better man for the truths I had to face. I just hated every second of being away from you. I love you and even after dealing with all my shit, you were still the only woman I wanted."

"Cal." Tears fell down my cheeks, hearing his words. I finally gave in and moved my hands to his chest, clutching at his sweater.

"I'm not saying I'm perfect and won't have things that trigger me, because I will. But they won't destroy me. They won't ruin me. Even if you still worked at Voyeur. Even if you were dating Jackson, I was going to fight for you tonight. I'm ready for you Oaklyn and I know I'm older and you're probably getting the short end of the stick, I'm asking you to have me. I'm asking t—"

I cut him off with my lips pressed to his. I didn't need to hear any more. Everything I needed to hear had been said and now, all I wanted was to feel him against me. To taste him. To have him listen to me. I pulled back and looked up at him, the most beautiful man I'd ever seen. My Clark Kent. "I love you too, Callum. So much."

He groaned and crashed his mouth to mine, digging his hands into my hair to hold me close. When his tongue licked at my lips, I opened, needing him closer. I burrowed my hands under his shirt to feel the soft skin stretched across his hard stomach, reaching around his back to cling to him. He thrust his hips and we both moaned at the feel of his length as it brushed against my stomach.

"I need you, Oaklyn. Please."

I nodded my head and he leaned down to grip my ass and lift me to him before kneeling and laying me out.

"Oh, wait," he said, pulling back. "I have a blanket in my car."

"No." I clenched my fists in his shirt and pulled him down between my spread thighs. "Fuck the blanket. I need you too much."

He smiled before returning to feast on my lips. His hand palmed my breast as he descended down my neck, leaving a wet trail of kisses. He never let his mouth leave my skin as he worked the buttons of my shirt open enough to bare my bra which he peeled back and latched on to my nipple. My back arched off the grass and pressed my breasts into his mouth. I gasped when he grazed his beard across the hardened tip, rolling the other between his fingers.

"I knew I liked that beard."

"I can't wait for you to feel it between your thighs, brushing against your sensitive pussy."

"Ung," I groaned, lifting my hips to try and get some friction and ease the ache.

"Stop teasing me, Cal. I want you."

He sat up and the cool night air pebbled my nipples even more as I caressed the wet tips. His fingers hooked in my leggings and panties and tugged them down and off. The grass scraped at my bare skin, but I didn't care. I'd be naked on coals if it meant I got to feel Cal inside me again. But I didn't have to endure because he shrugged his jacket off and told me to lift my hips as he laid it beneath me.

As he began working his buckle open, I rocked my hips up and spread my thighs, torturing him with the view. I moved my hands to my breasts and rolled the tips, tugging them until he slapped my hands away.

"Mine," he growled before latching on again.

The tip of his cock brushed against my opening and we both gasped at the connection. Then I shifted and reached between us to grip him in my palm and direct him to my core. He bit at my tip when I brushed the head of his cock along my slit before notching it between my folds.

"Fuck me, Cal."

He lifted up and held my stare as he pressed in one inch at a time. Agonizingly slow. Filling me up to capacity, all the way to the hilt.

"God, I missed this pussy."

"I missed your cock inside me."

He crushed his lips to mine and began fucking me. He thrust hard and fast, sometimes pulling back so he could watch my breasts bounce each time his hips collided with mine.

"Your tits are so perfect."

"They're small," I argued breathlessly.

His hand covered a breast. "They're perfect for me and my hands."

"I love you," I said.

He reached down to grab my thigh, pulling until it hooked up around his hip and he pressed his whole body to mine, grinding himself on me. "I love you, too," he said against my lips.

His words, the hard thrusts, the way he brushed against my hard clit set me off. I held on tightly to him and threw my head back as my whole body tightened, squeezing his cock to hold it deep inside me as my body exploded all around him.

"So beautiful. Like the most intense supernova every single time you come,"

He lost control of his movements then and pounded into me until finally he stilled, fully embedded inside me and came, his groans vibrating against my skin, sending little aftershocks of pleasure though my whole body as he filled me up.

"I love you so much, Oaklyn."

"I love you too." I brushed my hands through his hair and shifted to press a kiss to his damp temple.

He eventually slipped out of me and rolled to his side, but pulled me with him into his arms.

"I always imagined you when I thought of making love to someone under the stars."

Me. He'd imagined me, and it filled me with so much joy I felt like my heart would explode all over again from his words.

"So, what do we do now?" I asked, pressing a kiss to his chest as it rose on a heavy sigh.

"Now we be together."

"What about school?"

"We can't tell anyone, and we have to hide now. But Oaklyn," he began, shifting to look down at me. "When you're done being my student, I'm going to date the fuck out of you. Take you on the best dates. Show you off to the world and let them see I'm the luckiest man alive."

My cheeks hurt from smiling so hard. I loved this man so much and although the past month had been hell, I wouldn't change anything if it meant I was here in his arms at the end of all of it.

If it meant I got to spend every night with him under the stars.

Epilogue

Callum

"Look at those perfect tits bounce," I growled into her neck, watching her breasts sway with my every thrust in the reflection on the glass. "I wonder if everyone below can see how much you love having me inside you?"

"Cal," she gasped, her eyes pinching closed.

Her body was a glow in the glass. The sun setting over Sacramento city a backdrop to me coiling my body around hers.

I bit her neck and started fucking her harder. Her whimpers turned to moans and her fingers tried to dig into the glass. Leaning back, I gripped her hips and watched myself slip in and out of her tight, wet heat.

"Yes. Yes," she cried.

"Do you want them to watch you? Does that turn you on to have them see your pleasure?"

"Yes," she said again.

I leaned over her, pressing my chest to her back. Slipping one hand around the front, I moved my fingers between her legs and fingered her clit. Rubbing harder, I sucked on her lobe before pulling back with a nip at the tender skin.

"Me too," I breathed into her ear, detonating her orgasm.

I kept up my ruthless pace, focusing on her reflection, on the way her pussy squeezed me tight like a vice, on her moans.

And I came.

My eyes slammed shut as the muscles in my body contracted in pleasure, my hips pressed tight to her ass as I held myself as deep inside her as I could, feeling every last pulse on my cock.

I pressed one last kiss to the damp skin of her back as the ringing finally subsided in my ears.

"You don't think they can really see?" Oaklyn asked between her heavy breathing.

Laughing, I pulled out of her and groaned. "Probably not. But it's fun to imagine they can. You seem to come harder then."

Her hair breezed across my face when she whipped her head around to playfully glare at me. "I do not."

"Okay," I said, doubt heavy in my tone. "Now, come on. We're going to be late." I slapped her ass and then moved to the bathroom to get a washcloth.

"And who's fault is that?" she asked, stomping in naked, her dress in hand.

I turned with a wet washcloth and wiped it between her legs, eliciting a sharp inhale. "Yours for coming out in that dress. Practically begged me to fuck you."

I tossed the cloth to the side and placed a quick kiss to her lips.

"Now get dressed."

"I already was dressed before you pulled it off me," she said to my retreating back.

I waved my hand but continued to the sitting room of our hotel. Our suitcases still sat unpacked by the door, having just got in a few hours ago. It was hard to believe that twenty-four hours ago I was watching the love of my life walk across the stage to collect her diploma.

I'd sat in my academic regalia and kept my cheering to a minimum because she'd asked me not to stand and cheer like I'd wanted to. We were always safe with our relationship over the years, even after she was no longer my student. Although, we continued to keep a low profile not wanting to draw attention. Some people noticed in her junior year, but since there were no rules about a professor dating a student of the college, nothing happened beyond a few judgmental stares.

But we'd survived over three years and I could do whatever I wanted with her. Including fuck her in a high-rise hotel in front of the glass. I'd respected her wishes to keep my love for her to a minimum in public, but now all bets were off.

"Do you think you can keep it in your pants, Dr. Pierce?"

Oaklyn's arms slipped around my waist from behind and spread her palms across my chest. My own hand reached up to touch the diamond glittering on her finger.

"I can try, but we may need to meet up in the restroom later."

She laughed, moving around to my front and staring at the white-gold band shining bright against my black suit jacket. I'd asked her at almost midnight last night, after ravaging her, a sheet wrapped around her body as she dug in to takeout from Waffle House.

She'd made me happier than I'd been in the past three years when she'd nodded her head, tears running down her cheeks. Joy swelled so big inside me, filling every tiny space, I was sure I'd burst from it. Then I'd laid her out and made love to my fiancée until we'd passed out for a few hours before our flight to California.

"I think you can make it through dinner with your parents without a quickie in the bathroom."

"I guess I can try for you," I said before leaning down to kiss her.

We almost got lost in the kiss again, but she pulled back. "No, Dr. Pierce. We have reservations we need to keep."

"Fine," I grumbled.

She smiled up at me, my whole world in her eyes. "I love you," she said softly.

"I love you too." I had to swallow past the lump in my throat. She made me feel so much, so much happiness, that when the darkness came, it didn't put a dent in who I was. "Thank you for your patience and loving me regardless of the mess I was."

Oaklyn had been more than patient. She'd wanted me at my worst and waited for me to become my best. And I had. For her, I had continued therapy and truly gained a solid foundation to move forward with my future. Some days were still hard, but never as hard as when I was alone.

She sat with me in the dark and loved me through it.

I would spend the rest of my life loving her and I was sure it would never be enough. But I'd die trying. Hopefully when we were both old and gray, with a full life behind us.

"Always." One more soft kiss before her fingers linked with mine and led me to the door. "Now come on. I'm ready to show off this beautiful ring to your mom and dad."

"Are you sure no bathroom sex?" I teased.

"Maybe if you're good we can sneak up to the rooftop garden tonight and I'll let you make love to me under the stars."

"Fuck the bathroom. You under the stars is always my first choice."

The End.

Acknowledgments

First and foremost, as always, my family. My husband, who is always so supportive and is the main reason I can even do this adventure called writing. I love you. Then there are my beautiful girls who are my sunshine and I always push myself harder, just to make them proud. I hope you grow up stronger than Wonder Woman and Bat Girl.

Karla Sorensen: Thank you so much for all your pep-talks, all the times you held my hand and told me it was going to be okay. Thank you for being there when things got rough and encouraged me to keep going. I love you and am so blessed to have you in my life. #Dream-Team

Georgeanna and Rachel: You guys are my sanity and some of the best friends anyone could ask for. We may end up separated by miles, but you will always be my ride or die bitches. Thank you for being the best assistants and drinking partners at signings. Thank you for helping me plot this book over eight months ago on a long drive home. I love you both with everything I am.

To my betas: Julia, Michelle, Becca, and Serena. Julia, I can't thank you enough for squeezing me in. I know school is crazy, and yet, you always make time for me. Michelle, you swooped in and gave me such fabulous notes. They were constructive and positive. I may have gone back to them in moments when I questioned whether or not to light this book on fire. Voyeur is still alive because of you! Becca, thank you for managing to read Voyeur between all your work. I know how valuable your time is and can't thank you enough for always finding time to help me out.

Serena, as always, your comments give me life. The messaged updates have me smiling for days and laughing out loud. I love them and appreciate all your suggestions. You always go above and beyond and there are no words to truly express how much it means to me. Thank you, thank you, thank you. I love your bossiness and all the help you give me with my spelling errors on my teasers! Haha! Thank you!

Karen: I don't know how I got so lucky to have you edit my books, but my god, I am! I have so much more confidence in my work knowing that you have edited it. Thank you for all your hard work and still managing to make time for my books.

Alexis: Thank you for all your proofreading help. You always manage to catch the smallest details and help me deliver a clean book.

My reader group: You ladies are amazing, supportive, hilarious, dirty, wonderful, and a thousand more adjectives. I go to you when I'm down or frustrated and you always manage to build me up. Thank you for hanging out with me and putting up with my rambly live videos.

To all the bloggers of every kind: Thank you for sharing my work. You make this community go 'round. Thank you for all your support and kind words and pictures and teasers. I love that you are amazing enough to take time out of your busy lives to support us authors for no other reason than your love of books.

Thank you to all the readers in this beautiful community. I couldn't do this without you. You all are so supportive and amazing. Thank you so much for taking a chance on my books. I'm always beyond honored that you would spend the time and money on my characters and their worlds I've created. It is unbelievably amazing and I'm forever grateful.

Author's Note About the Cover

The cover photo was purchased from Alex Sens who runs Sensual Media. He also has a fun little dating adventure called Shooting Date, which is where this picture came from.

Basically, a person can schedule a time to get his/her photo taken with someone else. They don't meet until their photo session, like a blind date. And then they take these super sexy photos. How crazy and awesome is that?

So, the couple in this photo had just met and took this beautiful photo with all the emotion and I couldn't be happier that I stumbled upon this gem.

About the Author

Fiona Cole is a military wife and a stay at home mom with degrees in biology and chemistry. As much as she loved science, she decided to postpone her career to stay at home with her two little girls and immersed herself in the world of books until finally deciding to write her own.

Fiona loves hearing from her readers, so be sure to follow her on social media.

Instagram, Facebook, & Pinterest: @authorfionacole
Newsletter: http://eepurl.com/bEvHtL
Reader Group: Books, Wine, and Music with Fiona Cole
Amazon
BookBub

Other books by Fiona

All books are FREE on Kindle Unlimited

Where You Can Find Me
Deny Me
Imagine Me

Shame (Shame Me Not #1)
Make It to the Altar (Shame Me Not #1.5)

Voyeur
The Lovers
(Coming October 2018)

Made in the USA
Coppell, TX
26 April 2021